# 1

The police car

question. But it didn't lo , as it screeched
to a halt in front of him, the doors popping open and a fat Azerbaijani policeman jumped out, yelling at Berezin to halt—at least, that was what it sounded like. A second police car came up behind him a moment later.

The heavyset *Spetsnaz* trooper froze, staring at the police in front of him before looking over his shoulder at the police behind him. Flanagan slowed abruptly, holding Wade back with a hand. Something about Berezin's body language…

The Russian suddenly reached under his jacket and yanked out a PP-93 submachinegun, snapping it up without bothering to unfold the stock. A single burst sent the first policeman sprawling, blood spraying from his throat. Then Berezin spun, bringing the machine pistol around, and dumped the rest of the mag into the second Azerbaijani cop. The little 9mm fired fast, the *brrap* of its reports blending into a single, nasty sound. Only about half the rounds hit the policeman, but the last one punched through his eye, snapping his head back with a spurt of gore, and he sprawled over his car's hood and rolled off onto the street.

BRANNIGAN'S BLACKHEARTS

# ENEMY OF MY ENEMY

PETER NEALEN

This is a work of fiction. Characters and incidents are products of the author's imagination. Some real locations are used fictitiously, others are entirely fictional. This book is not autobiographical. It is not a true story presented as fiction. It is more exciting than anything 99% of real gunfighters ever experience.



Printed in the United States of America
http://americanpraetorians.com

**Also By Peter Nealen**

**The Maelstrom Rising Series**

Escalation

Holding Action

Crimson Star

Strategic Assets

Fortress Doctrine

SPOTREPS – A Maelstrom Rising Anthology

**The Brannigan's Blackhearts Universe**

Kill Yuan

The Colonel Has A Plan (Online Short)

Fury in the Gulf

Burmese Crossfire

Enemy Unidentified

Frozen Conflict

High Desert Vengeance

Doctors of Death

Kill or Capture

Enemy of My Enemy

**The American Praetorians Series**

Drawing the Line: An American Praetorians Story (Novella)

Task Force Desperate

Hunting in the Shadows

Alone and Unafraid

The Devil You Don't Know

Lex Talionis

**The Jed Horn Supernatural Thriller Series**

Nightmares

A Silver Cross and a Winchester

The Walker on the Hills

The Canyon of the Lost (Novelette)

Older and Fouler Things

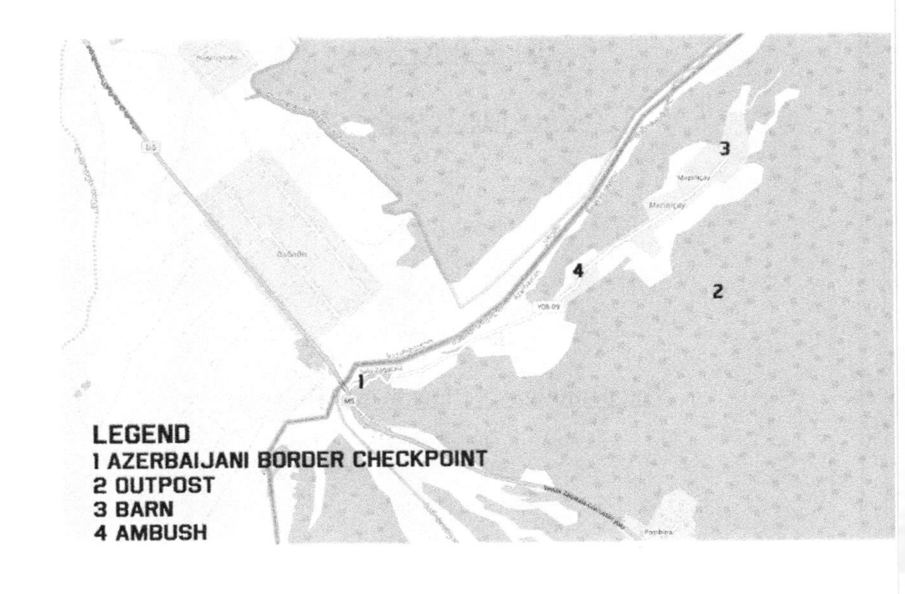
3
4
2
1
LEGEND
1 AZERBAIJANI BORDER CHECKPOINT
2 OUTPOST
3 BARN
4 AMBUSH

# CHAPTER 1

Night was falling fast over the rugged hills as Shamil Mashadov took a knee under the short, scrubby pine and looked back at his little strike force.

The fifty men were strung along the side of the mountain behind him, following the narrow goat path in single file. They blended in well, especially as the light failed. Much of that was thanks to the brand-new camouflage that the Emir had gotten them; the pixelated tan and green was every bit as effective as the American OCP, particularly amid the scrub and short trees of Paktika Province.

Most of the men behind him, except for Dilawar Safi, his Pashtun guide, were fellow Chechens, warriors of the *Aswad al Islam*. They were a long way from home, but what they would do tonight would be worth it.

Turning back toward their objective, he lowered the night vision goggles mounted to his helmet and scanned the valley below. The Americans had said that they would be gone from this part of Afghanistan months before, but, infuriatingly, they still had yet to withdraw.

Tonight, Mashadov and his brothers would teach the infidels that they should have fled long ago.

He lifted the encrypted Russian radio to his lips. "Timur, are you in position?"

It took a moment for Timur Kurbanov to answer. "Yes, brother. The mortars will be set up in another few minutes, and the machineguns are in place and ready."

"Good. We will be in position to attack in twenty minutes." Mashadov glanced at Dilawar. The Pashtuns—most jihadis, for that matter—were not very good at timing. *Insh'Allah*, the attack would go through, when Allah willed that it would go through. But Mashadov had been trained in the Russian-aligned *Kadyrovtsy*. Ramzan Kadyrov, like his father before him, might have been a traitor to the Faith and the true Chechen nation, but his friendship with Moscow had gotten them training and experience that they might otherwise not have had. And every man in Mashadov's strike force had either been in the *Kadyrovsty* or had been trained by those who had. Which made them more coordinated than many of the Chechens fighting the Jihad abroad.

Of course, Abu Mokhtar's vision and resources had facilitated even more training, as well getting them the top-of-the-line equipment they were using.

He stuffed the radio back into his load bearing vest and hefted the brand-new AK-203, lifting it to his shoulder and peering through the Elcan scope at the FOB below. It wouldn't take his hardened mountain fighters long to get close to the HESCO barriers that formed the outer perimeter.

The Americans weren't showing visible lights; the FOB was an only barely visible mass of blocks through the optic. But when he flipped his NVGs back down again, he could see considerably more.

Thanks to twenty years of war and ready access to the Internet, Mashadov knew quite well what he was looking at. He knew that the points of light surrounding the perimeter were the infrared chemlights hanging on the outer concertina wire, marking it for American infantry soldiers on night vision. He knew that the IR illuminators that the Americans were using from the guard posts would point him right to their positions. And he knew how to pick out the faint glow of the generator that was powering the Americans' operations center.

He could call that in to Kurbanov. But Kurbanov had his own observers, who knew how to pinpoint the right targets before they started dropping mortars on the infidels.

The mortars were just supposed to keep the Americans' heads down while Mashadov and his men closed the distance, anyway. This was going to be a much more personal fight.

If it had been anywhere but Afghanistan, that might have been strange. Mashadov had fought with the jihad in Syria and, though it had gone unremarked by most of the outside world, in Yemen. He had developed an antipathy for the Arabs there that was mirrored by his Pashtun brother only a few meters away. The Arabs didn't like to get in close to fight. The Pashtuns, however…they were a different matter.

Turning back to the column behind him, he pointed down the slope toward the low ground leading almost right up to the HESCO barrier wall. Then with a "follow me" gesture, he started down the hillside.

The scrub provided some concealment as they moved. The Chechen fighters slipped from bush to tree to boulder as they worked their way down the rocky slope, covered in tough grass. Their gear was all carefully secured, and they made no noise as they moved.

***

*What the fuck am I doing here?*

It wasn't the first time Specialist Colin Owens had asked himself that question. Or even the hundredth time. He'd lost track around the end of his first year in the Army.

He couldn't say that he was a *proud* member of the E4 mafia. Owens wasn't really proud of anything about being in the Army. He was doing his time until he could get out, grow his hair long, and do absolutely nothing if he felt like it. He hated the Army, hated his life, and really, *really* hated Afghanistan.

*We were supposed to be out of this shithole country* months *ago! Why am I still on midnight guard duty, on a fucking FOB in the middle of the mountains? At most, I should be sitting in a transient tent in Bagram, waiting to go home.*

He kept his thoughts to himself, even though he was pretty sure that Private Ortiz, his partner on watch that night, was of a similar mind. But Sergeant Merrill, their "Baboon Sausage," as Specialist Newkirk called their Platoon Sergeant, had a nasty habit of sneaking around the perimeter when their platoon was on security, and he really didn't want another ass-chewing for shamming, even if it was only talk.

So, he held his peace, wished for a cigarette, and stared at his sector, wondering how many minutes he had left before their relief got there. Which would probably be late. As usual.

As much as he hated the Army and everything about it, though, Owens wasn't so lost in his hate and discontent that he was completely ignoring the landscape around him. While they'd been shut up in FOB Mayne since they'd gotten there, and they hadn't been patrolling the area or interacting with the local populace much, they'd still been rocketed a couple of times over just the last week. Both times, the guard posts had reported people watching from the nearby ridgelines both before and during the attacks. Probably spotters. And despite himself, Owens didn't want to be the guy who missed a spotter and failed to warn the rest of the unit that they were about to get hit, just because he hated his life.

That was how he came to be looking at an open spot between a pair of distant pines just as a figure dashed from shadow to shadow across the grassy slope.

Owens blinked, squinting through his NVGs. The moonless Paktika night was so dark that he couldn't be entirely sure that he'd actually seen anything, even in the bright grayscale image projected by his dual-tube NVGs. It *might* have been his imagination. But he remembered the rockets coming in a few nights before, and so he decided not to take chances.

He picked up his rifle from where it was leaning against the sandbags, lifted it to his shoulder, then flipped on the IR illuminator and shone it toward the trees where he thought he'd seen the movement. "Hey, Ortiz," he said, without taking his eyes off the slope, "Get on the radio and call Sarn't Merrill."

***

Mashadov cursed as he saw the cone of infrared light stab over his head, illuminating the tree where Musa Anzorov had just taken cover. The Americans had seen something. They might have just lost the element of surprise.

Looking down the slope, he tried to judge how far they had still to go. He was crouched behind a boulder, less than half a kilometer from the wire, but that was still a long distance to cover under fire. And the mortars were not supposed to start firing for another ten minutes.

Yet Allah is beneficent. Even as Mashadov braced himself to charge the American perimeter, a series of distant *pop*s sounded, as the mortars started firing early.

The shells whistled down toward the American camp, and everything turned to pandemonium.

A series of bright flashes and earthshaking *whump*s marked the rounds' impacts. A siren started to sound in the middle of the camp, and that was Mashadov's cue.

Even as the mortars were joined by flickering streams of green tracers plunging down from strobing muzzle flashes up on the hills to the south, Mashadov rose from behind his tree and with a screamed, "*Allahu Akhbar!*" he plunged down the remaining slope toward the camp and the exterior wire.

If his plan had simply been to charge the FOB under cover of the mortar and machinegun fire, it would have ended messily and very quickly. But Mashadov was a thinker, and while he was perhaps slightly handicapped by his ideology, he hadn't let that influence his tactics as much as the hated Arabs had. He had a plan to get past the wire and over the wall.

He and the dozen or so men who made up his assault element threw themselves down behind cover a few meters short of the wire. He quickly got down behind his rifle and aimed in at the guard post above and to his left. The others would be aimed in alternately at the others.

So far, none of his assaulting fighters had fired a shot. So long as the mortars and the machineguns kept the Americans' attention occupied, they should have no warning about where the *real* attack was coming from, until it was too late.

Dzhamal Dudaev and Khanpasha Ismailov ran past him, lugging the satchel charges that had been carefully prepared days before. Dropping down on their bellies, they crawled the last few meters to the coiled concertina wire, which wasn't nearly as deeply emplaced as it should have been. Where there should have been two or three ranks of triple-strand wire, there was only a single coil, stretched out around the base.

At least Mashadov could be reasonably certain there wouldn't be mines. If it had been a Russian base, there would be.

Dudaev and Ismailov shoved their charges under the concertina wire. They'd brought poles to push them farther if need be, but with the Americans all either taking cover from the falling mortar rounds or focused on the machinegun nests higher up on the mountainside above them, they had been able to crawl right up to the wire. The charges slid underneath, and then they were reaching for the igniters.

***

Owens was trying to keep his head down as the mortars continued to rock the base, and machinegun fire hammered at the tops of the HESCOs to only a few feet away. *This is way worse than the last time. Fuck this place, man. Fuck the Army. Fuck all this noise.*

He never did know what made him turn back to the M240B mounted at the firing port. It was currently pointed away from the incoming fire, and there were plenty of pressing reasons to worry more about the actual falling mortar rounds than a possible—but so far invisible—threat outside the perimeter. But something prompted him to turn his attention back to his sector. Maybe it was simply the nagging worry that Merrill would somehow catch him out looking the wrong way.

He raised himself up just far enough to peer over the lip of the sandbagged plywood shack that served as a guard post. He remembered the movement he'd seen, or thought he'd seen, but figured that the attack was coming from off to the south. *Just a look, to cover my ass.*

But that look showed him two figures in the prone down by the wire, barely fifty yards outside the guard post.

*Oh, fuck.*

Owens might have been a shammer who hated his life, but he was still smart enough to know what was going on. The mortars and machinegun fire were just intended to keep their heads down. This wasn't simple harassing fire like the last couple of times they'd gotten rocketed.

While Owens might say that he wished he were dead about ten times a day, in reality, he really was attached to his own personal hide. He wanted to live to see the States again, not die in the middle of the night in fucking Paktika Province, Afghanistan.

Besides, American casualties in A-stan had been down to almost nothing for a couple of years. It would be embarrassing to be one of the first new ones.

"Contact!" he roared at Ortiz, while he grabbed the 240 and heaved it up, tucking the buttstock into his shoulder. Or he tried to roar. His voice cracked halfway through, and it was more of a cross between a scream and a squawk. But if his call was borderline incoherent and embarrassingly high-pitched, at least the stuttering roar of the gun as he slewed it to the side and opened fire on the two figures down by the wire got the message across.

Red tracers hammered into the dirt and the two men down on their bellies by the wire. The nearest IR chemlight swung wildly as bullets nipped through the concertina wire, and then was obscured by the cloud of dust kicked up by the long, thunderous burst of gunfire.

***

Mashadov flinched as the bullets chopped into Dudaev and Ismailov. They jerked and went limp. Dudaev might have tried to crawl backward, but quickly spasmed, the red tracers skipping into his body, and then he stretched out and went still, as the dust kicked up by the impacts clouded the two *shahidi*'s bodies.

Mashadov bit back the scream of hatred that he wanted to fling at the infidels. He had better than simply words to throw at them.

He signaled to Mokhmad Khizriev, off to his right. Khizriev rose up from behind his boulder, his RPG-26 already in his shoulder.

The *bang* of the PG round leaving its tube might have given away the true direction of the attack, except that another salvo of mortar rounds landed with a rippling roll of thunder at the same moment that the warhead slammed across the short gap and into the side of the guard post.

Owens hardly felt anything as the warhead vented its explosive fury on the interior of the guard post. There was a flash, a heavy *thud* that almost went unremarked in the cacophony of gunfire and explosions outside, and black smoke and dust billowed out of every opening before the plywood started to burn.

Then Mashadov and his fighters were up and moving.

He crossed to the bodies at the wire. Both men were dead; there was no way they could have survived almost point-blank machinegun fire. They had died *shahidi*, martyrs for the jihad. He would mourn them later.

Mashadov was more concerned with the breaching charges. They had wire cutters if they needed them, but the charges would be faster.

It took him a moment to realize that one of the dead men had pulled the igniter on his charge. Smoke was rising from the fuse.

"Back!" he screamed. "Get back!" His boots skidded on the grass and rocky soil as he spun around and almost fell in his haste to get away from the live charge. He got ten meters away and threw himself flat, covering his head with his hands.

Not everyone made it. One of his fighters was still too close when the breaching charge went off with a short flash and a loud *bang*, and went sprawling. He fell on his face and did not move.

Mashadov picked himself up and turned back toward the wall and the smoking gap in the wire, where rocks and dirt were still falling. With another roared, "*Allahu Akhbar!*" he surged to his feet and ran toward the HESCO barriers.

The Chechens flowed through the breach in the wire, firing from the hip and stitching bullets along the top of the double wall of HESCO barriers.

Then they were climbing the barriers, slinging rifles and grabbing the wire lip to pull themselves up, leaping down into the heart of the infidels' camp.

***

Staff Sergeant Merrill almost didn't realize what was happening until it was too late.

He'd heard the *boom* of the breaching charge going off, but it hadn't really registered as the mortars had kept howling down out of the night to slam into the south side of the FOB. Only when a bullet *snap*ped past his head, noticeably coming from the *east* did he figure out that something more was going on.

He turned in time to see dark figures piling over the wall on the east side, and smoke still pouring from the burning guard post. "Contact, east!" he bellowed, but his words were snatched away by the next salvo of mortar impacts, one round landing close enough to knock him off his feet.

More rounds *crack*ed overhead as fragmentation and debris pattered down on him. He rolled over and groped for his rifle in the dust and smoke, hardly noticing that his NVGs had been knocked away from his eyes. His fingers closed around the handguards and he dragged it to him, rolling onto his back and only then realizing that he couldn't see. Fortunately, his NVGs were still intact, and worked when he wrenched them back down in front of his eyes.

He got the tubes aligned just in time to see a figure looming over him. At first, he thought it might be another American; the high-cut helmet, night vision goggles, and streamlined gear, complete with integrated kneepads in the trousers. Only the Kalashnikov variant in the man's hands revealed that he wasn't an American.

Then the AK boomed, and Merrill saw nothing more, ever again.

# CHAPTER 2

"Dad, we need to talk."

John Brannigan looked up from his coffee cup and stared levelly at his son across the table. He wasn't particularly surprised or perturbed by the words; he'd known they were coming for a while.

Hank Brannigan had been out of the Marine Corps for about two months. He'd spent most of it up here, at his father's cabin, helping out where he could. He'd chopped wood, taken his turn at the cooking, and helped with several projects that Brannigan hadn't been able to get to, mostly on account of their needing a second pair of hands. Brannigan had welcomed his son and asked few questions. He knew what it was like, taking his first steps into the civilian world after the Marine Corps, and also knew that Hank hadn't parted with the military on necessarily the best of terms.

The younger man, lean and rangy, didn't look much like the Marine officer he'd been only a few months before. He'd let his hair and his beard both grow, though the latter was considerably scruffier. The elder Brannigan could easily have grown a bristling spade of a beard, but Hank had gotten his hair from his mother's side, and his maternal grandfather had gone clean shaven all his life for a reason.

Brannigan had a good idea that he knew what Hank wanted to talk about. It was a conversation that had been in abeyance since he'd gotten shot up on the Tourmaline-Delta platform. Hank had been a commissioned officer then, and while he'd guessed a few things, he hadn't wanted to put himself into the position of *knowing* that his old man was quite possibly running highly illegal mercenary operations in his retirement.

But Hank didn't work for Uncle Sam anymore, and from what Brannigan knew about his son's last tour, there was no putting off the conversation anymore.

"About what?" He cradled his coffee cup in his hands as he leaned on the hand-made table in the middle of the cabin's main room. The fire behind him crackled, though it wasn't that necessary, given the time of year.

Hank looked up at him with a furrowed brow, but Brannigan just watched him levelly. He had a pretty good idea where this was going, but he wasn't going to make it easy. He'd been in the business for too long.

Hank sighed when Brannigan didn't say anything more. "About work."

"Young man with your qualifications should be able to get all sorts of work." Brannigan took another sip of the scalding coffee. "Or are you asking about mine?"

"Yours."

Brannigan had to nod. At least Hank hadn't tried beating around the bush. That was good. John Brannigan had spent twenty-three years in the Marine Corps, a good chunk of that as an officer. He'd seen good officers and bad, and he'd seen the Marine Corps turn from emphasizing "leadership" to "management," resulting in an officer corps that he increasingly thought of as little more than politicians in uniform. He was glad that Hank hadn't picked up too many bad habits along those lines, though he was sure that there were some that had been unavoidable.

"What about it?"

"I know what you're doing." When Brannigan raised an eyebrow, Hank shrugged a little. "Okay, I don't know *details*. You've been too damned tight-lipped for that, and so has everyone else I know who might have any idea about where you're disappearing to every few months. But I've known the broad strokes ever since you wound up shot to shit a while back. I'm not blind. I *can* put two and two together. You're doing gunfighter work, somewhere. And I want in."

Brannigan just studied him coldly as he took another drink. "And why should I read you in?"

Hank blinked. "Why not? I'm a combat vet, I've been a platoon commander and a company XO. You said yourself that I could get all kinds of work with my background and credentials."

"You're still wet behind the ears to the crew I work with," Brannigan said bluntly. "Especially with all your experience being with shiny stuff on your collar."

"You were an officer," Hank protested. But when Brannigan just raised a sardonic eyebrow, he grimaced. "Yeah, I know."

He looked down at the table. "Truth is, I've been regretting taking that route for the last three years. Ever since my first platoon." At his father's sarcastic snort, he nodded, hanging his head a little. "I know, I know; you warned me. But I still hoped I could do better. I thought that I could leave the bullshit aside and actually *lead* like you taught me an officer is supposed to. But it doesn't really work that way, does it?"

"Not anymore." Brannigan kept his voice level, though some of the old resentment flared in his chest. He'd been where Hank was. Only he'd been fighting that uphill fight for a lot longer, until he'd finally lost.

Hank nodded again, tight-lipped. "Hell, they didn't even need me that much. My platoon sergeant could have run the platoon without me."

"Which is the whole point, and always has been." His father leaned back in his chair. "The platoon commander isn't there to *command*, son. He's there to learn from the squad leaders and platoon sergeant, so that he's not completely useless when he really *does* need to make decisions later on. Which is why I *told* you to enlist, first."

Hank slumped a little. He couldn't deny it; that had been something of a heated conversation at the time, with Rebecca trying to play peacemaker. Hank had finally insisted on going straight to OCS, and he had been quietly eating crow ever since.

"Fine. You're right. I'm not asking for a leadership position, anyway. I'm not *stupid*. I'll be a private, or whatever your equivalent is." He spread his hands. "What the hell else am I going to do, Dad? I got out because I was facing a three-year desk job if I stayed in. They were going to send me to a staff billet."

"As per." Brannigan was remorseless. "They aren't interested in what you want to do. They are concerned with the needs of the Corps, both kinetic and bureaucratic." He put the cup down and leaned back in his chair, folding his arms and staring his son down. "You weren't *planning* on joining up with my crew when you got out, were you?"

"Not precisely…okay, it was first on the list." Hank couldn't quite meet his father's eyes. "There were other possibilities, but I was really hoping…"

Brannigan sighed deeply. The truth was the small team of mercenaries that called itself Brannigan's Blackhearts probably *could* use another hand. They'd taken a beating over the last few missions. Don Hart had been killed in Chad, Sam Childress was still alive after being rescued from the Humanity Front, but would never fight again, Roger Hancock had been killed in Argentina, and he had no idea if Ignatius Kirk would be back after recovering from the sucking chest wound he'd taken on the same op. The team was getting a bit thin again.

And he knew that, despite their disagreement on OCS—which Hank seemed to have conceded, finally—he'd raised Hank well enough that he should at least be a dependable new guy. He might have picked up some bad habits that needed correcting, but Brannigan was confident that Santelli and Wade, at the least, would gladly square him away.

On the other hand, he had to face the fact that he really wasn't entirely comfortable with having his own flesh and blood going out with them. Not that he was worried about favoritism; he knew that Hank wasn't, either. He'd be *harder* on Hank than on any of the others, and not just because he was his son. Hank had more to prove and less experience, which made him something of a liability. A relative liability, perhaps, but a liability, nonetheless.

No, it was something much more primal than that. John Brannigan wasn't worried about risking his own hide out there. It was something he'd been doing for the better part of three decades by then. And with Rebecca gone and Hank full-grown, if he bought the farm, he wasn't too worried about it.

But Hank was his son, his only remaining family. Yes, he'd been in combat. Yes, he was a grown man and could make his own decisions. But if he went down on a mission with the Blackhearts, if Brannigan had to bury his own son because he'd led him to his death…

Before he could make a decision either way, the phone rang.

He turned a baleful eye on the infernal device. He'd moved up into the hills after Rebecca's death because he really didn't feel the desire to be a part of the modern world any longer. Only Hector Chavez's appeal, which had led to the job on Khadarkh, had brought him back in any capacity. Unfortunately, that had included getting a cell phone again. It didn't work all that well that far back into the boondocks, but his "business partners" had ensured that a repeater had been installed that meant he got signal. Only a handful of people had the number, but that was enough.

He scooped it up. "Yeah."

"We need to meet." Mark Van Zandt didn't comment on Brannigan's brusqueness. Van Zandt was used to it; neither man could be said to really like the other, though they had managed to put bygones in the past and develop a solid professional relationship. Van Zandt had been Brannigan's superior officer once upon a time, and had, in fact, been the one to supervise his forcible retirement. Now both of them were technically in the "private sector," though still doing much the same thing, if in a much more shadowy and riskier sort of way.

"Understood." It was just about that time, anyway. Brannigan had developed something of a sixth sense for when work was going to be coming their way. This had been one of the longest stretches yet between missions, but there was enough chaos out in the world that the Blackhearts particular services were usually in some demand. "The usual place?"

"Negative," Van Zandt replied. "We've got some other factors in play. Meet us at Kowacs' Bar and Grill in Alexandria, Thursday night at seven."

Brannigan grimaced. Alexandria, Virginia was not exactly his favorite stomping ground. For one thing, it was far, *far* too close to the Beltway. But the job was the job, and he'd been enjoying life in the mountains for several months. It was time to pay his dues.

*Someday I'll* actually *retire.*

"Understood. I'll be there."

"See you then." Without any further pleasantries, Van Zandt hung up.

"That sounded like a job." Hank made the observation quietly, almost hesitantly. At least he wasn't too eager or wheedling. Not that his father would have ever tolerated wheedling when he'd been a kid, never mind as a grown man and a former Marine officer.

"Maybe." Brannigan dropped the phone back on the table. He took a deep breath, eyeing his son. "I'm not going to make a decision on this right now. I've got to go get on a plane. I'll run it past Carlo and Joe. We'll make the decision together, before you go anywhere with us."

"What about Roger?" The question alone told Brannigan that Hank had figured out a lot. But not everything.

"Roger's dead, Hank."

The words were like a bomb dropping on the room. Hank stared at him for a moment, then swallowed, hard. He'd known Hancock as a kid; Roger Hancock had been one of Brannigan's platoon sergeants when he'd been a company commander, and they'd been friends even back then. To hear that one of his heroes had been killed, and he had never heard a word about it, was a shock.

"That's the life, son," Brannigan said quietly. "No big funeral, no obituary, sometimes no grave for family and friends to put flowers on. Just one day you're there, the next, you just don't come back. You disappear into a shallow grave in some foreign hellhole, where nobody except us will ever know. Roger wasn't the first, either."

Hank stared down at the table for a moment, processing it. "Who else?"

Brannigan stood up. "*If* Carlo and Joe decide you should come on board, then we'll talk about it. Right now, I've got to get a flight east."

***

Kowacs' Bar and Grill was about what he'd expected. Being in Alexandria, it was quite a bit more upscale than he would have considered standard for a "bar and grill," but there weren't many country sort of places in northern Virginia, and those that were tended to be kitschy and forced. He was just as glad that Van

Zandt hadn't wanted to meet in what he'd consider a high-class restaurant. Booths and tables were softly lit by hanging frosted chandeliers, the shadows made somewhat darker by the dark walnut and the even darker rugs underfoot.

He was dressed in simple business casual, but he still stood out. At six foot four and well over two hundred pounds of muscle, not to mention his salt-and-pepper hair and handlebar mustache, he filled the button-up shirt in a way that most men in the area didn't. He could feel the glances from men and women alike as he walked toward the back, where Van Zandt was waiting.

Four people were already waiting in the booth at the back. Van Zandt and Chavez were familiar faces, Van Zandt still trim, clean-shaven, and wearing a jacket and tie. Chavez was a little more rotund, his hairline still receding, and dressed similarly. Chavez had been a hell of a Marine officer before his heart had betrayed him, and he would have made a better general than Van Zandt, in Brannigan's opinion.

Behind Van Zandt, Brannigan saw a face less familiar, but one he'd met before. Clayton Abernathy was somewhere in his seventies, if he was gauging the man's age right, though his steely eyes were still bright and missed nothing. He didn't know exactly what Abernathy's deal was; he clearly had resources and his finger on the pulse of global events. Whether he was working within the intelligence community or on more of a "private" basis, Brannigan had not been able to figure out, and Abernathy himself had been remarkably close-mouthed about it on the few times they'd met.

The fourth man was considerably younger than the other three. Brannigan had never seen him before. He was dressed in similar business casual but was considerably softer in appearance than the other three. He also didn't look particularly comfortable.

Brannigan pulled a chair away from a nearby table and swung it around to the end of the booth before sitting down. He didn't exactly have his back to the wall, but he was sideways to the door, and could see most of the rest of one side of the restaurant. And he trusted Hector, at least, to be watching the rest.

"Okay, Mark," he said, with a nod to Abernathy and Chavez, who both returned it gravely, "what's the job?"

"You need to see this first." Van Zandt motioned to the younger man across the table. The newcomer looked uncertain, sizing Brannigan up, but when Abernathy shot him a hard look, he pulled a tablet out of the attaché case next to him, unlocked it, tapped a couple of icons, and slid it across to Brannigan.

Brannigan picked it up, seeing that the young man had brought up a video. With a glance at Abernathy and Van Zandt, who were both watching him with stony faces, he shrugged and pressed "Play."

The sound was turned down, and he didn't recognize the emblem that came up on the screen, but it clearly belonged to some Islamist group. A crossed sword and Kalashnikov were cradled in a crescent moon, with Arabic writing around them. Then the picture shifted to a night-vision image of what looked an awful lot like a Coalition FOB under assault.

Tracers zipped across the screen and muzzle flashes flickered in the dark. A series of explosions lit the night, noticeably *inside* the FOB's perimeter. Something was burning fiercely, lighting up the walls from within under a billowing plume of smoke.

Subtitles appeared underneath. Brannigan only skimmed them. He already knew the rough outline of what they would say. *Punishing the infidels...Allah's will...blah, blah, etc., etc.*

He looked up at Van Zandt and Abernathy. "Where and how bad?"

"Paktika," Abernathy said flatly. "And it was pretty bad. Not as bad as *Aswad al Islam* is trying to make it sound, but they still managed to kill about sixty men and women before they were driven off by danger close airstrikes out of Bagram. They still did enough damage that the FOB had to be abandoned. Which was the whole point, anyway, if we're taking Chechen Islamist propaganda at face value."

"These were Chechens?" Brannigan asked, looking down at the screen. He squinted. One of the assaulters looked awfully well-equipped.

"Most of *Aswad al Islam* is." The young man's voice was high-pitched and nasal. Brannigan couldn't help but think that it fit his appearance. "They're followers of Abu Mokhtar al Shishani."

"You said that name as if I'm supposed to know who it is." Brannigan fixed him with an icy stare. "I have a hard time keeping track of all the *kunyahs* floating around the jihadi world."

"He's the newest up-and-coming Chechen Salafist warlord." Van Zandt stepped in before the young man could get over his hesitation. "He came out of nowhere a couple of years ago, and since then, he's led some of the nastiest attacks against Russian interests inside and outside of Chechnya. He's on the edge of becoming the next Osama Bin Laden, and rumor has it that that's exactly his goal.

"Nobody knows for sure how large *Aswad al Islam* really is. What we do know is that they've got some serious resources, and that nothing recruits like success. If the indicators we've been getting are accurate, it looks like they could supplant Al Qaeda like ISIS never managed to. And now they've openly declared war on the US." He pointed to the tablet. "That was the opening salvo. I know you skimmed the propaganda, but at the end, they promise more to come."

"And that's what has Washington and Moscow talking." The young man leaned forward on his elbows on the table, apparently getting over some of his trepidation at being surrounded by so many older, more experienced men. "This group has spread like wildfire, and now the Russians are desperate enough that they're willing to work with us to try to counter them."

"They must be almighty desperate for that to happen," Brannigan muttered.

"They are," Abernathy said. "And if our intel is accurate, we know why."

"We have reliable reports that there are anywhere from four to five Russian 'suitcase nukes' in the wind somewhere in Central Asia. And the same reporting suggests that they are heading for Chechnya and Abu Mokhtar al Shishani's people." Brannigan had already pegged the younger man as an intel weenie, and the way he said it only confirmed his assessment.

"Great." Brannigan looked from Van Zandt to Chavez. "So, this is a nuke hunt?"

"Not quite." Van Zandt's face was immobile, but he was clearly a bit uncomfortable.

As Brannigan turned narrowed eyes on his former superior, now facilitator, Abernathy spoke up. "My boys are going after the nukes. If you're up to it, you guys get the dicier mission."

"What dicier mission?"

"As Mr. Grundy said," Van Zandt said, "Abu Mokhtar is unusually well-funded. He's been able to buy a lot of success lately. Word is that he's got a lot of the local authorities in the Caucasus and most of his other operational areas bought and paid for. Furthermore, as you probably saw in the video, his fighters are *extremely* well-equipped for jihadis. Nobody knows for sure how much he's worth, but he's got *very* deep pockets.

"The Russians have fingered one of his cash stores, in Azerbaijan. And they want our help to go get it."

"Why?" Brannigan leaned back in his chair. It creaked as he folded his arms across his chest. "It's in their backyard. Or are they finally admitting that their military is barely on the level of the US National Guard?"

"They're selling it as a gesture of détente." Abernathy's tone said just what he thought about that. "Though I think they want to bring us in mainly so that the finger isn't pointed at them if a Russian nuke goes off. 'Hey, we tried, and you know we tried.'" He spread his hands. "Certain people think this is an opportunity, not only to put the hurt on some terrorists, but also to get some inside information on Russian ops.

"However, some of those same people really don't like the idea of US SOF working in Azerbaijan with only Russian support."

"Which is where we come in." Brannigan let his voice turn grim, his expression getting slightly thunderous. "We're deniable, and therefore expendable."

"Not so much," Abernathy said, before Van Zandt could interject. "There *will* be assets in Georgia on alert, ready to pull you out if things get too pear-shaped."

Brannigan stroked his mustache as he thought about it. It wasn't quite the longest odds he'd ever faced; after all, they'd had *zero* backup on Khadarkh. But it was still one hell of a risk.

On the other hand, risk was what the Blackhearts thrived on, and there hadn't been work for months. The Humanity Front had gone quiet; even their 'legitimate' business was scaled back, and from what he'd been hearing, they'd done a fantastic job of compartmentalizing their terror campaign from the rest of it. Money laundering works, sometimes.

"Let me run this by the boys," he said. "I think we've been on the bench long enough that we'll probably go for it, as long as we've got a way out. Hurting terrorists is hurting terrorists, even if we've got to be buddy-buddy with some Russki thugs to do it. But I'll warn you; the bill's going to be steep."

Van Zandt looked slightly pained. The kid Abernathy had called Grundy frowned, as if just then realizing that this was mercenary work he was involved with. Abernathy's eyes crinkled knowingly. And Hector Chavez, who hadn't said a word, just looked at Van Zandt and smiled tightly as if to say, *I told you.*

Brannigan looked over as Abernathy waved the waiter over. He was hungry. The call could wait until *after* dinner.

# CHAPTER 3

Carlo Santelli straightened up, wiping his hands on a rag, and eyed his handiwork with some satisfaction.

It had taken a lot to get this particular specimen finished. Finding parts for a '67 Fury III had proved to be more difficult than he'd expected, but it had been worth it, especially since he already had a buyer for this particular car. And the man was eager enough for it that the price tag was going to more than pay for the parts, never mind the paint job.

He nodded with a sigh. This little side business had been working out better than he'd ever expected.

He'd needed to do something. It had been months since the Argentina mission, and while he and Melissa weren't exactly hurting for money yet, he'd needed to keep his hands and his mind occupied. And not just because he missed the action.

If he was being honest, he wasn't sure how much he really did miss the action, right then. He missed Roger Hancock more.

Roger had been short-tempered and volatile, but he'd been one hell of a professional soldier. He'd been one of the pillars of Brannigan's Blackhearts. And only after his death did Carlo Santelli realize just how much they'd all depended on him.

Because now that Roger was dead, Carlo was the next in the chain of command. And he wasn't sure he was up to the task.

It wasn't that he doubted his capabilities. He'd made Sergeant Major in the Marine Corps and had done the job well for several years. He'd been Brannigan's Sergeant Major, once upon a time, and that was why he'd been brought in in the first place. He had been one of the few men of his rank that the Colonel had trusted implicitly.

But command was another matter. He was getting older, and he was *comfortable* with the Sgt Major role. It was a support role. He had to worry about the men, their welfare, supply, and discipline. He didn't have to make the big decisions. He didn't have to be the one who made a call that might get another Blackheart killed. He just had to expedite and execute.

But if he was the second in command, he knew that that time when he was in charge of the whole team might come. It had already come for Roger once, when Brannigan had gotten shot up on the Tourmaline Delta platform. It was almost less a matter of "if" and more a matter of "when."

He didn't want a command. And he was dreading the call to go back out. Because if there was any lesson to be taken from the last several jobs the Blackhearts had taken, it was that any one of them could get his ticket punched at any time.

The door opened and Melissa stepped out into the garage, with Carlo Jr. on her hip. The little guy was growing fast, and he was already crawling around as fast as he could go, but she didn't want him scrambling all over his father's garage. "All done, baby?" she asked.

"All done," he said. "Now I've gotta give Kramer a call." He finished wiping his hands and tossed the rag on the workbench.

He was reaching for the phone when it rang. He hesitated, just for a moment, a bolt of adrenaline going through him. He could feel Melissa's eyes on him as he picked up the phone.

It was Brannigan. He hesitated a moment more, then hit "Accept" and lifted the phone to his ear.

"Yes, sir." He was proud that while his Boston accent might be as thick as ever, his voice was steady.

"We've got a potential job, Carlo," Brannigan said. "No details over the phone, as per, but start getting the word out."

Santelli didn't think he'd hesitated that much, but Brannigan caught something. Maybe he'd let out a breath a little louder than he'd intended.

"What is it, Carlo?" When he didn't answer right away, Brannigan pressed. "If something's wrong, you need to let me know. I need you, Carlo."

Santelli did sigh, then. He looked up at Melissa, who was watching him with concern in her eyes. But at the same time, he could see that she'd stand by him. How far they had come since just before Khadarkh, when he'd thought that their relationship was almost over. And he realized that he had Brannigan and the Blackhearts, in no small measure, to thank for that.

*And those words are my kryptonite.* I need you, Carlo. *He's got to know that I can't walk away now.* A lesser man would resent Brannigan for it. Santelli had known the Colonel for too long, though; he knew that that kind of petty manipulation was beneath him. He hadn't said that to pluck at Santelli's heartstrings and drag him along. He'd said it because he valued Santelli's work, as well as his friendship, and he was worried that something was wrong.

"No, I'm fine, sir. I'll start making calls."

***

Joe Flanagan wasn't comfortable. Social occasions were not comfortable places for him, and so he was leaning against the wall, a cup of coffee in his hand, watching the gathering.

Tall, rangy, with black hair and a thick but neatly-trimmed beard to match, he didn't exactly fit in with a lot of the people there. Most of them were Rachel's friends, after all. Few of his own, few as they were, would be coming to a pre-wedding party. He was only there because Rachel had begged him to come; she hadn't been the one to put it on, and she hadn't wanted to be there by herself.

Of course, she'd also had an ulterior motive, which was why she'd insisted that he had to invite Kevin Curtis.

Curtis was ordinarily the kind of man who would have been ecstatic at a gathering like this. A party with a three-to-one female-to-male ratio would be prime hunting territory to a tomcat like Curtis. But given that most of the women were, in fact, Rachel's friends, and therefore not particularly interested in…short-term liaisons…

Curtis walked over, a beer in his hand, and found a spot next to Flanagan. The two of them could not have looked more different. Flanagan was tall, rangy, and tanned, with dark hair and beard and piercing gray eyes. Curtis was over a foot shorter, with close-cropped hair and ebony skin. Flanagan was muscular, in a country boy, fighter sort of way, but Curtis was a bodybuilder, and probably weighed close to what his much taller friend did. "Man, this is *not* my usual play. You're lucky I like you, Joe."

Flanagan glanced at the beer. "Where did you even find that? There's no bar here."

"And that's another problem," Curtis said, waving the bottle to encompass the room. "Why is there no bar? What kind of social occasion doesn't have a bar?"

"In this case, a pre-wedding party," Flanagan said dryly, "intended to give the families a chance to get acquainted before the wedding."

Curtis frowned as he looked around. "Where's your family?"

Flanagan didn't look at him, but just took a sip of his coffee. "Don't have much anymore, Kev."

Curtis leaned back slightly and stared at him. "You mean I'm it? That's kinda sad, Joe."

Flanagan snorted. "You're telling me."

"Now wait a minute…" But a slow smile was starting to spread across Flanagan's bearded features. Curtis shook a finger at Flanagan. "Don't you turn that around on me like that! I am the best friend you ever had!"

"That's debatable." Flanagan still didn't look at Curtis, but he could still see his friend getting heated. His faint grin made his eyes crinkle as he took another drink. "I seem to recall all sorts of bar fights, late night rescues, and even almost getting stabbed by an irate Latina chick…"

"Details!" Curtis shot back. "Good friends go through tough things together!"

Flanagan looked down at him with a raised eyebrow. "Except that I don't recall ever being the *cause* of any of those tough times."

Curtis looked away, his face screwed up into a grimace, with a harrumph. "Well, you're sure the cause of this particular tough time," he muttered.

Flanagan openly chuckled at that. "You're in a room that's got way more women than men. Explain to me how that constitutes 'tough times,' oh Great Ladies' Man."

Curtis looked around the room with what might have been a look of discomfort and trepidation. "These aren't my kind of ladies, man." His voice was hushed. "Every one I've talked to has been…"

"Strangely wholesome?" Flanagan struggled to keep his expression bland and innocent. "Interested in something long-term, maybe marriage?"

Curtis stared at him in horror. "You knew about this?"

"Of course I friggin' knew about it, dumbass. It was Rachel's idea."

"You…you'd do this to me?!" Curtis' voice was starting to rise.

Flanagan leaned in, his grin turning wolfish. "Rachel thought that introducing you to some women who might be better for you than stabby Latina chicks might start you on the road to growing up and keeping out of trouble. Me?" He chuckled. "I just wanted to watch what happened."

Curtis huffed, taking a long swig of his beer. "You are a bad friend, Joseph."

Flanagan glared down at him with a raised eyebrow, and he winced. "Okay, I deserved that."

"What is this? Humility from Kevin Curtis?" Flanagan's glower eased and he downed the last of his coffee. "There might be hope for you yet."

He had to admit, though, that right then he felt more kinship with his shorter companion than he might have thought, in that environment. Rachel's family had pulled out all the stops, and there were probably a couple of hundred relations and friends of the family there. Far more people than he was usually used to or comfortable being around. And as he looked at the generally well-dressed, fresh-faced, slightly soft people chatting and mingling, all but ignoring him and Curtis where they leaned against the wall in the corner, he couldn't help but compare them to his teammates. There was a gulf between him and these people that he wasn't sure could ever be bridged.

Yes, his friends were rough men, and not always all that emotionally mature, as exemplified by his gambling, womanizing "brother from another mother" next to him. But they had seen things, gone through hardships together, that most of these people could barely imagine.

He caught Rachel watching the two of them, concern on her face. He gave her a faint smile, trying to reassure her that everything was fine. She returned it, with a touch of sadness. They'd talked about this, and she'd been so hopeful that he could mix with the rest of her family, not to mention her idea about trying to introduce Curtis to a woman who would be better for him than the booty calls he usually hung out with.

But sometimes the gulf is simply too wide to cross all at once. And Flanagan and Curtis had been on the other side of that gulf for a long time.

His phone suddenly vibrated in his pocket. Setting down his coffee cup, he pulled it out.

Curtis was looking over at him, his demeanor suddenly changed. “Who is it?” He sounded almost hopeful.

“It’s the Colonel,” Flanagan confirmed, as he started toward the exit.

“We’re saved!” Curtis exclaimed, looking up at the ceiling. “Thank you!”

Rachel watched the two men leave, her fiancé with his phone to his ear. Her eyes might have misted briefly, but then she turned back to her cousin, forcing a smile onto her face.

***

John Wade wasn’t sure whether he should be annoyed at the crowd of fat, useless people he was weaving his way through, or thoroughly appreciative of the cosplayer girls who were, in many cases, wearing next to nothing.

In the interests of not losing his mind and going completely postal, he decided that ogling the almost-naked girls was a much better option.

*Besides, I’ve got a hell of a good chance of getting laid, given the quality of the opposition here.*

Of course, he wasn’t at Max-Con for the people. Nor was Vincent Bianco, who had talked him into coming. Not that he’d had to talk too hard, after he’d shown Wade the score of Silver Age comics that he’d gotten there the year prior for a steal.

John Wade was a retired Ranger, and, anyone would agree, a hardass and intimidating as hell. Tall, fit, clean-shaven and with an icy blue stare that most people—even in the profession of applied violence—often found disconcerting. He was also a huge comic book nerd and collector, among other things.

He was pretty sure his collection was sitting at well over a million dollars' worth. But there were still a lot of issues he wanted to get.

And that was just the comics. Action figures were a whole different ballgame.

Vinnie Bianco didn't stand out quite as much in the con-goer crowd as Wade did, though that was really a relative sort of thing. Bianco stood even taller than Wade, and while he just looked big without being jacked, he was still packing a lot more muscle than most of the weebs and neckbeards that Wade was watching with distaste. His considerably younger-looking baby face and friendly manner, however, was far less stark than Wade's bristling demeanor and "fuck off" glare.

Bianco had found something; Wade saw him stop, towering over most of the people around him, bending down over a booth about another hundred yards ahead. Wade started working his way over, weaving between a pair of young men arguing over what he could only assume were anime characters—the names sounded Japanese, but Wade couldn't care less about most anime—and almost ran into one of the scantily-dressed cosplayers, who was getting a picture taken with a doughy, pale young man who looked like he wasn't sure whether to be excited or to faint at being that close to an attractive young woman in a state of undress.

The woman looked up at him in momentary annoyance, but that changed as she got a better look. The pudgy fan momentarily forgotten, she swiveled her head to follow him as he went by. He locked eyes with her and smiled, getting a dazzlingly sexy smile in return. The pale kid who was trying to put an arm around her without getting smacked looked like he was about to object until Wade pinned him with a basilisk stare that had given superior officers pause. The kid might have been living in a fantasy world most of the time, but he was still grounded enough to know not to fuck with the big guy giving him that look.

He winked at the cosplay girl, and turned back to join Bianco, who hadn't seen any of the byplay. Sure, he could have pushed things, probably even scored with her, but Wade was experienced enough with women not to press his luck under those circumstances. He'd planted the seed; if she was interested, he'd see her again. Most women he'd seen doing that sort of cosplay had been understandably standoffish, which was the other reason he wasn't going to overtly hit on her. *Got to play the right game.*

"What'd you find, Vinnie?" He didn't like raising his voice to be heard, but the dull roar of the crowds at the convention made it necessary.

Bianco grimaced, eyeing the plastic-wrapped issues laid out on the table. "Not what I was hoping for. This is all late 2010s stuff. It's crap."

Wade scanned the table. "Yeah, I don't see anything I'd even be interested in, much less anything I'm looking for."

"And what are you looking for?" Wade turned to find the girl he'd almost collided with at his elbow. She was looking up at him with her arms folded under her barely-covered breasts, her mouth quirked in a smile.

*Jackpot. That was even quicker than I expected.*

But before he could take advantage of the opening, he felt his phone vibrate in his pocket.

Not many people had his number. And those who did weren't likely to be calling him just to chat.

He held up a finger for the girl to give him a moment and dug the phone out. It was Brannigan.

He thumped Bianco on the shoulder and showed him the phone, then turned to the girl. "Sorry," he said. "As much as I'd love to continue this conversation, work just called. But I'd be more than happy to call you when I get back..."

She smiled again and reached for his phone. He handed it over. He'd call Brannigan back.

# CHAPTER 4

"How'd you even find out about this?" Santelli eyed the small studio from across the street warily.

"The dumbass tried to recruit me." There was wry contempt in Mario Gomez's voice. Which was more than Gomez usually expressed; he was a quiet man, and rarely spoke, much less showed much emotion. "I guess he thought the quiet guy would make a good wingman, or something."

Santelli shook his head, frustrated. Even so, this was more the kind of problem he was used to as a Senior NCO. This was the sort of thing he'd wrestled with for years as a First Sergeant, and later as a Sergeant Major.

"Well, let's go corral our wayward prodigal." He wasn't sure if he was using that combination of words right, but it sounded right. Santelli knew he wasn't the most eloquent or well-read of the Blackhearts, but like most men of his background, he tried.

At least he had never flubbed things to the level of one First Sergeant he'd known, back when he'd been a Corporal himself, who had tended to say, "It would be the who of you," when he'd meant to say, "It would behoove you."

Of course, if he'd messed it up, Gomez wouldn't say. Which was simultaneously a comfort and a source of irritation. Santelli could never quite read Gomez. The most he'd ever seen the man open up had been when most of his immediate family had been murdered, and even then, it had been a mostly quiet, cold rage.

That quiet, cold rage had led the Blackhearts south of the border, where they'd slaughtered most of an entire upstart cartel in the process of rescuing Gomez's sister. The half-Apache former Recon Marine had been grateful, but as always in his wordless, cool way, his black eyes as unreadable as ever.

What bugged Santelli about him was that he'd known Marines who acted much like him, who had been perennial discipline problems, mainly because they held pretty much everyone around them in contempt. Many of them had been Hispanic, too. It was part of the *machismo* that suffused the Hispanic culture, especially the Mexican one. Now, Gomez wasn't Mexican. He was half Tex-Mex, half Mescalero Apache. And he'd never been a discipline problem, so far as Santelli knew.

Maybe it was the Apache part that raised Santelli's hackles. He didn't know. Joe Flanagan was almost as quiet as Gomez, most of the time, and didn't have the same effect. But Joe didn't have that air of a predator lying in wait all the time. Gomez did.

Santelli shook his reverie off as he got out of the rental car. He hadn't wanted to use a taxi for this, and Gomez had been entirely willing to throw in for the rental when he flew up from New Mexico. After their phone call, Gomez had been more than willing to come along.

Together, the two men, Gomez standing a head taller than the slightly rotund, balding former Sergeant Major, walked across the street to the studio.

George Jenkins had pulled out all the stops. The sign for "Dynamic Defense Concepts" had been professionally painted on the glass doors, along with the SEAL trident right below it. As they walked in, the lobby looked professional enough, with a reception desk—currently unoccupied—plants tastefully arranged on the counter and the floor, and all sorts of the kind of posters and notices one might expect from a professional dojo.

He'd dropped a pretty penny on this operation. Unfortunately, if what Gomez had said was true, all with ulterior motives that were getting Santelli pissed off all over again.

The two of them walked right past the reception desk and pushed through the doors that led back into the dojo proper. The single large room was equipped with a full-coverage martial arts mat, several striking dummies, stacks of kick pads and foam and rubber weapons, and a full wall of mirrors. Two doors on the far side bore men's and women's locker room signs.

The mats were currently occupied by about a dozen women, ranging from their early twenties to a couple who looked to be very fit fifty-somethings. Jenkins was at the front, running them through some very, *very* basic defensive moves. He was dressed in track pants and a skintight brown t-shirt, his sandy hair longer than the last time Santelli had seen him.

He saw the two men come in and faltered for just a moment. Santelli's lips thinned. Jenkins had never been good at disguising his emotions. He'd been caught, and he knew it.

Gomez took up station by the door, leaning against the wall with his arms folded. Being Gomez, he was almost guaranteed to be strapped, probably with that CZ P01 he tended to favor, regardless of the fact that they were in Colorado Springs, and there was no way that Gomez had a Colorado concealed carry permit. Again, being Gomez, he wouldn't give a damn.

He wouldn't need a weapon for this. But Gomez was always prepared.

Santelli planted himself in front of the door, his meaty arms folded, watching Jenkins. The younger man was noticeably more self-conscious as he continued to run the women through the drills, and several of his students were also distracted, casting glances over their shoulders at the two men standing silently and ominously by the door. The fact that Jenkins was obviously trying to ignore them only made the discomfort of the situation that much more acute.

Finally, as it neared the bottom of the hour, Jenkins stopped, looking at the clock. More of the women seemed puzzled; he hadn't moved from his position at the head of the dojo since the two Blackhearts had come in. Santelli was pretty sure he knew why, based on what Gomez had told him.

"Okay," Jenkins said. "I'm afraid I'm going to have to cut it a few minutes short this week, but we'll try to make up for it next week. I'll see you then; I've got to go here soon."

Gomez didn't make a sound, but Santelli snorted, drawing several curious glances. Most of the older women in the crowd could obviously tell something was wrong; the one with undyed, salt-and-pepper hair was watching carefully, her gaze moving from Santelli to Jenkins, her brow furrowed. She was evidently putting some pieces together.

Of course, she might be putting the *wrong* pieces together. Santelli knew he often resembled a Mafia goon more than a professional soldier. His callsign *was* "Guido," after all.

The rest of the class started packing up and heading for the exits. Santelli was tempted to call Jenkins out right then and there, but he refrained. "Praise in public, correct in private" had long been a mantra of his, and he wasn't going to put that aside now, no matter how much Jenkins' attitude often made him want to put the man on blast in front of the whole world.

Jenkins wasn't a bad soldier, not really. He just wasn't nearly as good as he thought he was, and his status as a former SEAL didn't mean he could get away with as much as he thought he could, either.

The women in the class filed out past Santelli, who didn't move, casting curious glances at him. A few tried to approach

Jenkins, but he waved them off, as he was obviously simultaneously trying to watch Santelli and Gomez while avoiding eye contact.

They waited until after the last of the women had left. That happened to be the graying older woman, who had paused as she passed Santelli, studying him long enough that Santelli had greeted her politely. Only after the door shut behind her did the two of them start to cross the floor to where Jenkins was fiddling with a stack of kick pads, trying to look busy.

"Have we got a job?" he asked, still not looking either man in the eye.

"Yeah, we do," Santelli said. "Which is the only reason I'm not conducting some wall-to-wall counseling right now."

"I don't know what you're talking about, Carlo." Jenkins stood up and turned to face him, clearly trying to get some of his bluster back.

"*Sure,* you don't," Santelli sneered. "Which is why you got nervous as soon as we walked in, dismissed the class early, and didn't try to keep any of the hotter young chickies back for some 'special training.' Am I about on course?"

Jenkins tried to look surprised and offended, but Santelli had faced enough junior enlisted in trouble to know when he'd scored. "Drop the act, George. I know what you've been up to with this little studio. Gomez told me. Now, as long as you're actually training them, I suppose it's not technically *illegal* to be using your martial arts/self-defense classes as your own personal dating service, but it's sure unethical as hell. And if we didn't need you for a job, I'd break both your legs and let you try to pay the rent on this place from a fucking wheelchair."

Jenkins didn't seem to have an answer to that. He knew Santelli well enough to know that there would be no good answer, and that the thickening of an already thick Bostonian accent was not a good sign. In a previous life, Santelli probably would have just thrashed him, taking him out to the woodline and making him do pushups, jumping jacks, flutter kicks, and eight-count bodybuilders over and over and over until he puked or just collapsed in a puddle of his own sweat. Now?

These days, Jenkins could have no doubt that Santelli would follow through on his threat of grievous bodily harm.

"Now, pack your shit and be out to the usual place by tomorrow evening," Santelli snapped. "I'd suggest you close this place up and get on it, before I decide we don't need you that bad." He turned on his heel and started to leave. Gomez stayed where he was, his arms still folded, watching Jenkins with those cold, black eyes of his.

Santelli paused at the door. "Oh, and Jenkins?" He looked back over his shoulder to see the former SEAL still standing there, looking a bit shell-shocked. He was not the best-liked of the Blackhearts, and this wasn't going to help anything. Oh, Curtis might give him a high-five, and Javakhishvili would probably just shrug. Even Wade might, except Wade already detested Jenkins. "I'm not going to make you close this place down, but let me find out that you're picking up your students again and I'll fly out here from Boston and kick your ass. *Capisce?*"

Jenkins just nodded jerkily. Another man in his position, and with his demonstrated attitude, might have gotten pissed and tried to bow up or otherwise get defiant. Jenkins, however, had seen Santelli in action, and knew where he stood with the Blackhearts. He'd overstepped himself, he knew it, and he was regretting it.

If he hadn't been so pissed, Santelli could almost have pitied him. Jenkins was That Guy. He was the guy who never could quite seem to do the right thing.

But right then, as he left "Dynamic Defense Concepts" behind, he couldn't quite find it in him to feel pity for the little scumbag.

***

Tom Burgess was playing cards with a skinny, sour-faced old man named Barry in the front room when Brannigan came up the steps. Burgess, tall and rangy, with his long, still-dark hair drawn back in a ponytail behind his neck, stood up as Brannigan walked in. Barry started to do the same.

"Sit down, Master Guns." Brannigan waved him back down. "You shouldn't be standing up for me."

"Force of habit, Colonel." Barry gave him a wrinkled grin. "After all, it ain't every squad leader who gets to see one of his boots become a battalion commander."

Burgess' eyebrows rose. Even having been a part of Brannigan's Blackhearts for a little while, he'd still only been on two jobs, only one of them overseas, so he was still getting to know all there was to know about his new teammates. And Barry hadn't been all that forthcoming about the past, being far more interested in playing Spades.

In retrospect, it made some sense that Brannigan and several of the Old Fogies would know each other. After all, the Old Fogies were Ben Drake's network, and Brannigan had known Ben Drake from his early days in the Marine Corps. They were all retirees, most of them old Staff and Senior NCOs, too old to go running and gunning—much, anyway; several of them had reaped their share of souls when Burgess had gone along with Roger Hancock, Mario Gomez, Carlo Santelli, "Herc" Javakhishvili, and Ignatius Kirk to rescue Sam Childress from the mercenaries who had snatched him out of the hospital on behalf of the Humanity Front.

The fact that he was there playing cards with Barry was a direct result of that rescue mission. And the state of several of those involved was a sobering thought.

Roger Hancock was dead. Kirk had just gotten out of his third surgery for the sucking chest wound he'd taken in the Argentina job. And Sam…

Burgess hadn't known Childress before the rescue. And it was looking more and more like he never would; at least, he'd never know the man he'd been before he'd been shot in the spine in Transnistria.

"Is Sam awake?" Brannigan asked quietly.

Burgess nodded. "Herc's with him. Barry and I were on front door duty."

Brannigan nodded, visibly steeling himself before walking into the back rooms.

The house looked like a regular farmhouse on the outside, and even in the living room and kitchen. Only once a visitor got into the back rooms did its real purpose become evident—the farm had been converted into a secret hospital, well-equipped and staffed, effectively a black site for certain men who had been wounded in combat somewhere that American combatants weren't supposed to be.

Burgess followed Brannigan toward the back as another of the Old Fogies, a burly man named Fred, who had been on the rescue op, came in from outside to join Barry. The Old Fogies had been running pretty continuous security on the hospital since Childress had been brought in, in no small part due to the fact that their guardianship in the civilian hospital where he'd been after Transnistria had been penetrated by the killers who had been sent after the stricken Blackheart. These old men were the kind who took such things personally.

Childress was sitting up a little, propped up by pillows and the tilt of the bed itself, when they came in. Paralyzed from the waist down, he couldn't easily sit up under his own power. He'd briefly taken over as the Blackhearts remote intel specialist, rapidly teaching himself a lot of the cyber stuff on the fly. But that had been before he'd been snatched.

He looked over toward the door as Brannigan and Burgess entered, his face strangely vacant. His gawky beak of a nose was still a little crooked; it had been all but smashed flat when the

Humanity Front's mercs had worked him over. But that was far from the worst damage.

He frowned as he forced his eyes to focus, looking from Brannigan to Burgess. Burgess could almost see the gears struggling to turn as he tried to remember who he was looking at. Javakhishvili, long-haired, blunt-featured, and scruffy-looking as always, had looked away for a moment. He'd known Childress for longer; he'd been there when he'd taken the bullet that denied him the use of his legs, and he had tried his damnedest to help him along the long road of suffering that had followed.

Recognition finally dawned in Childress' eyes. "Sir." He started to stir, like he was about to try to stand up. "You came." His words were slightly slurred, and they came slowly.

Brannigan was a professional; he kept most of the pain off his features as he took Childress' hand. The two of them had been through a lot; Childress had been on the Khadarkh job and every mission since until Transnistria. He was an original Blackheart, and he had been one of Santelli's problem children in the Marine Corps before that. He'd been a bit of an impulsive loudmouth; he'd rarely been wrong, but he'd lacked the judgement to know when to just keep his mouth shut, even when he had been right. He'd been a good man to have along, and he'd been taking care of his aunt with the money he'd earned with the Blackhearts.

Burgess knew enough of the story, having been guarding Childress off and on for months. He also knew that Brannigan had taken over making sure that Anna Childress was well taken care of, since Sam had been hit.

"How are you doing, Sam?" Brannigan asked gently.

"I'm…I'm all right sir. Getting a…a little stir-crazy in here. I…" He trailed off. "I do get headaches sometimes."

That was an understatement. The brutal beating that he'd received at the mercs' hands had cracked his skull, and he definitely had permanent brain damage because of it. It was clearly deeply painful for Javakhishvili to watch, and Burgess could see that it was bothering Brannigan a lot. The big man's jaw worked, and he blinked a couple of times. He'd been by several times since Childress had woken up, but it never really got any easier.

"I wondered when you'd come." Despite his slow and halting speech, there was hope in Childress's voice. "When are we going to go back to work, sir?"

That was the worst part. Brannigan had come by only a couple weeks before, but Childress evidently didn't remember it. His short-term memory was in bad shape. He'd even struggled to recognize Brannigan when he'd come in. It had been the same last time.

"Soon, Sam." Brannigan's voice had gotten a little thick. "Real soon. Now, I need to borrow Tom and Herc for a bit. That all right with you?"

Childress blinked a little, and he looked over as if just noticing Javakhishvili sitting there. He frowned a little again. It was clearly causing him a lot of effort to put things together in his head. "Yes, sir. Sure. Just…just don't be too long before you come and see me again? I…" His voice faded away again, as if he'd lost his train of thought.

"I'll be back soon, Sam," Brannigan said. "I promise." He caught Javakhishvili's eye and tilted his head toward the door. He clearly didn't want to make things harder for Childress by talking about another mission in front of him.

Javakhishvili patted Childress on the arm. "Take it easy, Sam." Even after years in the Navy and as an American PMC contractor, he still retained a little bit of his Georgian accent from his formative years on the Baltic Sea coast. "We'll be back soon."

The three of them stepped out of the room and headed back to the front of the house, as one of the nurses slipped into Childress' room behind them. Brannigan stopped just inside the living room, looking at the ceiling and taking a deep breath.

“At least he’s alive, Colonel,” Javakhishvili said. “He’s better off than Don, or Roger.”

“Yeah,” Brannigan said. “Yeah, you’re right. It’s still…damn, I hate to see him this way.”

“It’s rough,” Burgess said. “Hell, it hurts me, and I didn’t even know him before.”

Brannigan took another deep breath, then looked at each of them in turn. “Okay. Back to business. We’ve got a mission. Briefing is at the usual place, in…” He checked his watch. “Eighteen hours or so. You boys able to make that?”

Javakhishvili nodded, turning to Barry. “Hey, Barry. Are you guys going to be okay if Tom and I take off for a while?”

“Finally get some peace and quiet around here,” Barry grumbled, without looking up from his cards. Fred had joined the Spades game. “Though I’m going to have to step up my Spades game; Fred’s harder to beat than Tom.”

“They’ll be fine,” Javakhishvili said. “Barry tries to be a hardass, but he’s a big teddy bear, and acts like Sam’s his son. We’ll see you there, Colonel.”

# CHAPTER 5

"So, there it is, gents," Brannigan stood by the campfire with one boot on a log round. The rest of the Blackhearts were sitting on logs or rocks around the fire. The campsite was one of their usual briefing locations; it was next to impossible for anyone using electronic means to snoop on them, and nobody was going to get close enough to listen in without being spotted or heard. "That's the situation."

Javakhishvili spat. "Russians." He looked around the group darkly. "Never trust Russians."

"Not planning on it, Herc." Brannigan let out a faint chuckle. "I remember Transnistria just as well as you do. And if this was just the Russkis trying to hire us, I wouldn't even have made the call.

"But even Abernathy thinks this is something we need to deal with. And whoever that hard-eyed old man is, I've never gotten the impression that he's given to many visits from the Good Idea Fairy. I saw the footage of these Chechens hitting FOB Mayne. They're ruthless, they're well-trained, they're using sophisticated tactics, and they're well-equipped. If they get WMDs..."

"They'll use 'em," Wade said grimly. "Went up against some Chechens in Iraq. Yeah, there were lots of rumors about Chechen snipers or Chechen fighters going around, and most of them were probably fake, but these were definitely Chechens. They were the toughest, most ruthless bastards we ever saw over there. Made the Iraqis look like teddy bears." There were a few snorts from some of the older men around the fire. "Yeah, I know, low bar to clear. But these fuckers were *vicious*."

"Okay, I get wanting to keep backpack nukes out of Chechen hands." Flanagan stirred the fire with a stick. "But why go after the funding first, and with the Russians, at that? It's not like we've been particularly friendly with Moscow over the last few years. Especially after some of the dustups in Syria, not to mention some dead *Spetsnaz* in Transnistria a while back. Why not go after the nukes themselves?"

Hank looked up at that. He was still a little separated from the rest, sitting a few feet off to one side. Most of those who'd known Brannigan before knew who he was, but no one had commented on his presence, so far.

"Abernathy says that his boys are on the nuke hunt." That prompted a few raised eyebrows, and Brannigan could well understand why. Nobody knew exactly what Abernathy's game was, or why Van Zandt deferred to him, but it had become evident not long before the Argentina mission that the Blackhearts weren't the only secretive group of hitters in the game. "We get the heist mission because we're presumably somewhat more deniable than they are." The corner of his mouth lifted slightly. "He hasn't said as much, but I suspect that more than a few of his guys are still on Active Duty, somewhere."

He looked around at the group. Most of them looked thoughtful. Santelli was staring at the fire. Something was still eating at him, and they were going to have to talk it out. Brannigan watched him pensively for a moment.

*Maybe it really is time for Carlo to retire. He'll hate it, once he stays back, but this is getting harder and harder for him every mission. I know that if Hank was Carlo Junior's age again, I'd have a hard time leaving, possibly never to return.*

His eyes moved to Hank. The younger man was watching his new colleagues, studying them, his face blank, but with a hint of uncertainty and trepidation in his eyes. He looked like he wanted to say something, but he was too nervous to venture his opinion. Brannigan held his peace.

*You wanted in, son. Now you've got to earn your way.*

"Well, hell, as long as it pays." Wade took another sip of his beer. "I figure that if I keep doing this long enough, eventually I'll be able to afford a copy of *Detective Comics 27*."

Brannigan wasn't sure of the reference, but Wade hadn't been shy about his hobbies. Whichever issue that was, he was sure it probably cost a mint.

"What if the Russians turn on us?" Hank asked.

"You mean what do we do *when* the dirty fucking Russians turn on us?" Javakhishvili spat in the fire as if to punctuate the rhetorical question.

"We do have contingency plans in place." Brannigan held up a hand to placate Javakhishvili a little. "Van Zandt is going to have people in Georgia, and they'll be monitoring the situation as best they can. We'll have emergency comms to contact them, as well."

"And if we're on the other side of Azerbaijan?" Burgess asked quietly.

"Then it'll be one hell of an E&E." Brannigan let his voice turn grim. It wasn't a happy thought. "Some of us will remember Burma." That got a few reactions. The only way out of Burma had been into China. *That* had been dicey, and Brannigan still didn't want to think about how many different ways that extract could have gone wrong. The fact that Van Zandt's mysterious office had all sorts of contacts in the intelligence community had been the only reason they hadn't ended up in a Chinese forced labor camp for the rest of their natural lives.

Especially since they'd just slaughtered a North Korean special operations unit that had been working with ethnically Chinese Communists in northern Burma.

He glanced up at the night sky through the trees. "It's getting late. Since this is a liaison mission, there's not a lot of planning we can do on this end, not even logistically. We're going to have to fly commercial, so there's a pretty strict limit on what we can take with us." There was some muttered discontent at that; it meant they were going to have to rely on local acquisition to get weapons and gear. That was nothing new to the Blackhearts, but it had worked out badly more than once. "Hector's getting flights right now. We'll do some drills in the morning; knock some of the rust off. Until then, get some rest."

Most of the Blackhearts started to move off to tents or the lean-tos that had been erected a while back, when they'd first started using this particular site to do briefing and planning. Brannigan caught Santelli's and Flanagan's eyes, and nodded toward the treeline.

Hank looked like he wanted to join them, but Brannigan just shook his head fractionally. This wasn't the time. And Hank was the new guy. He was going to have to get used to being the low man on the totem pole all over again.

The three men walked into the shadows under the trees, away from the fire. Flanagan was as easygoing and composed as ever, but Santelli, despite himself, looked nervous.

Brannigan leaned against a tree, facing the two of them. "Okay, gents, time to get this sorted out. This is our first mission since Roger went down. He was my 2IC, and he did a damned good job of it when I got shot up off the coast of Mexico. But he's gone, and that means we need a new one."

It was hard to see in the dimness, but Flanagan might have been frowning a little. He was probably wondering why he was a part of this conversation. Being Flanagan, he had to be putting two and two together, and he probably didn't like it.

Santelli was shifting his weight from foot to foot, staring at the tree roots beneath Brannigan's boots. His nervousness, that Brannigan had sensed over the phone, was coming to the fore again.

*Is that it? It's not that he's afraid to go back out, but he's afraid to be thrown into the command position?*

"What's the problem, Carlo?" he asked quietly. "You've been nervous about something ever since we talked on the phone."

"It's nothing, Colonel" Santelli said, though he still didn't look up. He took a deep breath, then, and finally did look Brannigan in the face, though it was too dark to really make eye contact. "I'll do what you need me to do."

"Are you sure?" Brannigan asked. "Because I know this has been getting harder for you. You're a married man and a father, now. If you need to stay back..."

That might have been a tightening of Santelli's mouth he saw. The former Sergeant Major did stand up straighter. "No, sir. I mean...it might feel like the right thing at first, but as soon as you boys headed out..." He shook his head. "No. I wouldn't be able to live with myself."

"So, what *is* the problem?" Brannigan pressed. "Be honest with me Carlo. I can't afford to have you in two places at once. Especially if this turns out to be as dicey as I expect it might be."

Santelli immediately looked uncomfortable again. "Well, sir..." He hesitated, looking down at his hands in the dark, "I just... It's losing Roger, sir. And I know what you want to talk to me about. And I don't know if I can fill his shoes."

Brannigan nodded. That was a problem he could handle. "Well, I'm not sure I agree with you there, Carlo. I think you're selling yourself short. You've stepped up more than once out there. But I'm not going to drop that on you if you don't want it."

He turned to Flanagan, who was standing there with his arms folded, still silent. "Joe?"

Flanagan let out a long sigh. "Why did I know you were pulling me over for this, John?" He shook his head. "I got out as a Sergeant."

"And how does that matter a damn?" Brannigan countered. "I've known Corporals with more leadership ability in their little finger than entire General Staffs. Hell, I can think of a couple of Lance Coolies who'd qualify."

He stared Flanagan down. "The truth is, there isn't a man here—okay, I can think of a couple of notable exceptions—but regardless, most of the Blackhearts could step up in a pinch. Several already have. Wade's certainly got the experience, but he's a belligerent son of a bitch and really doesn't want it in the first place. Bianco's too friendly. Javakhishvili's not a good fit. Curtis…well. The less said about him in a leadership role, the better." Both of the others got a bit of a chuckle out of that. "Double for Jenkins. Burgess hasn't been with us long enough. You're quiet, but you're not as quiet and standoffish as Gomez. You've already been an element lead, and you've done it well. The rest of them respect you—yes, even Curtis. Face it, Joe. You're the best fit if something happens to me." He was pretty sure that both men had noticed that he hadn't mentioned Hank, but there was no way in hell that his son was going to be in the running for a long, long time. Blood or not, Hank was the FNG, and he was going to have to earn his keep with the other Blackhearts before he was ever tapped for much more.

Of course, that could happen quick, given the type of missions they tended to run.

Flanagan still didn't look comfortable. "Can I think about it?"

Brannigan clapped him on the shoulder. "You've got until drills tomorrow morning to get used to it."

***

The lead element moved down into the valley, slowly and carefully.

Gomez was on point, with Brannigan behind him, followed by Bianco and Wade. Javakhishvili and Jenkins took up the rear, with the follow element in a loose echelon about two hundred yards behind and to the left.

The target was a trailer down in the valley, with several guards stationed around it. The trees thinned as the hillside descended, finally giving way to a grassy meadow about fifty yards from the trailer itself.

The lead element was still about a hundred fifty yards from the target when all hell broke loose.

A string of what sounded like gunshots rattled out from the trailer with a series of flashes. Something heavier went off at the treeline with a flash, an ugly black puff of smoke, and a thunderous *boom.*

Brannigan went down hard, dropping to the pine-needle-covered ground behind a tree. The rest of the lead element started returning fire, quickly cutting down the guards outside, but another burst rattled from beneath the trailer.

"Kodiak is down!" Wade yelled. "We are pinned down and need support!" The incoming automatic fire wasn't slackening, despite the return fire that was now rocking the trailer, bullets punching through the thin fiberglass walls.

Farther up the hill, Flanagan didn't hesitate. "Push up and left!" He was already moving that way, along with Burgess, Santelli, and Curtis. Hank had suddenly found himself on point, but he'd stopped to wait for orders, and had to hurry up and catch up as Flanagan almost passed him.

At first, it almost seemed as if the trail element was moving away from the contact instead of pushing to relieve the pressure on the pinned point element, but Flanagan knew what he was doing. He pushed them another hundred yards, putting them almost fifty yards past the pinned-down lead element and on-line with the trailer.

He didn't yell orders. He didn't need to, at least not for the three other seasoned Blackhearts. They were all watching their relative position as they ran, gauging angles and figuring out when they'd have a solid line of fire on the enemy without running the chance of accidentally firing on their comrades. They ran just far enough and started to drop to a knee behind trees, Curtis being the first one to get down in the prone. Under most circumstances, Curtis' weapon of choice was a belt-fed machinegun, so he'd be the primary base of fire.

Hank had already been ahead of him when Curtis dropped. Unsure of the SOP, he was about ready to keep going. He wasn't entirely sure how far they were going to push, but Flanagan reached out and grabbed him before he went too far, pulling him down to cover behind a fallen log at the edge of the meadow before finding his own position about three yards farther back, where he could see the other three easily.

Then the entire element opened fire on the trailer. It rocked under the impacts, puffs of dust and shattered fiberglass kicking out from the bullet holes as they punched right through it. A moment later, the fire coming from the trailer stopped.

Flanagan wasn't given to loud, motivational noises. He didn't say anything. He just vaulted over the log and sprinted toward the trailer, his rifle held ready to engage if any bad guys showed themselves. The others followed, Hank once again a few steps behind.

Flanagan reached the corner of the trailer, paused just long enough for Santelli to catch up, and then was moving on the door. He yanked it open and went in behind his rifle, turning hard left to cover the bullet-riddled rear corner, while Santelli heaved himself up behind him, turning right to cover his back.

"Clear!" Flanagan called hoarsely. His chest was heaving, and his throat was burning a little from the sprint, but he was still in control. "Coming out!"

He and Santelli stepped out of the ruined trailer, to find Hank, Burgess, and Curtis on security at the corners. "Collapse on Alpha," he barked. Without dropping security, the five of them moved back to the treeline.

"Friendlies!" Hank called, having moved back into the point position as they'd moved away from the trailer.

The trail element moved into the ragged perimeter set by the lead. Burgess, Santelli, and Curtis pushed out onto the perimeter, but Hank required a nudge. Not much of one, but he was clearly still trying to figure out where to fit in. *Too much time in an officer billet.*

"Kodiak's KIA," Wade told Flanagan as he took a knee near the center. "Everybody else is up and up."

Flanagan nodded. "Grab his weapons and ammo. We'll fall back over the ridge and reconsolidate."

"End-ex," Brannigan said, sitting up. "Not bad. Nobody tripped over themselves." He looked around at the Blackhearts coming in from the perimeter. "Nobody got wrapped around the axle about chain of command, either."

"I think I put the fear of God into the ones who might have," Santelli said, eyeing Jenkins in particular.

"It was a trial, taking orders from Joe, I do have to say," Curtis said. "You'd better not get shot for real, Colonel."

"If he does, I'll shoot you next, make sure you don't have to endure the misery," Flanagan said. "That work?"

"No, it does not, Joseph," Curtis replied indignantly. "You'll just have to take the bullet for the Colonel, is all."

"You're the one complaining," Flanagan replied. "Seems to me that it's your problem to try to fix."

"Are you two done?" Santelli demanded. "Holy hell. Like an old married couple."

"Let's police up the brass and the targets." Brannigan hauled himself to his feet. He looked up at the angle of the sun. "I think we can run a couple more scenarios before dark."

***

As they picked up the targets around the ancient trailer that Brannigan had towed out there to act as a training aid a couple of years before, Brannigan came up to Hank, who was still picking up brass out by the treeline, noticeably keeping his distance from the rest. "How'd it go?"

"About as well as you'd expect from the greenest boot in the team." Hank didn't look up but kept picking up brass, his jaw clenched. "I had to be ushered around like a fucking private who didn't know what the hell he was doing."

"I warned you that you were going to be the low man on the totem pole for a bit," Brannigan told him. "You've got about twenty-four hours to make up your mind if you can swallow your pride and accept that you're the boot here, or if you want to go try to find another contract somewhere. Because once we're wheels up, there's no turning back."

Hank looked up at him then. He smiled a little. "You haven't changed a bit, Dad."

Brannigan didn't return the smile. "This has nothing to do with being your father." He wondered inwardly how much that was true. *Am I going to be harder on him, just in the hopes that he quits and stays back? Do I want him to quit, to reduce the risk that he'll be killed?* "It has everything to do with being your commanding officer on a very small team that's about to go halfway around the world, into enemy territory, with allies we can't trust, to conduct a very dangerous mission. One weak link at the wrong time, and none of us are coming back. So, again, if you're not sure you're up to it, you've got an extremely short time to figure it out. Because there's no safety net once we leave." He turned to leave, heading back to the trailer. "Think real hard on it, son."

He could feel Hank's eyes on his back as he walked away. He didn't regret the speech. Hank was a grown man. And it had all been true. This wasn't a gentleman's club that Hank was trying to join. Not a family business.

It was a chance to go into hell with no guarantees of coming back. And with a lot less backup than he was used to.

That message had to get across to him before they left. And he hoped that what he'd said had gotten through.

Damn, but he hoped it had gotten through.

# CHAPTER 6

Brannigan watched the coast glide past under the Aeroflot Boeing 737's belly with decidedly mixed feelings.

The closest he'd ever been to Russia had been the Transnistria mission. Most of his career in the Marine Corps had been focused largely on the Middle East, Africa, and parts of East Asia. But the military he'd come up in had been shaped by the Cold War, and distrust of Russia had been deeply ingrained. While he'd never had orders to that effect, he'd started getting his Marines ready to deploy to Georgia and fight the Russian Army during the Russian-Georgian War in '08. Nothing had come of it, but he'd been ready.

Sure, President Pavlenko had publicly distanced the Russian Federation from the Soviet Union that had preceded it. He'd made a lot of noise about the failures of Communism. But Brannigan had never been able to put aside the fact that Pavlenko had been GRU, and had continued many of the Soviet Union's nastier practices, including making political opponents disappear, not to mention the subversion and low-intensity warfare aimed at forcibly bringing Eastern Europe back under Moscow's wing.

His last couple of encounters hadn't improved his opinion of the Russians. The first being a deal with Russian mobsters in

Dubai that had gone south when they had left the Blackhearts stranded at sea on extract from Khadarkh. The second had involved going toe-to-toe with *Spetsnaz* in Transnistria, which had been a glorified Soviet-era time capsule.

*Seventy years of Communism had an impact. Most Slavs you meet these days don't seem to have much of a soul left.* It had actually been Ben Drake who had told him that; Ben had gotten around after his retirement, which was a part of why his network was so extensive. Only part of the reason, of course; Ben's many, many years in the Corps had given him a list of contacts a mile long.

Sochi was a pretty modern-looking place, right on the Black Sea coast. He peered out the window, watching the shining white domes of two stadiums—probably built primarily for the Olympics a few years before—and the line of high-rise, beachfront apartments and hotels, facing a marina sheltered from the sea by a long, blue-walled, concrete jetty. As the plane descended, the trees behind the beachfront properties got thicker, forming a veritable forest that surrounded the airport.

It all looked very clean and inviting in the seacoast sunshine. Far different from the gray misery of Transnistria, or what he knew *most* of post-Soviet Russia looked like.

*The publicity effort for the Olympics must not have worn off yet.* He knew that he wasn't being entirely intellectually honest. But he didn't like or trust Russians, and flying in all but alone and unarmed had him in a bad mood.

*Herc's wearing off on me.*

He found himself tensing up a little as the plane coasted down to the strip, the trees blocking off the view of all but the hills to the south and a couple of the high rises. The long flight was almost over, and now all the unknowns came into play. He wasn't flying on his own passport, but on a product of Abernathy's resources, that identified him as "Tom Stauer." Abernathy's people were pros; he was sure it would pass muster. But it was still an American passport, and there might well still be trouble, just thanks to general Russian bloody-mindedness.

He kept his expression carefully controlled as the descent ended with a jolt and a squeal of tires. The engines roared and he was pulled forward as the pilot reversed thrust and braked to slow the aircraft's headlong rush toward the end of the runway.

Taking his eyes off the window, he scanned the rest of the cabin. Most of his fellow passengers were Russian; he'd heard a lot of the language on the flight, but there were plenty of Westerners and Chinese as well. He was the only one of the Blackhearts aboard; Hector Chavez had been careful to spread them around as much as possible, so that it wouldn't appear to anyone who didn't need to know that a group of Americans, all male, all vaguely military in appearance, was coming into the country all at once.

Brannigan wasn't sure just how necessary that precaution was under the circumstances; after all, they were going to be working directly with the Russians, so trying to disguise their arrival *from* the Russians was something of a fool's errand. On the other hand, he was sure that there were other powers watching Sochi International Airport, and they didn't need to know who was coming in.

Which probably included the US State Department.

And if the jihadis had spies around—and given Sochi's relative proximity to Chechnya and Dagestan, they just might—the less they could figure out, the better.

Good security habits were good security habits, regardless of whether or not they seemed to be applicable to the immediate situation.

He still felt naked as the plane pulled up to the gate and the fasten seatbelt sign went out. He watched and waited as the other passengers started to file off, all of them ignoring each other, absorbed in their own conversations or their phones. Once his row was empty, he slid out and stood up, almost grazing the ceiling with his head, pulling his small overnight bag out of the compartment and shouldering it before he walked out. He got a couple of looks as he went, including a smile from the pretty Russian flight attendant standing at the door. He was, after all, big enough to draw some attention.

He glanced around as he stepped off the skybridge and into the terminal. The airport's interior was spacious as all hell, the vaulted ceiling held up by an angular webwork of girders, about two stories overhead. The entire outer wall was glass, letting in plenty of sunlight, which glinted off the polished floors. He looked around for directions, finally picking the sign for Customs, in English and Russian, out of the mass of commercial signage above restaurants and duty-free shops.

Glancing at his watch, he did some math. He was the first one on the ground; he'd made sure of that. Not that he had any way to warn the rest if things went sideways, but it had always been his policy as a leader to be the first one on the ground, last one off. He'd take the bulk of the risk, as much as he could. Flanagan and Javakhishvili should be next, landing on separate flights, about five minutes apart, provided they were still on schedule. The rest would be straggling in over the next hour and a half.

He eyed the sign for Customs, debating. *Get it over with now, or wait for the rest, then tackle dealing with Russian authorities?* He was supposed to meet their liaison at Customs; he had detailed instructions for making the meeting. But he was hungry, and they were going to have to wait for the rest, anyway.

Yet, as he glanced at his watch again, he frowned, and changed his mind. *Don't want Joe or, Heaven forbid, Herc making contact first. I'd better go take care of work first. Horse, saddle, self.*

He turned toward Customs, following the signs and weaving his way through the crowds. There wasn't a lot of difference in airport crowds, anymore. They all wore generally

Western clothes and were all on smart phones of some sort. If there were a few more people speaking Russian or Chinese, it was little different than walking through a Middle Eastern airport, if slightly cleaner.

There were two lanes at Customs, a "green" lane for those with nothing to declare, and a "red" lane for those who did. He turned toward the green lane, scanning the stony-faced, dark-blue-uniformed Federal Customs Service officers waiting at the checkpoint. They didn't cut impressive figures, most of them. The lead officer was morbidly obese, sweating in the lights over the checkpoint and breathing heavily through his mouth even though he wasn't exactly exerting himself.

*There.* That *guy is out of place.* The trim man in a suit standing off to one side was definitely not some FCS officer just getting through his day, marking the hours and minutes off until he could, maybe, collect a pension. His bland, slightly babyish face couldn't completely disguise the hardness in his dark eyes as he scanned the crowds. There was a deliberation to his observations, too; he wasn't just curiously watching people. He was looking for something. And Brannigan thought he knew what.

*Here goes nothing.*

He walked toward the checkpoint, reaching up to straighten his dark green ball cap. The gesture caught the man's attention, and those dark eyes flicked to the cap, then to his face. While the man kept his expression stony, Brannigan caught the flicker of recognition in his eyes.

The man stepped forward, shouldering past the obese FCS officer with a low word. The sweaty man started, as if only just then noticing the man in the suit, then looked over at Brannigan. His eyes widened slightly, until Brannigan locked gazes with him, at which point he hastily looked away.

*Doesn't want to have anything to do with whoever the secretive man from the government is meeting. Probably smart.*

"Mr. Stauer?" The man in the suit spoke good English, with only a faint accent. When Brannigan nodded, the man held out his hand. "Akim Innokentivich Krivov." His handshake was firm, with just enough pressure to suggest that he was a lifter, and somewhat tempted to test his strength against Brannigan's. That was something Brannigan had come to expect from Americans more than foreigners, but if Krivov was what he thought he was, he guessed he could understand. He returned the handshake with just enough responding pressure to act as a warning. *Just try it, bud.*

Krivov didn't react to the hint of a crushing squeeze. He glanced past Brannigan's shoulder. "I was told there would be ten or eleven of you."

"The rest are coming," Brannigan said. "Logistics and timing being what they are, we had to spread the flights out a little." Not strictly speaking the truth, but what the Russians didn't know couldn't hurt them.

Of course, Krivov just nodded, with just enough amusement in his expression to indicate that he knew exactly what was going on and why. So, they weren't fooling the Russians.

"Come with me. I will send someone to collect your friends." He held out a hand to usher Brannigan past the Customs checkpoint. "There is a secure area where we can discuss matters."

Brannigan motioned for Krivov to lead the way, which he did, with a shadow of a half-smile. Brannigan was already starting to dislike that expression; it reminded him of their linkup in Transnistria, with one of Erika Dalca's underworld contacts. It was the expression of a man who knew more than he figured his companion did, and Brannigan didn't like it one bit.

They turned into a door behind the checkpoint, Krivov holding it open for Brannigan, while he turned to another couple of men in suits and spoke in rapid-fire Russian. Both men eyed Brannigan, doing the sort of sizing up that professional soldiers sometimes do when they know they're in each other's company.

One was short and squat, built like a powerlifter, with blunt Slavic features that showed the scar on his cheekbone and an oft-broken nose quite prominently. The other was taller, though athletically built, and with Asiatic features. Both wore their hair cropped short.

The powerlifter grunted a short, "*Da, Mayor.*" Then the two of them stepped out, leaving the room to Brannigan and Krivov.

There wasn't much in the way of furniture; a simple desk with an office chair behind it, and two benches of typical airport seats. There was a camera on the wall, and a monitor on the desk, but besides that and the two doors, one opposite the one that he and Krivov had entered through, the walls were blank.

Brannigan lowered his overnight bag onto the seat next to him. "Okay, Major Krivov." He faced the *Spetsnaz* officer squarely. "What do we need to discuss?"

"For now, only the next step." Krivov leaned against the desk and folded his arms. "How soon will all of your team be here?"

"Another hour or two," Brannigan replied. "There were only so many flights, and my employers didn't figure that a charter flight would be...prudent."

Krivov might have snorted slightly at that. "Once they are all here, I will take you across the airport, to a secure compound, where we will board the next flight, courtesy of the Russian Air Force. From here, we will go to our staging area in Dagestan."

"Dagestan, huh?" Brannigan decided to try to feel the other man out. "I'm guessing that's pretty familiar territory for you. *Spetsnaz*?"

"You are a perceptive man, Mr. Stauer," Krivov said easily. "Yes, I have deployed to Dagestan before. I assume you have been to Afghanistan? Maybe Iraq?"

"It's a safe bet," Brannigan replied, "given what we've been hired for and recent history being what it is."

Krivov really did smile wryly at that. "Of course."

"I'm wondering about something, Major." Brannigan studied the other man. "You seem awfully relaxed for a man who's welcoming foreigners—Americans, at that—into your country's backyard to conduct a mission that I would have expected to be right up your unit's alley."

There might have been a flicker of expression on Krivov's face, but it was quickly shut down. He shrugged. "I am a soldier, Mr. Stauer. I follow orders. I am ordered to be your liaison with Russian forces and…other elements. So, I will do it."

"Of course." Brannigan left it at that.

A couple of minutes later, the door opened again, and the Asiatic *Spetsnaz* trooper came in with Flanagan and Javakhishvili. The latter was looking even less impressed than usual, and eyed Krivov with visible distrust.

"So, is this our contact?" he asked. "Or our handler?"

"Our contact," Brannigan said. "And he speaks pretty good English, Herc." Javakhishvili just grimaced.

"So, Major," Brannigan continued, "since you're just following orders, have those orders explained just why your country agreed to get us involved?"

There might have been a tightening around Krivov's eyes. "Your guess is as good as mine, Mr. Stauer. Moscow has not seen fit to tell me. But I would imagine that it has something to do with distancing us from military operations in Azerbaijan. Especially given certain recent events." The clashes between Russian-backed Armenia and Turkish-backed Azerbaijan were still fresh in everyone's mind. That had gotten dicey before the latest cease-fire.

"They could have 'hired' Wagner to do that." Suspicion was written all over Javakhishvili's face and dripped from his voice. But once again, Krivov only shrugged.

The conversation sort of stilled after that. Krivov had little to tell, and the Blackhearts didn't want to talk a great deal around him. Santelli, Wade, and Jenkins were the next ones in, followed by Gomez, Curtis, Bianco, and Burgess over the next hour. The atmosphere in the little room got steadily more tense in the brittle silence. With little to say, the silence got steadily more oppressive.

Finally, Hank straggled in, the last to arrive, flanked by the other two Russians. "That's it," Brannigan said.

Krivov was looking around at them. "You did not pack much."

"Commercial air travel with the kind of equipment we will probably be using tends to get difficult," Brannigan replied. "And we were told to talk to you about gear."

"Of course," Krivov replied. "We will have weapons and equipment for you in Dagestan."

"Great. Russian gear…" If Krivov heard Javakhishvili's muttered imprecation, he gave no sign.

Krivov led the way out the opposite door, past the desk. They found themselves in narrow corridor, and the *Spetsnaz* Major started walking briskly toward the far end as the Blackhearts fell in with him, the other two Russian soldiers bringing up the rear.

He led them through several doors and back rooms of the airport, passing the airport personnel going about their regular tasks that kept the airport working and the planes coming and going. They got a few glances, but enough were quickly averted that Brannigan began to suspect that they knew that the Russian military was doing *something* around the airport, and they'd been cautioned to mind their own business.

They came out under an overhang, where several vehicles were parked, including a panel van and two white UAZ Patriots. Krivov opened the panel van doors and ushered them in. Brannigan took the front seat, while Krivov moved to the lead UAZ. A moment later, they were rolling quickly across the tarmac, weaving between taxiing aircraft, heading for the far end of the airport, where an An-26 was parked next to a fenced compound. Netting woven into the cyclone fence obscured the inside of the compound, but Brannigan could guess what he'd see there, anyway. Military compounds have a certain continuity, no matter who built them.

The vehicles pulled up behind the Antonov, which already had its props turning. Krivov got out of the UAZ and waved, so Brannigan piled out and pulled the panel van's side door open. "Looks like this is our ride, gents."

The Blackhearts piled out, each man getting his bearings quickly before moving toward the aircraft. There wasn't much hesitation, as bad-tempered as Javakhishvili looked. Like it or not, they were committed. The only way out of this was going to be through.

He just hoped that this wasn't going to go as badly as the last time they'd worked with Russians.

Brannigan counted each of his men on, Krivov standing by his side. The other two Russians had boarded first. Finally, the two of them walked up the back ramp, found seats on opposite sides of the cargo compartment, and strapped in.

The rising whine of the An-26's engines made conversation impossible. Each man was isolated with his thoughts as the ramp closed, and the bird sat there, the engines spooling up. Brannigan watched Krivov for a moment before turning his attention to the rest of the Blackhearts as the aircraft started to taxi with a lurch.

Flanagan had his head back against the fuselage behind him, his face icy calm and composed. Curtis was fiddling with something in his hands, occasionally glancing around as if he wanted to say something, but then being silenced by the noise. Jenkins was even more fidgety.

Javakhishvili was watching Krivov like a hawk, unblinking. He'd been fine in Transnistria, but that had been a bit different. It was *Russians* Javakhishvili didn't like or trust. Ordinary, run of the mill gangsters he could deal with. He'd just stuck his head inside the jaws of the lion that had just about devoured his country back in '08, before he'd become an American citizen, and he clearly didn't like it.

Wade was watching each of the Russians in turn. If possible, it seemed like his steely blue eyes would burn a hole through whatever he stared at, but that was just Wade.

Gomez, like Flanagan, was composed, his head back and his eyes closed. Or not; Brannigan thought he caught a glint between the quiet man's lids. He was watching their hosts like a hawk, but he was being far more subtle about it than Wade.

Santelli was leaning on his knees, his head bowed, his meaty fingers intertwined in front of him. While he'd been relieved of the strain of being the next in line for command, he hadn't been especially enthusiastic about the mission, either.

Bianco had pulled a comic book out of his pack and was reading it as if this was just another flight somewhere. Which, Brannigan supposed, it was. Burgess looked like he was asleep already, though he was probably playing possum just as much as Gomez. Burgess had been around, especially in Eastern Europe.

Hank was by far the most visibly nervous, as hard as he was trying not to show it. He was fiddling with his fingers, fidgeting as he kept looking back at Krivov and forward at the powerlifter-looking Russian, who was sitting just outside the cockpit. Brannigan frowned a little; Hank should have known better, from his upbringing as much as his officer training. But, he supposed, this was a whole new experience for the young man.

Then the engines roared to a fever pitch and the plane lurched forward, rapidly picking up speed before the nose tilted up and the wheels came away from the tarmac.

For better or worse, they were on their way to Dagestan.

# CHAPTER 7

Makhachkala was also a coastal city, but it seemed to Brannigan that that was about where the resemblance to Sochi ended. While he couldn't see a lot in passing—the An-26 was descending toward the airport almost ten miles south of the city itself—what he could see outside the little viewport, spread out between the rising massif inland and the Caspian Sea coast looked somehow more Middle Eastern than Russian.

Given that most of Dagestan was Muslim, there was probably a reason for that. There was quite a bit more green than most of the Middle Eastern cities he'd been in, except for Turkey, but there was just something about the atmosphere that didn't look quite as shiny and touristy as Sochi had.

Then the plane was turning away from the city itself, the Caspian stretching blue outside his window, and they were on final approach.

The airport was considerably smaller than Sochi's, with a single runway and a straight, rectangular terminal, the walls gleaming with blue glass. The Antonov touched down with a faint shriek of rubber on the tarmac, slowing and stopping about halfway down the runway, then turning toward the terminal as it rolled onto the taxiway.

The pilot didn't taxi to the terminal itself, however, but turned right, toward the short row of hangars. A few moments later, the bird lurched to a stop, the engines starting to spool down, and the ramp cracked open.

Krivov got to his feet and started down the ramp, holding out a hand to tell the Blackhearts to wait. At the bottom, he looked toward the hangars, then nodded, waved, and turned back to beckon them to follow him.

The team filed off, followed by the two other plainclothes *Spetsnaz* soldiers. Krivov led the way toward the hangars, Brannigan catching up to him with a couple of strides.

He looked around as they walked across the tarmac. This half of the airport had clearly been taken over by the Russian military; there were two Su-35 Flankers parked at the edge of the taxiway, and a pair of Mi-38 helicopters next to another An-26 and a massive An-12. A pair of UAZ 469s raced along the fence, apparently on patrol.

A growl overhead drew their eyes, and he glanced up to see a single Mi-28 Havoc circling the airport. The Russians weren't taking chances. Given the resurgence of the Chechen jihad, that shouldn't be surprising. Dagestan had never been *quite* as kinetic as Chechnya proper, but it had certainly seen its fair share of violence.

Krivov was making for the nearest hangar, ignoring the Havoc attack helicopter overhead. Brannigan kept pace with the shorter man easily, and they stepped through the cracked main doors, into the shadowed interior.

The hangar had been converted into an operations center. One corner was occupied by easels, maps, and radios, surrounded by a cluster of men in Russian Army uniforms, the mostly green digital camouflage marked with the multicolored patches on breast, shoulder, and cap. Another third of the hangar was taken up with supply and equipment crates, while cots were lined up at the far end.

Krivov led the way over to the maps, snapping to attention in front of a shorter man with heavy jowls and a massive gut straining the front of his uniform blouse. The triangle of three silver stars on his collar identified him as a *Polkovnik*, a Colonel. Which, Brannigan mused, probably accounted for his slovenly appearance and lack of physical fitness. He was the top dog; he didn't need to be in fighting shape anymore.

It was an attitude he'd encountered before, and he'd always detested it. He supposed that he shouldn't be that surprised to find it among the Russians, given some of what he'd learned over the years.

Krivov saluted crisply, and the Colonel returned it sloppily, distractedly. "*Polkovnik* Pichugin, Mr. Stauer and his team," Krivov said by way of introduction. Pichugin nodded, studying Brannigan and each of the Blackhearts in turn as he pulled a pack of Sobranie Black Russians out of his shoulder pocket, tapped one out, and lit it. Vile-smelling smoke wreathed his head as he sized Brannigan up.

Brannigan, for his part, had to adjust his assessment slightly. As slovenly as his appearance might be, the *Polkovnik*'s eyes were sharp and observant. He was visibly taking in every detail as he held out his hand. His handshake was firm, and there was more strength in his meaty hand than Brannigan might have expected.

"Welcome to Dagestan, Mr. Stauer." His accent was heavier than Krivov's, though still decipherable. "Though I should tell you that not all of my men are terribly happy about your presence here."

"Not surprising," Brannigan replied. "I don't think *I'd* be that enthused if Washington brought Russians in to help with a situation in the Caribbean, either. But the situation is what it is." He tilted his head curiously. "Though I wonder, Colonel. Why *did* your government bring us in?"

Pichugin would have made a hell of a poker player. His stony expression didn't move a whit as he spread his hands, the cigarette tilting upward in his mouth. "Moscow does not tell me, Mr. Stauer. They just tell me that you are coming. And I do not speculate."

*He's lying.* Brannigan couldn't read the man well enough to be able to say *why* he felt it, but he sensed that if Pichugin wasn't flat-out lying, he at least withholding the whole truth. Which, he supposed, was the man's prerogative, but that didn't mean he had to like it.

*At least it tells me where we stand.*

There was something of an awkward silence after that, as Pichugin offered him the pack of cigarettes. Brannigan declined. He still smoked a pipe from time to time, and there had been a time when he would have killed for a dip, but if the smell of that Black Russian was anything to go by, he wasn't inclined to partake. *If I smoke one of those, I'll probably have lung cancer* tonight.

"So, what exactly is the mission, and what part are we going to play in it?" Brannigan asked. It wasn't exactly his first time doing joint operations with local nationals, though in his Marine experience, the Americans had usually taken the lead. He wasn't really expecting that to happen this time.

Pichugin grunted and turned toward the biggest map. "First thing is to find the target."

Brannigan held up a hand, feeling an uncomfortable feeling creeping up his spine. "Wait a minute. You don't know where the cache is yet?"

"No." Pichugin looked up at Brannigan out of the corner of his eyes. It gave him a shifty look that Brannigan didn't like. From the look on Flanagan's face, he didn't like it, either. "Abu Mokhtar's security is too tight. He is smart. But we believe that we know who might know where it is located. My men will conduct..." He hesitated, then turned to Krivov. "*Razvedka?*"

"Scouting," Krivov translated.

"Scouting, yes." Pichugin nodded. "Your team will conduct the pick-up."

Brannigan's eyes narrowed. That sounded suspiciously like the usual "joint" op where the Americans did the bulk of the work and the locals took the credit.

It also didn't sound like a particularly Russian solution, particularly not in Russia's own backyard. "Really? You want us out front?"

"Yes." Pichugin seemed to consider something for a moment, then straightened and looked him in the eye. "Understand, this is Azerbaijan where we will be operating. Russians could cause international incident." He looked around at the Blackhearts. "You are not obviously Russians. Since American forces have not been much in this part of the Caucasus, then the Azeris might not immediately jump to conclusions, especially with black and brown faces." He shrugged. "Is not completely 'deniable,' but should cause enough confusion."

Brannigan traded a glance with Flanagan and Santelli at that. It made a twisted sort of sense, but it was thin. He had a nasty feeling that there was another reason why they wanted the Blackhearts out front, and it wasn't going to be a good one. That much he was sure of.

*I think I know why we didn't get much in the way of details before now. And I like that reason even less.*

"Wouldn't your boys have a better feel for the area?" he asked lightly.

Another shrug. "We have not been in Azerbaijan in very long time." *That* was almost certainly a lie. Maybe they hadn't been over the border *officially*. But if he were a betting man, Brannigan would have laid good money on the Russians having made a few excursions into the predominantly-Muslim Azerbaijan, especially with the Chechnya situation flaring up again, never mind the continuing standoff between Azerbaijan and

Armenia happening down south, which had gone hot several times over the last couple of years.

"So, you don't know where the cache is. Do you know where the nukes are supposed to be exchanged?" There were some unreadable looks between a couple of the other Russian officers. "Seems to me that hitting the exchange would be killing two birds with one stone. Take the nukes out of play and get the money at the same time. Rather than hunting around Azerbaijan for the cache, or somebody who might or might not know where it is."

But Pichugin shook his head again. "That is not the plan," he said flatly. "We will find this man." He pointed to a blurry digital photo of a weaselly-looking man with a thin mustache, dressed entirely in black. "He is Azeri *mafiya*, and he is associated with the Chechens. Our contact assures us that if anyone knows where Abu Mokhtar's caches in Azerbaijan are, this man knows."

"And how do you know your contact is trustworthy?" Flanagan asked.

"We have worked with him before," Krivov said. "He is Russian, not Azeri. He has contacts all over the world, including among the black-asses." That was a particularly Russian slur, usually aimed at Muslims, rather than any particular race. He looked over toward the cots and said something to one of the younger Russian soldiers standing at attention nearby. *Probably Pichugin's aide.* The kid snapped to attention, turned on his heel, and walked back to a curtained-in enclosure at the far end of the hangar.

The Blackhearts watched as the kid said something, and a figure came out of the enclosure and followed him back toward the operations center, smoking a cigarette. As he got closer, Brannigan's eyes narrowed, and he felt Flanagan and Santelli stiffen next to him. He shot Curtis a warning glance. The shorter man caught it at the last moment, and his mouth closed with a snap.

The shorter man had a flat face, with faintly slanted eyes and a pug nose that had clearly been broken a few times. His dark hair was going slightly gray, as was the stubble of a beard on his jaw.

He was also familiar as hell, and Brannigan was momentarily glad that Roger Hancock wasn't with them. Roger probably would have killed him on sight.

"Anatoly," Pichugin said, "tell our friends about the man they are going to pick up for us."

"Yes, *Anatoly*. Tell us." Brannigan hoped that the momentary stress on the man's name—or alias—hadn't been noted by the Russian soldiers, but none of them reacted. So, while he hadn't quite been able to help himself, he hadn't quite given the game away, either.

The short, flat-faced man shrugged. "His name is Etibar Akbarov. He was a small time Azeri gangster until a few years ago, when he became something of a facilitator. Now he is a major go-between for Chechens and international smugglers. He lives in Quba. I happen to know where."

"And you have no idea just how he suddenly became a 'facilitator,' *Anatoly?*" Brannigan asked.

Another shrug. "Business is business. Some are better at it than others." That familiar grin flashed, just for a moment. Brannigan fought down the cold rage burning in his chest.

"So, if he's a business partner, it should be easy enough for you to have him come to a meeting," Brannigan suggested.

"He does not leave the country anymore," the flat-faced man said easily. He glanced at Pichugin. "He has become somewhat paranoid about Russians."

Brannigan raised an eyebrow as he glanced at the *Polkovnik*. "Meaning that you tried to grab him already, and it didn't go well."

"That is a fair guess," the man going by Anatoly said, taking a long drag on his cigarette. "At any rate, he is even wary of me now. Will not make contact. But I have people close enough to him that I know he will be in Quba in two days. We can grab him then."

"*We*," Brannigan muttered. "Right." He folded his arms across his chest. "So, Pichugin's teams are going to spot him, you're going to stay back here, and we're supposed to waltz in there playing tourist and snatch him?" He stared at Pichugin. "Am I getting the gist of this plan right?"

"That is basic plan, yes," Pichugin replied.

"You have to understand, these Russian Army guys always *look* like Russian Army," 'Anatoly' said cheerfully. "Most of them do terrible job of playing tourist. But you Americans…" He grinned again. "Born tourists, all of you. And something close to twelve or fifteen thousand of you visit Azerbaijan every year."

"If you think we're going to pull a snatch-and-grab with just cameras and board shorts, you're out of your mind," Wade snarled.

"We will have equipment for you," Pichugin said. "It will be waiting for you at a safe house in Quba."

"And I will not be staying back here," the flat-faced man said. "I will be coming with you. I know him better than that shitty photograph, after all."

Brannigan smiled a little at that, though there was no warmth in it, and he saw a flicker of what might have been the barest hint of fear in the man's eyes. "That sounds like a good idea. That way we can be certain."

*Certain that you don't walk away and leave us high and dry, holding the bag,* Anatoly.

"I am sure it has been a long day, after long flights." Pichugin waved toward the cots in the back. "We will let you rest; start detailed planning in morning. After all, Akbarov will not be in Quba for two more days."

Brannigan just nodded his thanks, keeping his eye on the flat-faced man. The other Blackhearts waited for a moment, until he waved at them to head back and grab some real estate. They started drifting back toward the cots, their bags over their shoulders. The flat-faced man got hard looks from Santelli and Curtis, though Flanagan had managed to keep his own expression guarded. Hank, Jenkins, and Bianco all looked at him curiously as they walked past.

Wade met Brannigan's eyes for a moment, then glanced at 'Anatoly.' Brannigan shook his head fractionally. *Later.* This wasn't a conversation he wanted to have with Pichugin and his cronies around.

Not that they probably wouldn't find out eventually, anyway. Presuming they didn't already know that 'Anatoly' and the Blackhearts had a history.

# CHAPTER 8

Brannigan waited until the last of the Russian officers had left before he turned on the flat-faced man. Santelli, Curtis, and Flanagan, the only other Blackhearts remaining from the Khadarkh mission, flanked him.

"You get around, don't you, *Anatoly*?" he rasped. "Or is it *Dmitri*? Presuming either one is your real name."

The man who had first introduced himself to Roger Hancock in Dubai as Dmitri took a long drag on his cigarette and shrugged. "To some people I am Anatoly, to some I am Dmitri. To others, I have an entirely different name. In this business, one cannot be too careful."

"Of course," Santelli snarled. "You've got to be careful that the people you fucked over and left to die can't find you easily."

Dmitri turned a bland eye on the irate Bostonian. "Is that what you think happened? That I made an agreement, then went back on it because there might have been some risk, meeting a single small boat in middle of the Persian Gulf at night, kilometers away from anything?"

"You had the money." Flanagan's voice was flat and hard. "Seems like it was easier for you to just go home, while we foundered out at sea. Or all died on Khadarkh."

"My friends," Dmitri said, though without any of the wheedling tone that Brannigan might have expected. "That is not what happened. It was a mistake, I assure you." He turned over his shoulder toward the little curtained-in enclosure where Pichugin's aide had fetched him. "*Grigori Ivanovich! Idite syuda!*"

The curtain stirred, and a tall, gawky-looking man with a hooked nose and prominent Adam's apple came out, looking sullen. He wore a patch over one eye.

Dmitri looked up at Brannigan, taking another long drag off his cigarette, and jerked his head toward the one-eyed man. "It was going to be a late night after a long day. So, I set in rest plan. This little *suchka* was supposed to wake me up to come get you. He drank half a bottle of vodka and passed out, instead." He turned a poisonous glare on the other man, who looked like he wanted to flinch. Brannigan honestly wasn't sure how much of either reaction was an act or not. "So, I took his eye."

Flanagan's eyebrows went up at that. Curtis swore under his breath. Even Santelli looked a little shocked. Brannigan, however, didn't necessarily believe that any of Dmitri's story was the truth, and maintained his look of studied skepticism.

Dmitri turned back to them. "If you want to take the other one, I can only ask that you wait until after this operation is finished."

The matter-of-fact way that he said it, as he finished his cigarette and dropped it on the concrete floor at his feet might have put a chill through Brannigan, if he hadn't already been pretty sure of what kind of man Dmitri was. A man didn't become a *brodyaga* in the Russian *mafiya*, much less one who operated internationally, without a particularly ruthless streak.

And, if he was being frank, Brannigan and his Blackhearts were pretty ruthless men, themselves. The three men standing beside him had slaughtered the Suleiman Syndicate thugs who had tried to double-cross them with little more than rocks, sections of pipe and rebar, and bare hands, and that had been before they'd ever met Dmitri. And they'd killed a *lot* of people since then. Including a well-equipped bunch of psychopaths-for-hire who had made Dmitri look like just the kind of friendly, easygoing man he tried to appear to be.

"So, you woke up late, shrugged and said, 'Oh, too bad,' is that it?" Brannigan asked.

"It was far too late to come make rendezvous," Dmitri replied with another shrug. "By that time, you were either dead or had made other arrangements." He smiled. "I am glad that you made other arrangements."

"Sure you are," Brannigan said coldly. "And I'm thinking that maybe we ought to be thinking about making 'other arrangements' again. Before we *have* to."

If the implied threat rattled Dmitri, he didn't show it. He just spread his hands. "And I might not blame you. If I were in your place. But think about it. You are in Russia, on a Russian Army installation. I am telling you the truth, but even if you do not believe me, how do you think the Russian Army will react if you kill me? You are a very long way from home."

Brannigan smiled at that and leaned in close. The smile never reached his eyes. "Never said we'd do you here," he said quietly. "We have our reasons for getting into these situations, but it's not because we're stupid."

Dmitri didn't seem to have an answer to that. Unfortunately, Brannigan knew that he didn't need one, right then and there.

He was right. They were wholly in the Russians' hands, and if the Russkis were going to keep Dmitri close, then there wasn't a damned thing the Blackhearts could do to him. They were good, but they weren't exactly in the best of spots right then.

Dmitri smiled again; if there was any unease in his expression, he kept it well-hidden. Of course, if he was telling the truth about what he'd done to Grigori, then he was hardly a man who was unused to threats and brutal violence. Being in the Russian *mafiya*, he had to be plenty dangerous himself, and Brannigan and the other Blackhearts had always known that. He was hiding behind Pichugin's *Spetsnaz* right then out of convenience, not inability.

He backed away, maintaining that smile, and then turned and headed back toward his corner of the hangar, barking at Grigori to follow him. The one-eyed man flinched and obeyed.

*I wonder what else he's done to that kid?*

The Blackhearts watched him go, those who had joined after Khadarkh a little more curiously from the cots where they were setting in. There was murder in Santelli's eyes.

Brannigan put a hand on his old Sergeant Major's shoulder. He felt him sigh a little as he grimaced and turned away. "There'll come a time, Carlo."

"Yeah, I know, sir," Santelli replied. "I'd just be a lot more comfortable if it was sooner rather than later."

"I know." Brannigan stepped past him and headed for the cots. "But he's not wrong. If we lift a hand against him here, we're going to have Pichugin's guys on our heads in a heartbeat. And from there, it's a tossup as to whether they kick us out, in which case it's mission failure, or they just make us disappear."

"They're Russians," Javakhishvili said darkly. "They'll err on the side of 'make them disappear.'"

"Who's your friend, boss?" Wade nodded toward the curtain where Dmitri had disappeared.

"An old contact." Brannigan set his bag down on an empty cot and sat. "When we were in Dubai ahead of the Khadarkh mission, we had to locally source our weapons and gear.

The first attempt you probably already know about. The Suleiman Syndicate tried to double-cross us at the first meeting, which didn't go so well for them. Afterward, Roger made contact with some of the Russian Mafia, who have their fingers in just about every pie in that city." He looked toward the curtain. "Dmitri, there, was the contact we bought the weapons from, who also facilitated our insert."

"Ah," Wade said. "Small world, huh? Didn't he leave you high and dry when it came to extract?"

"He did," Santelli confirmed. "Took the money and disappeared. He *says* it was a mistake. I don't trust him."

"He's a Russian mobster," Brannigan snorted. "There's probably not a trustworthy bone in his body, no matter how much he protests that he's telling the truth."

"Well, I've got to hand it to you guys," Wade said conversationally. "I'd probably have wrung his neck if he'd done that to me."

"Won't deny I was tempted," Brannigan admitted. "But he made the very accurate point that we're here on Russian sufferance, and they probably wouldn't take kindly to one of us killing their primary contact with the target individual."

"Which brings up another problem." Burgess's voice was quiet. "Namely, that we're in Dagestan, on Russian sufferance, and none of this sounds anything like the mission we were briefed Stateside."

"It does bear a passing similarity," Flanagan said. "We *did* have the finance mission, while the…other guys got the nuke intercept. But you're right; the fact that the Russians didn't even blink when the Colonel asked about where the exchange was supposed to happen…"

"Maybe they don't know any more than we do," Hank suggested. "I don't imagine that their intel is perfect, either."

While he made a good point, he still got bemused glares from several of the other Blackhearts, and subsided. "Thanks,

New Guy," Jenkins said acidly. "We'll take that under advisement."

"Shut up, George," Santelli snapped. "You keep demoting yourself, so don't get too full of being senior, or you might end up lower on the totem pole than young Hank there by virtue of being a jackass."

"Hank's right, though," Bianco said. "I smell a rat."

"Is it really any different from just about any other job we've taken on, though?" Wade looked around at the rest with raised eyebrows. "I mean, hell; we jumped into fucking *Burma* and E&E'ed into *China*. And let's face it, we were committed as soon as we got on that Antonov in Sochi. The Colonel's right: if we decide to quit now, they've got no reason to just let us go home. I mean, what are we gonna do? Walk into the US Consulate in Makhachkala and ask for help? Oh, yeah, there isn't one. Where *is* the nearest US Consulate, anyway?"

"Probably Tbilisi. Which would mean walking out of here and across the Russian/Georgian border. I'm sure that would be a pleasant, easy stroll." Flanagan laughed humorlessly. "We'd only have to hike through Chechnya and South Ossetia, probably. No trouble at all."

Wade waved a hand at Flanagan. "So, our best bet for the time being is to play the game. After all, didn't these Chechens kill a bunch of Americans already? Enemy of my enemy, boys."

"That Chechens are the Russians' enemy just means that we have a common enemy, not that we're friends," Javakhishvili grumbled.

"Nobody said we were friends," Brannigan told him. "We're going to keep our eyes open and our weapons close at hand, this entire time. And we'll have an E&E plan for every place we go." He let the corner of his mouth lift. "Including here." He pulled a satellite phone out of his bag, just far enough that the others could see it. "Once we're a little more settled, I'll set up a rendezvous with Van Zandt's contact in Georgia. Yeah, there's a lot of contested airspace and touchy frontiers between here and there, but he'll be able to get *some* kind of transportation out this way. Even if it's gotta come from Turkmenistan. We discussed that a bit before we left." He let the phone drop back into the bag. "Like I told our friend Dmitri, we've got our reasons for getting into these situations, but it's not because we're stupid."

"Well, that's all well and good," Santelli said, "except for the part about keeping weapons close. Because last I checked, we came here without any."

"I'm guessing that's what those are for." Gomez pointed to the equipment cases stacked near the cots. "I don't see any of the Russians setting up in here, so those are probably ours."

"You'd think," Javakhishvili said. "But never underestimate the Russian capacity for making simple shit hard."

"They're not secured," Wade mused. "And they're not being guarded."

"Worth checking them out, anyway," Flanagan said. "Better to beg forgiveness than ask permission, right?"

"Except where the people you're begging forgiveness from are the Russian military," Santelli muttered. "Somehow, I don't expect them to be reasonable. It's not in their nature."

"Somebody's talking sense," Javakhishvili said.

"I'd rather be begging forgiveness with a gun in my hand, if it's all the same to everyone else," Brannigan said. "And Wade's got a point. If the stuff in there was meant for someone else, where are they?"

Wade surged to his feet. "Enough jaw-jacking, fuck." He stepped over to the nearest crate and flipped the catches open, lifting the lid. "Okay, that's what I'm talking about."

He lifted a black rifle out, pulling back the charging handle to peer into the action. "Looks like AK-103s," he said. He tossed the rifle to Flanagan and started rummaging through more of the crates. "One per case, along with ten mags and a chest rig."

He snorted. "Cheap knockoffs of old AK chest rigs. Same shit we saw all over the place in Iraq."

"Beggars can't be choosers, I guess." Flanagan grimaced a little as he turned the weapon over in his hands. The furniture was all black synthetic, but it was still basically not far removed from the AKM, the modernized version of the AK-47 that had been around since 1959. It was even chambered the same, in 7.62x39mm.

"Are you hating on Kalashnikovs again, Joe?" Wade asked, as he hauled the case down and started into the next one. "Looks like only one weapon and loadout per case."

"Look, the AK-12s weren't bad, but they weren't great, either," Flanagan said, as he hauled the rifle and its case over to his cot. "I've used a lot better, is all I'm saying. Not least being the ACE-52s on the last job."

"We all have," Wade countered. "Is there ammo anywhere in this heap?"

"Over here," Gomez pulled out an ancient-looking wooden crate, wrapped in rusting metal bands, the wood discolored and the stamped Cyrillic markings all but illegible. "I hope somebody's got a multitool."

"And hope that nobody rat-fucked the crates for the spam can openers," Wade muttered, as several multi-tools were produced out of several of the Blackhearts' luggage. How exactly they'd been disguised to get them through security wasn't a question anyone was going to ask. Some were "travel-safe," but several obviously weren't.

"More importantly, are there any RPKs or PKPs?" Curtis peered over Wade's shoulder at the weapons cases. "Mama Curtis' baby boy was not meant to carry a peashooter like a noodle-armed pleb."

"Sorry, doesn't look like you get to waste ammo this time." Wade leaned back and looking the cases over. "No belt feds. You're going to have to aim like the rest of us."

"That is *not* why I prefer firepower, John," Curtis sputtered. "See how y'all are laughing without good suppressive fires…"

"Is it all AKs?" Santelli asked.

"Looks like it," Wade answered. "Better than nothing."

"Truer words were never spoken," Brannigan said. "Break everything out and start jamming mags. I want every man armed and loaded out before anybody goes to sleep."

Because when he was dealing with Russians, he wasn't going to take any chances. Especially if it got around that the Blackhearts had left some *Spetsnaz* bodies in the snow in Romania a while back…

# CHAPTER 9

Brannigan put his eye to the narrow gap in the corner of the Kamaz cargo truck's canvas topper. Unfortunately, the view was as limited as ever; the truck was parked in the trees on the south side of the city, and Brannigan's side was facing the fields and the mountains to the south. The view hadn't changed since the last five times he'd looked.

Turning back to the inside, he glanced around at the other Blackhearts. They weren't geared-up for a hit; they were still in a city that was not, technically, a war zone. Each man wore an AK chest rig under a cover shirt or jacket, his limited first aid kit and radio stashed in pockets and strapped to belt or ankle.

They were all quiet and mostly still. It was go time, and each man had his game face on. The only real exceptions were Jenkins and Hank; Jenkins was fiddling with his rifle, looking around and trying to peer out the back. Hank kept his face composed, but his fingers were rapidly tapping on his rifle's black plastic forearm.

Krivov was up near the front with Brannigan, pointedly not looking at him, listening to his radio through the wireless earpiece he wore. He was on a different channel, so Brannigan couldn't listen in, even if he understood Russian, which he didn't, at least not enough.

Somewhere in the city, a team of three or four of Krivov's *Spetsnaz* were prowling the streets in two cars, looking for Akbarov. The fact that he hadn't heard sirens yet told Brannigan that they *probably* hadn't been burned.

But a glance at his watch also told him that they were behind schedule. Dmitri had assured them that Akbarov was supposed to have left his apartment for a restaurant an hour ago. But Krivov hadn't given them the "Go" signal yet.

He watched the Russian officer carefully. Krivov was leaning against the wooden hoop behind him, his elbow on the metal frame behind the bench seats, his chin resting on his fist. His aloofness might have been simply because he was trying to focus on the radio traffic coming from the recon team.

Brannigan hoped it was. The possibility that this was all a double-cross wouldn't leave his mind, and if Krivov just didn't want to give anything away…

"Are your boys seeing anything?"

Krivov looked up at him then, a faint frown creasing his features. He still looked distracted, and Brannigan could faintly hear traffic in his earpiece. "Akhbashin thought that he spotted him thirty minutes ago, but Simosin says that no one has left his apartment."

"Which one was in position first?" Wade asked from where he sat next to Brannigan.

Krivov shot him what might have been an irritated glance; it was hard to read his flat features in the shadows under the canvas. "Simosin."

"And he's sure there aren't any other exits that he didn't spot?" Brannigan pressed.

Krivov looked even more annoyed. "Simosin is experienced. No one has left the apartment."

Brannigan just nodded, though he wasn't sure he entirely believed it. The Russians weren't likely to admit that they were screwed up six ways from Sunday to a bunch of American contractors, but he'd seen enough in Transnistria to suspect that even the *Spetsnaz* didn't quite live up to the superman reputation they tried to maintain. And with only four of them on the ground, the likelihood that Akbarov had slipped past one of them was even greater. Brannigan had run surveillance before. Four men was about as bare-bones as you could get.

Wade was watching Krivov closely. Brannigan had to hand it to the Russian; Wade's pitiless, icy stare tended to unnerve people, but Krivov seemed utterly unaffected.

The Russian stiffened a little, sitting up straighter on the bench. "Berezin thinks he sees him."

"I thought Simosin said nobody had left," Brannigan said dryly.

Krivov ignored the observation. Apparently, he didn't have *quite* as much faith in Simosin as he'd made out.

*Gotta save face in front of the Americans. Even if they know you're full of shit.* The more things changed, it seemed, the more they stayed the same.

Krivov was frowning, and he leaned forward to knock on the back of the cab. "Berezin is on Heydar Aliyev Avenue." He looked almost worried. "If it is Akbarov he sees, he is over a kilometer away from his apartment, and moving away from the restaurant."

Brannigan shared a glance with Wade, who looked every bit as unimpressed as Brannigan felt. The truck lurched into motion with a rattling rumble, turning back onto the road and pushing east along the treeline.

"So, the intel's already bad," Hank said quietly.

"Intel's *always* bad, sonny," Santelli replied. "It's just a matter of *how* bad."

Krivov was still barking into the radio. Javakhishvili was listening, the frown on his own heavy-browed face getting deeper. "Wait," he snapped. "Is there no one in front of him?"

Krivov waved at him as if to dismiss the question, but Brannigan leaned forward. "He got past your entire team?"

"It is possible," Krivov said. "Berezin is trying to confirm his identification."

"So, we're changing position based on a possible, without positive identification?" Wade stared hard at Krivov, then looked at Brannigan again. "Just what kind of amateur-hour bullshit did we get into this time?"

If looks could kill, Krivov's would have put a bullet between Wade's eyes, but the former Ranger was unfazed. He just returned Krivov's glare, his knuckles tightening around his AK-103.

"There are only four men on surveillance team." Krivov's accent apparently got a little thicker when he was pissed.

"Exactly my point," Wade snarled.

"Enough," Brannigan snapped. The mission was still the same; they were just going to have to adjust on the fly. It wouldn't be the first time. "Can we get ahead of him in this thing?"

"We are trying." Krivov banged on the back of the cab again. The truck lurched again, swaying alarmingly as they went around a corner. "Streets are tight here."

"Then maybe we shouldn't have brought a damned troop truck," Flanagan muttered. If Krivov heard that, he gave no sign.

The Russian was listening intently, barking directions to the driver up front, occasionally banging a fist on the cab for emphasis. Brannigan wasn't sure what that was really going to accomplish, but he held his peace. Things were already tense enough between the Blackhearts and their Russian "allies."

Then Krivov suddenly stiffened, putting his hand to his earpiece. Brannigan could hear what sounded like rapid-fire talk over the radio, but even if he'd understood Russian, he probably couldn't have made out the words.

Krivov was suddenly banging on the cab again, barking orders into the radio even louder and faster. Javakhishvili cursed.

"We were rushing to try to cut off the wrong guy." He leaned back against the side of the truck bed, disgust written across his features. "Simosin just watched him walk out of his apartment."

"Is that so?" Wade snapped acidly, staring at Krivov. "So, now we're *all* out of position."

"He does not know we are coming for him," Krivov said flatly. "We can still maneuver and get back into position. We still have time."

A few muttered imprecations passed between Blackhearts, but fortunately none of them, not even Wade, called Krivov out on it. They really didn't need to get into an international pissing match in the back of the truck, while still on mission.

The Kamaz's driver wasn't the most graceful or subtle. They lurched to a halt in a few yards. Brannigan had to throw up a hand to keep from being thrown against the cab, and Wade stomped a boot down on the deck beneath them, bracing himself before he was thrown into Brannigan's side. Hank and Curtis weren't quite so well prepared; they both almost went sprawling. Then the driver threw the big vehicle into reverse with an audible grinding of gears, and they were backing up.

Brannigan just hoped they didn't hit anything. That would only make an already bad situation that much worse.

He studied Krivov as best he could in the gloom under the canvas as the driver started what felt like a thirty-point turn, grinding the gears and stomping on the brake hard enough to make the whole truck rock with every movement. The *Spetsnaz* major was holding onto one of the canvas canopy's hoops with one hand, his other hand to his ear, pointedly ignoring the Blackhearts' tangible hate and discontent. He was trying hard to be outwardly professional, which had to be difficult when the op he was supposed to be ramrodding was clearly turning into such a shit-show.

"He is not going to the restaurant." Krivov frowned, his muttered words barely audible over all the noise the truck was making. "He is walking toward the park."

Unless Brannigan had completely lost his bearings—which he was pretty sure he hadn't—the park was immediately to their northwest. In fact, they should be right at the southeast corner.

"Can we grab him in the park?" Wade asked.

"Might be a *bit* more high-profile than we planned on," Brannigan said, before Krivov could express his opinion of that option. From the look on his face, he didn't like it at all. "Better to get eyes on him and tail him to somewhere a bit more sheltered."

"Preferably without getting spotted, ourselves," Burgess murmured.

Krivov looked over at them. "We will stay in this vehicle until we are in position to make the intercept, as planned."

Brannigan felt Wade start to bristle. The shaky alliance they had with the Russians was one thing; the Russians giving orders was something else. Even so, *some* unity of command needed to be maintained, and despite Krivov's tone putting his teeth on edge, he understood the point.

"If we go running out there with rifles and chest rigs, it's going to give the game away," he said. "Let's keep it nice and calm and low-key, track him until we can snatch him without anybody seeing, and get out of here." He really wasn't sure how much he believed in the plan, himself, but it was better than starting a fight with Krivov in the back of a troop truck that was trying very hard to look like a farmer's "drive to town" vehicle.

Krivov kept listening to the radio, staring at the floorboards while Brannigan watched him with an increasingly thunderous expression. He could hear the tinny background noise of radio chatter in Krivov's earpiece. There was a lot going on, but you wouldn't know it, sitting in the back of that truck.

"How about an update?" he asked Krivov, the tone of his voice as he leaned forward being more along the lines of, *Updates, asshole!* "We can't exactly get ready to take this guy if we don't know what's going on."

Krivov didn't look happy about it, but he glanced around the inside of the truck, apparently becoming aware of the extremely unhappy stares he was getting from trained killers with more firepower than he had on him.

He grimaced. "Akbarov is not going to the park." His English had become a bit clearer. "He has turned east along Zaur Cəfərov. Berezin is walking south to intercept him, and Akhbashin is trying to get eyes on him before he gets out of Simosin's view."

"Just make sure they're acting slow and casual, before one of them runs right at him and gives the game away." Santelli got another sharp look from Krivov for that, but the fireplug of a Bostonian was completely unruffled, only meeting Krivov's gaze with a heavy-lidded look of his own that all but dared the Russian to make an issue out of it.

Krivov didn't pass that along, though Brannigan frankly would have been surprised if he had. Instead, he turned away and went back to listening to the radio, as the driver got the Kamaz turned around and started back toward the park.

Brannigan was wondering now if they weren't simply heading in the wrong direction again; if Akbarov wasn't going into the park, then they were simply retracing their steps to a position farther away. But if Krivov thought of that, he didn't correct the driver. And Brannigan didn't figure that the driver was going to obey *him* if he tried to get him to stop until they had a better idea of where their target was going.

Krivov tilted his head as he listened, a faintly quizzical look on his face. "He is stopping in…the Damir Bank? Strange."

"Maybe he needs cash," Brannigan speculated. "Maybe he needs to transfer some money to his jihadi buddies before he goes to get tea."

"Akhbashin is moving to watch the door," Krivov reported.

For several minutes, they just waited. The driver probably would have kept driving west, past the park, because it took Krivov banging on the cab again to get him to stop with another brutal lurch.

Brannigan wondered if this guy hadn't been the source of one of the many dash cam videos of horrible driving and hair-raising wrecks in Russia.

Time stretched in the relative silence that followed. The tension inside the back of the truck seemed to ratchet up as the seconds ticked by without report. Whatever Akbarov was doing inside the bank would presumably take a few minutes, but the waiting seemed to go on longer and longer. Had he found a different way out? Had Akhbashin missed him? Had it all been another wild goose chase, with Simosin and Akhbashin following the wrong guy, like Berezin had been earlier?

Finally, Krivov broke the silence. "Akhbashin sees him at the door. He is coming out."

Brannigan looked around at the Blackhearts and made a "settle down" gesture. They were getting a little *too* keyed up and ready to go. They couldn't just grab Akbarov on the street as he was walking out of the bank, even if they hadn't been several blocks away. But at least they hadn't lost him.

A burst of loud, tinny, undecipherable Russian blasted in Krivov's earpiece.

"*Tvoyu maht!*" Krivov spewed a stream of angry Russian into the radio and banged on the cab again. Once again, grinding gears and wrenching the wheel over, the driver rammed the truck into motion, trying to bring the massive vehicle back around to the east again, stomping on the brake halfway across the road.

"He just saw Akhbashin as he came out of the bank," Krivov snarled. "I do not know what gave him away, but Akbarov is running."

# CHAPTER 10

The driver was obviously excited; his driving was even more erratic than before. The lurch as he nearly went into the ditch on the north side of the road just about sent the Blackhearts sprawling, regardless of how braced they were. Jenkins' rifle clattered to the floorboards, and he snatched it, just in time to get thrown the other way as the driver ground the gears into reverse, yanking the truck back with another sickening sway to point east along the wooded road.

"We're not going to catch Akbarov if this idiot wrecks us!" Brannigan snapped at Krivov, but the Russian ignored him.

With a coughing rumble, the driver gunned the Kamaz down the road, once again throwing the men in the back around. Muttered curses flew around the back as the canvas flapped, the truck picking up speed.

"Where is he?" Brannigan demanded.

"He is running east, into residential areas," Krivov replied. "If we can get ahead of him, we can cut him off."

The driver certainly seemed intent on getting ahead of him; they were moving fast, plummeting down the road to the east. It was all the Blackhearts could do to hold on. The road wasn't exactly smooth, and the Kamaz didn't exactly have the best suspension in the world, either. Brannigan was starting to feel bruised all over from the bouncing, and he wondered if his spine hadn't already been compressed a couple of inches from the impacts when the truck hit a rut or a pothole.

"He is on his phone," Krivov reported, just after another particularly jarring impact, "he might have friends coming."

"Great." Not that anything else had gone right so far in Quba. "Tell this jackass to slow down; he's not going to outrun a truck on foot, and we're just going to attract more attention if we're treating this like a damned Formula One race in a cargo truck."

Krivov shook his head. "We must finish this quickly, before Azeri police get involved!"

Brannigan leaned toward him, holding onto the front of the troop bed. "Do you think they're *not* going to notice a truck suddenly barreling down the road at the same time that a foot chase just started?"

"We have people monitoring their radios," Krivov retorted.

"Oh, that makes it all—" Wade cursed as another bump lifted him completely off the bench seat. "That makes it all better, don't it?"

Brannigan didn't have time to ask the question. The four-man Russian surveillance team couldn't have been actively monitoring the Azeri police nets. Krivov obviously wasn't doing it. That meant that there were more Russians in the city, Russians that he hadn't been told about.

But even as he was about to say something, the driver hauled the wheel over, almost lifting the left-hand tires off the pavement as he dragged the Kamaz around the corner.

And promptly slammed head-on into an oncoming car.

At least, that was what Brannigan assumed had happened, once he got his brains un-rattled from being suddenly thrown against the front of the bed with a catastrophic *bang*.

The impact had thrown everyone in the back forward, and Brannigan momentarily had the breath crushed out of him by the combined weight of Wade, Curtis, and Burgess as they all halfway piled on him, pressing his ribs against the front of the bed. He heaved the others back, fighting to get air back in his lungs as he probed his side, hoping he hadn't just cracked a rib. He'd fought through worse, in his day, but it wasn't something he ever *wanted* to do again.

"What did we hit?" Santelli asked thickly. They weren't moving, so whatever they'd hit, either the driver wasn't in any shape to keep driving, or the vehicle wasn't.

"I don't know, but we need to move." Brannigan started to push his way toward the tailgate.

Flanagan grabbed him by the arm. "We don't want to be running around in broad daylight looking like a plainclothes *Spetsnaz* team."

"We don't want to be sitting here in a wrecked truck with this kind of weaponry and equipment, either." Brannigan shot an accusing glance at Krivov, who was picking himself up from underneath Santelli. "Doing this in broad daylight was already stupid, but now we've got a short list of shitty options. Everybody out!"

Gomez and Hank were the first ones on the ground. In retrospect, Brannigan thought that he shouldn't have had Hank at the rear of the truck; the kid wasn't utterly incompetent, but he didn't have a lot of special operations experience. He'd been a grunt platoon commander, and that left a few things to be desired if the goal wasn't just "smash everything in that direction."

But he'd performed decently in the train-up, brief as it had been, and he didn't disappoint now. Past the tangle of bodies and weapons, Brannigan saw him drop off the tailgate and set up on the corner, across from Gomez, his AK held muzzle down along his leg, mostly hidden from view by his body and the bulk of the truck.

*Good lad.*

The Blackhearts disentangled themselves quickly and piled out. Brannigan and Krivov were last. As his boots hit the dirt, Brannigan looked forward and saw the front of the truck crumpled against what looked like a Lada in even worse shape. And more people were starting to come out of the woodwork. They needed to scram, fast, quick, and in a hurry.

"Get out," he said. "Scatter. Keep to the trees and the deeper woods as much as you can. Stay the hell away from people as much as possible." He caught Flanagan's eye. "Take Burgess and Wade," he said. "See if you can get ahead of him. The rest of you, with me. Rendezvous point is our fallback rally point, as planned." He got a look from Krivov at that; they hadn't discussed a fallback rally point with the Russians. Which had sort of been the whole point…

Sirens were starting to whoop somewhere deeper into town, and they were beginning to get some looks from the locals on the sides of the road. It was time to get scarce. Hopefully, they could be gone before the Azeri authorities started putting the pieces together.

"Move," he snapped, keeping his rifle as close to his body as possible as he faded into the trees to the south of the road.

***

Flanagan had already vanished, plunging into the line of woods on the other side of Mashadi Azizbayov Street, with Burgess and Wade close behind. The wreck was starting to smoke, but he couldn't be sure someone hadn't noticed them running across the road.

He was cursing under his breath as they jogged through the trees, trying to keep their rifles close to their bodies. If the Russians hadn't insisted that daylight was the best time, when they knew where Akbarov was going to be…

*Where the hell do they think he is during the night, given that they had somebody set up on* his frigging apartment?

If ever there was a reason not to have taken this job, the Russians seemed hell-bent on reinforcing it.

But Brannigan's Blackhearts were not men given to a lot of bitching and moaning that they shouldn't have been where they were. They all had plenty of experience getting in over their heads. The situation was what it was, and they were just going to have to adjust on the fly and get through it.

To do anything else amounted to suicide, and none of them were the suicidal type. Regardless of how suicidally insane some of their operations appeared to be.

He pushed another hundred yards or so before he dropped to a knee behind a tree. While the wooded band along the southern border of Quba was narrow, it was thick. They had a good amount of concealment to hide in.

Wade and Burgess joined him, dropping down on the other three corners of a triangle, their weapons held close but ready. "How the *fuck* is this supposed to work?" Wade asked. "Long guns in broad daylight, no wheels if we can even make the grab before we get swamped by local cops..."

Flanagan was already thinking it over. He had been since they'd bailed out of the truck. "We need to stay back in the trees. We'll be the backup plan, maybe a blocking position. If we stay out of sight, we might be in position to cut him off while the others move in on him."

"You think that's going to work?" Burgess was breathing a little more heavily than the other two. "What are the rest going to do? We didn't exactly plan this part out."

Flanagan cursed under his breath again as he scanned the trees, listening to the whoop of Azerbaijani police sirens in the distance.

***

Brannigan paused in the woods, looking back toward the wreck at the intersection. Azerbaijani police lights were flashing through the gaps in the trees, but they didn't seem to be coming into the woods yet. So, the Blackhearts had a moment to catch their breath and figure out what to do next.

*We're several blocks south of his last known sighting and out of position. We're going to have to move fast if we're going to catch this guy. And then we've got to somehow get out of here with him.*

He looked over at Krivov, who had, fortunately, accompanied them into the trees, leaving his driver to fend for himself. Which was kind of shitty, but in the interests of mission accomplishment, Brannigan was actually kind of glad.

"Where is he, and where's he headed?" he demanded.

Krivov listened to the chatter in his earpiece again. "He is heading for the bus station. Berezin is trying to get ahead of him, but he is fast." Which implied that Berezin wasn't *as* fast.

Brannigan sighed in frustration, looking around at the other six Blackhearts scattered around the trees. "Ditch the weapons and the chest rigs."

"What?" Jenkins asked. Hank snapped his head around to stare at his father in some disbelief.

"Ditch 'em!" he hissed. "We're not here to get in a firefight with the Azeri police. We'll have to do this the hard way. We're tourists until we get eyes on Akbarov. Then, once we spot him, we can move in on him." *Presuming we can get between him and the bus station. If he gets on a bus, he's gone, and we've got nothing.* He keyed his own radio. It was a Russian job, like all the rest of their equipment, so Krivov's people were probably listening in, but that was kind of a given at that point. "Woodsrunner, Kodiak. Ditch your weapons. We're going to have to try to be a little more subtle."

"Roger," Flanagan replied. "Where's the quarry?"

"Heading for the bus station," Brannigan replied. "He should be just north of you."

"On our way," was Flanagan's answer.

***

Wade and Burgess had heard the call just as clearly as Flanagan, and both men were already divesting themselves of their chest rigs, their rifles already on the ground. "Waste of good guns and ammo," Wade muttered. "And now what are we supposed to use for the rest of the op?"

Flanagan was thinking the same thing, but he didn't say anything. If the Russians decided to get difficult about it, they might be in trouble.

*What am I thinking? We're already in trouble.*

But right then, Brannigan was right. Their best chance was to strip out of their weapons and gear and try to cut Akbarov off without attracting too much local attention. Tourists were one thing; armed tourists were something else.

He shoved his AK-103 into the roots before slipping out of his leather jacket and shouldering out of his chest rig. The chest rig and his limited belt kit, aside from his knife, went on top of the rifle. Then he swept some fallen leaves over the whole thing before straightening, pulling his jacket back on.

He couldn't see much past the trees, but he thought he knew roughly where they were, which was almost due south of the bus station. "Come on," he said, heading toward the road at a jog. Burgess and Wade had divested themselves of their paramilitary gear almost as fast as he had, and they were on the way in a moment.

Threading through the thick woods, they still made good time. Until they hit their first check.

Azerbaijani houses looked more European than Middle Eastern, despite the Islamic influences. They tended toward peaked roofs and didn't have the balconies that were fairly common in the Mideast. However, instead of fences or open yards, they appeared to be mostly set in walled compounds, which was more Middle Eastern. Flanagan, Wade, and Burgess came out of the trees and right up against a wall.

"Son of a bitch." Wade's voice was flat and emotionless, but since it was Wade, Flanagan could still hear the frustrated rage simmering underneath.

"Up and over," Burgess said, scanning to their right and left. There didn't appear to be any alleyways between the residential compounds that they could slip through; as far as they could see, each wall butted up right against the next. "Just hope they don't have dogs."

Flanagan reached up and chinned himself over the top of the wall. The yard inside was expansive and luxurious, with a paved courtyard centered on what looked like a fountain, though there was no water in it. More importantly, there were no people, and no sign of dogs.

He heaved himself up, hooked a foot on the top, and vaulted over. Wade and Burgess followed, as Flanagan moved to the shadow of the wall alongside the driveway and hurried toward the exit. None of them wanted to be inside that compound for long; if the house's owner was inside, and they got spotted, it wouldn't matter that they'd ditched their weapons and chest rigs.

The gate was shut, but once again it was a simple matter to get over the wall; it wasn't that high, and there were no spikes or barbed wire on top. There were, however, security cameras pointed at the gateway. Flanagan dropped off to one side, trying to stay out of the camera's range. He couldn't be sure if he'd accomplished it, but by the time anyone looked at the footage, they should be far away.

Or so he hoped.

Back on the street, it was a short dash to the intersection and the next street leading north. He jogged quickly over and started up toward the bus station and their quarry, picking up speed as he stretched out his long legs, hoping that a man running down the street, trailed by two more, wouldn't be alarming enough for someone to call the cops.

***

Brannigan was making his way north rather more sedately, though more by necessity than anything else. The only way to get past the wreck without jumping fences was to go up the side of Mashadi Azizbayov Street, right past the scene, and hope that the police or the bystanders in the vehicles that had stopped behind the crash didn't recognize them as the men who had piled out of the back of the crashed Kamaz.

He walked past the smoking vehicles and the Azerbaijani police car, its lights still flashing, and rubbernecked and gawked. The traffic cop didn't even seem to notice him. Almost everyone else on the road was focused on the wreck; those who weren't were ignoring everything else and just trying to get past and get where they were going.

The mission may have gone south, but to everyone else in Quba, it was just another day. As long as nobody was shooting and nothing was exploding, it would likely remain that way. Which gave them options.

Except that the clock was still ticking; if Akbarov got on a bus, they were back to square one.

Krivov was somewhere behind him, but he didn't dare look back to check on where. He was supposed to be just another rubbernecker and tourist. Fortunately, there were supposed to be a few in Quba; the city's historical sites were one of Azerbaijan's big tourist draws. There was no way that he was going to pass for a local, even before he opened his mouth.

He walked as quickly as he could without being obvious about past a large estate or compound, dominated by a yellow-sided, five-story building. Only when he got to a tree-shaded corner did he pause, looking around as if trying to get his bearings. He was supposed to be a tourist, after all.

Krivov came up next to him. "He spotted Berezin and turned back," he murmured. "He is moving south through residential areas, away from the bus station, now."

"Have the cops figured out what's going on yet?" Brannigan asked. The sirens that had sent a jolt of adrenaline through him a few minutes before had died away; they must not have been actually connected to the Blackhearts current operation, or Akbarov's flight.

Krivov listened some more before he answered. Neither man had looked at the other while they spoke. "Berezin thinks that some of them are following him. But he is running and following Akbarov, so he can't be sure."

"He'd better hurry up and get sure," Brannigan growled. "If he burns this whole op…"

He knew that it wasn't the end if Berezin did get burned. If anything, it might help; if Akbarov thought that his pursuer had been rolled up by the police, he might get careless.

A man could hope.

Krivov looked around, frowning. "I think that he has passed us," he said suddenly. "We should have seen him by now."

"Woodsrunner, Kodiak, the quarry might be heading your way."

"Roger," Flanagan replied. "Just saw movement near the intersection ahead; looked like somebody running, but I couldn't see if it was our boy or not. He went around the corner. If it's him, he's a block west of us."

Brannigan swore under his breath as he looked back the way they'd come. The nearest entry into the neighborhood to the east was almost a quarter of a mile behind them, and all too close to the wreck and that Azerbaijani police car.

"Gamer, grab Ventura and see if you can circle around the west, come back at the wreck from there," he called over the radio. "Our boy is running for it, and he might have just slipped past Woodsrunner and Angry Ragnar."

"Roger," Bianco replied. Somewhere behind him, he knew that the big man was crossing the street toward a side street or alley with Jenkins in tow.

He just hoped that they could spread the net wide enough that Akbarov couldn't get out of it before they were all in position.

***

With the realization that Akbarov had gone the wrong way, Flanagan had slowed to a walk. Wade and Burgess were with him; three tourists together, even all male tourists, looked *slightly* less suspicious than three strange men, all going the same way, all looking the same way, but separated by infantry dispersion of two to five meters.

"There's that dumbass Russki," Wade muttered. Sure enough, the man running down the street toward the corner ahead of them was recognizable from Makhachkala; big, burly, with hardly any neck and a beetling brow and permanent scowl on his jowly face. He looked more like a thug than a soldier, which, given what Flanagan knew about the Russian Army, might not be all that far off.

He was also being followed, and sirens were suddenly whooping from behind the three Blackhearts, too.

"Oh, shit," Wade muttered. Flanagan felt a jolt go through him at the sound. Were the cops coming for the three men who had run through a local's compound? Or were they looking for Berezin?

The police car sped past them, which answered that question. But it didn't look good for the Russian, as it screeched to a halt in front of him, the doors popping open and a fat Azerbaijani policeman jumped out, yelling at Berezin to halt—at least, that was what it sounded like. A second police car came up behind him a moment later.

The heavyset *Spetsnaz* trooper froze, staring at the police in front of him before looking over his shoulder at the police behind him. Flanagan slowed abruptly, holding Wade back with a hand. Something about Berezin's body language…

The Russian suddenly reached under his jacket and yanked out a PP-93 submachinegun, snapping it up without bothering to unfold the stock. A single burst sent the first policeman sprawling, blood spraying from his throat. Then Berezin spun, bringing the machine pistol around, and dumped the rest of the mag into the second Azerbaijani cop. The little 9mm fired fast, the *brrap* of its reports blending into a single, nasty sound. Only about half the rounds hit the policeman, but the last one punched through his eye, snapping his head back with a spurt of gore, and he sprawled over his car's hood and rolled off onto the street.

Then the first cop's partner was returning fire, yelling into his radio. Berezin ducked and ran back the way he'd come, reloading as he went.

The Blackhearts ran for the nearest alley and ducked down as more sirens started up in the distance. The game was on, now.

# CHAPTER 11

Flanagan sprinted for the corner, his long legs pumping, wishing he still had a rifle in his hands. That Russian had just turned *everything* on its head. Right up until the last couple of minutes, they might have been able to run this quietly, despite all the setbacks. If Berezin had just kept his head and played things off, he might even have gotten away from the Azeri police with a bribe, and they could have tightened the noose until they cornered Akbarov and got him out of the city.

Not anymore. Now the police would be out in force, and from what little Flanagan knew about Azerbaijan, they were going to lock Quba down, hard.

Now it was a race.

He slowed near the corner itself, watching his surroundings carefully so that he didn't go barreling into an untenable position, whether it was a police patrol or Akbarov himself waiting in ambush. Wade and Burgess were right behind him; they'd had no trouble keeping up.

The street was lined with trees and bushes, framing the homes that nestled between the greenery on either side. A few cars and microbuses were parked on the pavement, and a couple of older men were standing outside one of the gates a few dozen yards north. They were staring quizzically up the street, looking away from the three men who had just come out of the alley.

The man running toward them, dressed in a checked shirt and dark blue trousers, was looking over his shoulder. When he turned back around, Flanagan got a good look at Etibar Akbarov. He looked a lot like his photo.

Unfortunately, Akbarov saw the three men spreading out across the street at the same time. Wade had moved to the other side, and Burgess was stepping out next to Flanagan. They had stopped running; there was no need when their quarry was coming straight at them.

Akbarov could not have recognized them, but something about the three of them must have set off alarm bells in his already-panicked head. He skidded to a halt, looked around him frantically, and dashed for the fenced, wooded yard on the west side of the street, jumping and vaulting the fence as Wade cursed and started after him.

"Hold it! Wade!" Flanagan pointed to the opening of a side street or alley a block south. "You and Burgess go that way, try to cut him off! I'll follow him!" He glanced at the three Azeri men watching the excitement, hoping that they were still too far away to take note that the men chasing the guy in the checked shirt were speaking English. That would definitely give the game away.

But there was no way to avoid that risk, except to let their quarry go. He dashed toward where Akbarov had disappeared into the trees. None of them except Javakhishvili spoke Russian, never mind Azeri. They just had to hope that they could grab Akbarov and get clear before the police started putting two and two together.

It was a short run to the trees. The fence was considerably lower than the wall he'd vaulted earlier, and a line of low bushes was growing around and through it. It wasn't all that easy to get over, as the wire wanted to bend and the bushes caught at his jeans, but he managed it, using one of the posts as a fulcrum as he threw his legs over. Branches dragged at his back leg, throwing off his balance, and he staggered as he hit, half-rolling over and only managing to stay somewhat upright because he was still holding onto the fencepost.

He heaved himself up, spinning to face the wooded yard. He couldn't see Akbarov at first, but as he sprinted out of the thicker stand of trees, he spotted him nearing the far side, closing in on the next line of bushes that lined the street beyond.

Akbarov pushed through the bushes without a backward glance, even as Flanagan put on speed and sprinted after him.

***

Brannigan wasn't looking back when Akbarov burst out of the bushes, but Javakhishvili let out a yell, and he turned to see the man starting to run south down Mashadi Azizbayov. He could only see his back and the checkered shirt, but there probably wasn't anyone else busting through hedges and running like the hounds of Hell were on their heels in Quba right then.

Javakhishvili was already running after him as Brannigan started, yanking on Krivov's arm and pointing him across the street. Their Georgian medic almost collided with Flanagan as the lanky, black-bearded man burst out of the hedge behind Akbarov, pausing just long enough to spot the fleeing jihadi. It slowed both men enough that Akbarov was able to get another dozen yards ahead, though he was clearly starting to slow down.

Brannigan passed the two of them at full tilt. He was a big man, and while he wasn't all that fast off the starting blocks, so to speak, once he got going, it wasn't a good idea to get in his way. Krivov was already on the other side of the street, pounding down the pavement.

Akbarov glanced over his shoulder, his eyes wide, and started to put on more speed. Then he saw the flashing lights up ahead, where the police were still investigating the wreck of the Kamaz.

He stutter-stepped, slowing as he looked around frantically. Clearly, the Salafist jihadi with connections to the Chechens didn't want to get rolled up by the still predominantly secular Azerbaijani police. He suddenly turned and dashed across the street, jumping to grab the top of the wall just behind the spare hedge that encircled the grounds surrounding the five-story yellow building.

His feet scrabbled at the concrete as Krivov closed in on him, then he was over. He dropped out of sight, as yells erupted from the security checkpoint at the north corner.

"Gamer, Ventura, this is Kodiak." Brannigan keyed his radio as he slowed, trying not to attract too much attention from the cops, himself. "Looks like he's coming to you. He just jumped the fence and cut across near that yellow five-story building we passed."

***

"Roger," Curtis gasped as he ran around the corner and up the cracked, crumbling concrete street. Jenkins was already ahead of him, but had kept going down the dirt road along the treeline, where they'd been waiting in the Kamaz before everything had gone south, and had to skid to a halt, turn around, and run back.

*I* hate *running*. He'd promised himself after getting out of the Marine Corps that he wasn't going to ever do it again. He'd lift weights and bang girls for his cardio. Sure, there'd been some running that he'd had to do on ops; fire and movement didn't happen at a leisurely pace. But that was different. That wasn't chasing some skinny Azeri punk through a damned city, trying to run him down as he kept changing directions.

He pounded up the street, trying to remember just where the five-story building Brannigan had talked about was. He knew that he was *supposed* to be navigating at all times, but he was the machinegunner, damn it! He had been watching for threats, not taking notes on every damned old building in the city.

There. That must be it. The walls did look sort of yellowish, and it was the tallest building around. He slowed, looking at the nearest intersections and wondering if he should try to get closer, or move up to see if Akbarov ran out in front of him.

*What if he cuts in behind us, and I'm looking the wrong way?* He chewed his lip. "Is he heading north or south?"

"He's heading west," Brannigan said. "We do not have eyes on at the moment; he jumped the wall into the compound."

*Shit. That's no help.* He hesitated. He didn't want to be the one to screw this up.

Of course, he was also, as far as he knew, the only black man in the city, currently breathing heavily and sweating, standing in the middle of the street, looking like he was trying to figure out where to go next.

Jenkins raced past him, heading north. He almost called the former SEAL back, but he still wasn't sure which way to go.

Then Akbarov burst out onto the road ahead. He'd angled north.

He glanced over his shoulder to see Jenkins bearing down on him. Jenkins might not have been the top operator in the Blackhearts, but he was still fit, and he was closing the distance fast. Akbarov stumbled a little, catching himself as he tried to change direction quickly. That was when Curtis, who was starting to run again, spotted that he had something in his hand.

Before he could yell a warning, the Azeri twisted and flung a chunk of brick at Jenkins' head.

Jenkins saw it coming and ducked, losing his own balance in the process as he tripped over a crack in the road. He landed hard, rolling to mitigate some of the impact, but Akbarov was already moving, putting on more speed as he raced north. Curtis put his head down and forged after him, cursing under his breath.

"He's heading north on…" He realized that he didn't know the name of the street, and there were no signs, even if any of the rest had memorized the street names. "Shit." He keyed the mic again. "He's running north!"

***

Flanagan's lungs were burning as he kept running. He heard sirens and whistles behind him, somebody yelling what was probably "Stop!" in Azeri, but he kept going. Then another burst of gunfire rattled across the neighborhood dwindling behind him.

*They're probably not even yelling at me. They're more worried about that crazy Russian and his submachinegun.*

In a way, that was an advantage. But the more Berezin shot the place up, the more proactive the Azerbaijani police were going to be about locking it down.

*But I'll take it if it keeps them off my back for a few more minutes.* How they were going to get out afterward was another matter altogether.

He hit the corner at a dead sprint, leaning into the turn. Past the rasping of his breath in his own ears, he could hear pounding footsteps as Wade and Burgess kept pace.

Unfortunately, the road he'd taken to try to cut Akbarov off wasn't a straight shot. He sprinted to the next corner, coming around as a big Azeri dog jumped against the other side of the fence, barking viciously. He'd seen it coming, so he didn't flinch, though he heard Wade swear behind him as he went around the corner again.

"He's heading north on…" Curtis' voice in his earpiece cut out for a second. "He's running north!"

Flanagan was breathing too hard to demand more details, but he thought he could figure it out. He ran for the next corner and the main north-south road. Unless both Curtis and Akbarov had bounded a lot farther west than he'd expected—and Akbarov had already been starting to flag a little when he'd jumped the wall—then that should be the road their quarry was running north on.

He came around the corner fast; he didn't want to give Akbarov any more warning than necessary. Unfortunately, even then, he'd misjudged how fast the little man was moving.

Akbarov was gassed. That much was obvious at a glance. His run was more of a fast jog than a sprint anymore. Only the fact that Jenkins was limping a little and Curtis wasn't much of a runner was keeping him in front of his pursuers. It also put him farther away than Flanagan wanted.

Even as Flanagan picked up speed, charging down on him, Akbarov looked up and saw him coming. With a pained grimace he stumbled, turned, and jumped for the fence between the apartment building he'd just passed and the four-peaked house on the corner.

A massive, jowly mountain of black and tan fur threw itself at the fence, barking furiously. The deep, thunderous barks almost drowned out the pop and crackle of gunfire half a mile away.

Akbarov fell backward as the mastiff slammed its paws against the fence, snapping and snarling at him. He hit hard, sprawling on his back with an impact that must have knocked most of the wind out of him.

That was all the opening the Blackhearts needed. Flanagan and Wade were on him in a moment, Flanagan grabbing a wrist and flipping him over, twisting his arm behind his back as he put a knee on his neck. Akbarov was screaming and cursing in Azeri and Arabic, as Wade hastily searched him while Burgess and Curtis caught up.

"Shut the fuck up," Wade snarled. He stood up, Akbarov's cell phone in his hand. "He's clean. For certain values of the term."

Flanagan could smell the little man's acrid sweat, so he didn't need any clarification. He stood up, pulling Akbarov to his feet with him.

The jihadi promptly spat at Curtis and tried to kick Flanagan. Flanagan deftly blocked the kick with the edge of his boot sole before kicking him in the back of the knee, forcing him back down onto the ground and cuffing him, hard, on the side of the head.

"None of that," he growled. He looked up at Wade. "We need a way out."

"Kodiak, Angry Ragnar," Wade called over the radio. "We've got him; we need an extract plan." The sounds of gunfire seemed to be receding, but that didn't mean that all the police were necessarily going to be drawn after Berezin, especially if someone had just seen them take Akbarov down. And someone probably had, since they'd just tackled him in broad daylight in front of an apartment building.

"Head south and get into the trees if you can," Brannigan answered. "Boris and I are going to try to acquire alternate transport."

# CHAPTER 12

Brannigan fell back a few feet and grabbed Krivov by the arm. "We need wheels. Where's your other team?"

Before the Russian officer could even speak, Brannigan cut him off, already seeing the denial in his face. "Don't fuck with me, Krivov. Where. Is. Your. Other. *Team?*"

The *Spetsnaz* officer looked like he was going to argue for a moment. But as Brannigan tightened his grip and, in the process, made it evident that he didn't need the rifle he'd left behind when they'd bailed to end Krivov's life, he reconsidered.

"They are in a vehicle to the north, halfway between Quba and Qusar," Krivov finally said. "They are monitoring the Azerbaijani communications." He held up a hand, trying to wrest his arm out of Brannigan's grip. "Wait." He bent his head, listening to his earpiece, or at least attempting to make it look like he was listening to it.

"*Chyort.*" He looked up and tried to pull away toward the south. "The Azerbaijani police are requesting assistance from Khachmaz. They are going to try to lock down the city."

"Then we've got less time than we hoped," Brannigan growled. "Get your team down to the south side of Quba to pick us up."

"They cannot," Krivov protested. "There is not room in the vehicle, even if they could get past the Azeris, who are moving every unit out onto the streets."

Brannigan grimaced as he and Krivov hastily crossed the street and ducked into a side street that appeared to lead west, if in a jagged, zig-zag sort of way. "Then we have even less time. Move."

He was already wracking his brain for a solution to the thorny tactical problem in front of them as he moved, walking fast but without breaking into a run. With all hell breaking loose on the streets of Quba, running would only attract some very unwanted attention.

They were a little less than a quarter mile from the woods, where they had a better chance of hiding. It wouldn't be perfect; eventually the police would sweep the woods as well. But they also had weapons cached back there, and if things got dicey enough, they might need them.

But if they got to the woods and got the AKs back, then what? They'd still be on foot, deep in hostile territory, with a detainee. Akbarov might not be all that well-liked as a jihadist in officially-secular Azerbaijan, but that would be small comfort when the men who had infiltrated the country with smuggled weapons and kidnapped him were captured.

"Can you hotwire one of these microbuses?" he asked.

Krivov glanced at one of the GAZ vans parked alongside the street. "Of course. It is not difficult."

Brannigan scanned their surroundings again. They were getting looks. There were still people on the street; only a few had gone inside when the gunfire had started. Brannigan vaguely wondered at that, as he had in just about every other country where he'd seen the local populace flatly ignore the shocking violence happening just a few blocks over.

He supposed that in a place like Quba it was a combination of disbelief and denial. They were so used to their daily lives that any disruption was simultaneously unthinkable and so dangerous that they didn't *want* to believe it was happening. It was "over there," after all. It wasn't on their block.

But it meant that the Blackhearts and their Russian allies would be observed wherever they went in the city. And that could prove disastrous. He had no idea just what kind of relationship the locals had with the Azerbaijani National Police, but it was a rare occurrence that a local would cover for strangers who might have been involved in violence in their neighborhoods, whether they liked the cops or not.

Every step they had taken since Akbarov had started running was going to be documented later on. They had to get out of Quba fast.

"All Blackhearts except for Woodsrunner and Angry Ragnar," he called over the radio, "head south to the woods and retrieve the weapons if you can. Boris and I are going to get alternate transport. Rendezvous is at Point Victor One." They'd assigned alphanumeric designations to every major intersection and point of interest in the city prior to insert, just in case some kind of coordination like this became necessary.

Naturally, it had. *No battle plan survives contact with the enemy, indeed.*

"Let's go." He ignored the frowning look he was getting from Krivov at the use of "Boris." The nickname kept Krivov's actual name off the radio, and he wasn't going to explain the characters of Boris and Natasha to the humorless *Spetsnaz* officer, anyway. "I want to find a van that's not right out in the open."

***

Akbarov was starting to recover from Flanagan's blow to the head, and he was beginning to struggle again. Flanagan twisted his wrist behind his back, forcing him to bend over as the joint went farther than it was supposed to. It only had limited effect, as he screamed, far louder than the pain would have justified, and dropped to his knees, yelling in Azeri.

"We're starting to attract attention, buddy," Wade said, scanning their surroundings. Flanagan risked a glance up to see faces pressed to windows, and a few peering out from gates and starting to step out onto the street. Then Akbarov was twisting and fighting again, and he had to focus on keeping the man restrained.

"Come on, you jihadi bastard," he muttered, wrenching their quarry back up to his feet. Akbarov seemed to have figured out that being dead weight was his best chance; he was a skinny little man, and he didn't have anything like Flanagan's wiry strength. Instead, he was going to drag his feet, fall down, and scream and yell until somebody came to help him.

Flanagan thumped Akbarov at the base of the skull with an elbow, and the man quieted and went limp. He wasn't quite unconscious, but that spot was often called the "Reset button" for a reason.

Hefting Akbarov up, he started to drag him down the street, all too conscious of how many eyes were watching them as well as the big dog still barking at the fence behind them. Wade had moved around to Akbarov's other side and slipped under his other arm. Unless someone had seen the struggle a moment before, it would look like two men helping a sick or injured friend.

Except for the fact that everyone on the street had to have heard Akbarov screaming, and more than a few had witnessed the fight.

With Akbarov's toes dragging behind them and his head lolling, they started moving quickly down the street. But it was probably already too late; more people were coming out onto the street, and none of them looked friendly.

As Akbarov started to lift his head blearily, Wade keyed his radio. "We might need some help, here."

***

Santelli was cursing under his breath, dredging up old obscenities that he hadn't heard or used in years, and probably inventing a few along the way. He was sweating under his light jacket; the rush to get away from the wreck and spread out to try to head Akbarov off hadn't been fun, and he wasn't a spring chicken anymore. The weight he'd put on after Argentina was starting to tell on him, as well, and he was cussing himself for getting fat more than anything else.

He hadn't gotten too deep into the city; he'd been heading east, after Flanagan, Burgess, and Wade, before the call had come in that Akbarov had changed directions. He'd stayed in the trees, and he'd just turned up the west side of the compound dominated by that tall, yellow building when he'd seen Akbarov jump the fence and run off to the west.

Santelli had already been puffing by then. *I really need to PT more. Got so wrapped up in the car business that I let it slide.*

He'd started after Akbarov, putting his head down and pumping his legs as his muscles and his lungs alike burned. He hadn't gotten far before Wade had called and announced that he and Flanagan had caught their prey, though.

Now the Colonel was telling everyone to head back to the trees and grab weapons. With a deep breath and a glance at some of the looks he was getting from the locals in their backyards, he turned and started forging back south again, thankful for once that he hadn't gotten all that far.

*You're getting old, Carlo. If the fuckin' Altiplano didn't kill you, why are you sucking wind here?*

He jogged back into the trees, pointedly not looking over his shoulder until he was in the woods. *If you don't look guilty, maybe you're not.* It was thin, but when they were all by themselves and everything was going to crap, every little bit of confusion and misdirection might help.

He really didn't like this kind of op. He was a fundamentally straightforward man, who would have preferred a quick smash-and-grab in the middle of the night. Get in, grab Akbarov, and get out. Preferably at about two or three in the morning, when nobody would be up and about to see or interfere.

Then he wouldn't have had to worry about trying to blend in in a foreign country where he didn't even begin to speak the language.

Once he was in the trees, he got behind a trunk and only then dared to look back behind him. No one was following him, and he was mostly masked from the houses back there by the trees. He started to breathe a little more easily.

Then he saw movement. Someone was coming. He got farther back behind the tree trunk, at least as much as a man of his size could; none of the trees were all that thick. They were slender and close together.

A moment later, he got a better look at the advancing figure jogging into the trees. At first, he hoped that the man was too big for an Azeri, though he hadn't really seen enough of the locals to know what their average size was. He just tended to assume that most people were smaller than Americans. It had been a rule of thumb that he'd seen borne out year after year in the Third World.

He was right; the big man looking around as if he was trying to get his bearings resolved into Vincent Bianco. "Vinnie!" he hissed. "Over here."

Bianco joined him quickly. The big man was still looking around, an embarrassed frown on his face. "Carlo, I don't know where the hell we left the guns," he whispered.

"Over that way," Santelli said, jerking his thumb over his shoulder. "Wait here a second until we can gather anybody else who's coming in, then we'll go get 'em."

But a moment later, Wade's voice came over the radio again. "We might need some help, here."

"Shit." If the capture team was getting cut off, they were really screwed. "Come on."

The two of them started weaving through the trees, heading back east toward the wreck and the spot where Santelli, at least, remembered caching the weapons. He was hoping beyond hope that no one had investigated the woods after they'd bailed from the wreck.

Hank Brannigan came out of the trees near them with a hissed, "Friendly!" Santelli was gratified that not only had the kid remembered to try to deconflict, but he also hadn't been taken by surprise. None of them had; they were all still on their toes.

He would have expected the Colonel's son to at least know what he was about in the bush, but then, the kid had been a junior officer. Who knew what kind of bad habits he'd picked up?

"There." He pointed a stubby finger and ran down into the hollow that dipped toward the creekbed running along the south side of Quba. His AK-103 and chest rig were right where he'd left them, their hasty covering of leaves undisturbed. He threw on the rig and picked up the rifle, as the others spread out to find their own kit.

More footsteps crunched in the carpet of old leaves under the trees. Santelli faded behind a trunk, his rifle held ready, until he saw that it was Jenkins, his head down and looking at the roots of the trees. Unfortunately, their resident SEAL wasn't doing quite as well as the former shavetail.

Which was being unfair to Hank, he knew. Hank had done a full five years and gotten out as a Captain. He wasn't a mere butter-bar. He was still vastly inexperienced compared to the other Blackhearts, but not a babe in the woods.

"Jenkins!" He didn't dare raise his voice too much, but he didn't want the man to just blunder into them, either.

Jenkins jerked his head up, just as Curtis came out of the trees behind him. "Friendlies," Curtis called, a little too loudly. The two of them hurried past him, Jenkins having the good grace to look a bit sheepish at having been caught with his head down. He knew that Santelli had seen him; he'd made eye contact just before Curtis had passed him.

Santelli had no idea where Burgess, Javakhishvili, or Gomez were. Presumably, Brannigan was somewhere in the city with Krivov, and Wade was with Flanagan and their captive.

"Hurry up and get geared up, we don't have all day!"

***

The crowd on the street was growing, watching the action as Akbarov started to revive from the blow to the back of his head. Both Blackhearts were holding his wrists securely, so there was only so much he could do to fight, but as his head cleared, Flanagan felt his lungs fill as he got ready to yell.

There weren't any good options. They were still being watched, but if Akbarov started screaming bloody murder again, it was only going to make the situation worse. Flanagan cut him off with an elbow to the stomach, hard. It was a little awkward at that angle; he didn't get quite as much force behind the blow as he'd wanted. He still felt and heard the wind get knocked out of Akbarov's chest with a grunt.

But people had seen it. The growing knot of men standing at the intersection up ahead, ranging from a few who looked barely out of their teens to several older, thickset men in dark jackets with gray at their temples, didn't look happy. They hadn't moved yet, and Flanagan and Wade had dragged Akbarov over to the other side of the street, but they were talking amongst themselves, all eyes on the two Blackhearts and their human cargo.

"This ain't good, buddy," Wade muttered. "I don't think they're going to let us just walk past."

"I don't think so, either, but what other choice do we have?" Flanagan grumbled in reply. Both men had kept their voices low, hoping that the English words didn't travel far.

The crowd's motionlessness didn't last. As the two Americans and their captive got within half a block, they started to drift across the street, blocking the way. Flanagan could see a couple of cudgels and bricks, but he was less worried about those than he was the couple of Makarovs he could see near the front of the crowd. This was about to get ugly, and he didn't know what to do about it. Even if they let Akbarov go—which would make all of the pain and effort worthless—he didn't think this crowd was going to just let them walk.

"Let me do the talking," Wade said quietly.

"Can you speak Azeri?" Flanagan asked.

"No, but I'll think of something."

"Well, think fast," Flanagan muttered. Akbarov was still wheezing and gasping for breath, all the fight gone out of him for the moment. But Flanagan didn't think that was going to last.

The crowd was in front of them now. The men in front had their faces set, hard, each radiating hostility. One of the older, thickset men said something in Azeri. It was a question, but that was about as much as Flanagan could make out.

"Our friend is very drunk." Wade was falling back on the excuse more than one American soldier, Marine, or sailor had used in more than one liberty port. "He gets a little crazy when he's had this much." Flanagan hoped that none of them knew Akbarov. Saying that a Muslim was drunk wasn't impossible—in fact, he'd known a few nominal "Muslims" who'd gone to mosque every Friday, then gone home and downed a fifth of whiskey. But it was unlikely. Especially for a Salafist working with the generally extreme fundamentalist version that had burrowed itself into Chechnya in the '90s.

He could already tell that they weren't buying it. And why would they? Gunfire elsewhere in the city, the cops going nuts, and they'd just watched them beat this guy who'd been screaming for help in Azeri. They knew a kidnapping when they saw one.

He was really wishing that they hadn't left their AKs behind. Not that they would have necessarily helped, but having a weapon would have made this little trainwreck a little less no-win.

*We're going to have to drop him and run. Find another way to get the information. And we're going to have to do it soon, before we're too close and they can stop us.* It galled him to just give up when they had the package in hand, but it was what it was.

Then a familiar rattle of Kalashnikov fire, along with the *snap* of bullets flying by overhead, changed the equation.

The little mob flinched almost as one; the bullets had been fired over their heads, but not *far* over their heads. Another burst rattled out, accompanied by a yell, and then they were scattering, running for cover wherever they could find it.

As the crowd cleared the street, Flanagan looked through to see Santelli and Bianco crouched at the T-intersection at the far end, pointing their rifles up the street.

"Good timing," Wade grunted, as the two of them surged forward, dragging Akbarov, who was starting to struggle again as his lungs recovered from the blow to his solar plexus.

"Still ain't out of the woods yet," Flanagan replied.

The pair of armed Blackhearts ran up the street toward them, as other figures with weapons filtered through the trees behind them. "Come on," Santelli called out, apparently unconcerned about the locals hearing English on the street. "We need to get off the streets before the local cops lock this place down." He wasn't wrong; Flanagan could already hear sirens entirely too close behind.

"On your six," Brannigan's voice crackled in his earpiece.

Wade slowed first, turning and looking back. "Where?" Flanagan asked; he couldn't see past Akbarov, who was starting to plead in Azeri. He turned his attention briefly to their prisoner. "Shut up."

The blue UAZ minibus pulled up next to them and the side door slid open. "Get in," Krivov snapped. "We do not have much time."

# CHAPTER 13

Santelli and Bianco ran to the back of the UAZ van and each took a knee, their weapons pointed out toward either side of the street. "All Blackhearts, come north and rendezvous on the street," Santelli called over the radio. When that drew a look from Brannigan, which he seemed to sense rather than actually see, Santelli said over his shoulder, "They're all right behind us. We might as well load up here, instead of stopping somewhere down the road."

And the rest were indeed coming out of the woods, black Kalashnikovs in hand and chest rigs either worn or slung over their shoulders. Gomez and Curtis were each carrying an extra AK or two, bringing the unarmed Blackhearts' weapons along with them. The gunfire had already rendered any attempt at staying low profile moot. They were being watched, and the police were going to be on site at any moment, but the cat was out of the bag, so they ran toward the van, weapons out and heads up.

He and Bianco stayed in place as the UAZ rocked under the impacts as each man got in next to them. None of the Blackhearts were small men; even the shortest were heavy with muscle, and the weapons and gear added weight.

"Get in!" Wade was suddenly bellowing at him from the partially open window. Sirens were whooping in the distance, and while the street had been suddenly cleared by the gunfire and the openly displayed weapons, they were going to be in a world of hurt if they didn't get moving.

Heaving himself to his feet, Santelli ran around the back of the van, grabbing the extended hand sticking out of the door without looking, and hauled himself inside.

It had been Hank who'd pulled him in. "Go, go, go!" the young man yelled, far too loudly, given how close he was to Santelli's ear. But he was young, it was his first job with the Blackhearts, and he was obviously amped to the gills with adrenaline. This was an entirely different animal to leading a platoon in conventional combat.

Santelli held on for dear life as Brannigan stomped on the gas. The door was still open, and it would have been embarrassing—not to mention probably fatal in the long run—to fall out right then and there. But the UAZ wasn't exactly a high-powered machine, and there were a lot of bodies inside. More than the vehicle was designed to carry.

The van accelerated slowly, with more of a chugging slow roll than a surge. But it was moving, and Santelli leaned over Hank to get himself all the way inside so that Bianco could shut the door.

It was hardly the most comfortable ride; the interior was already heating up from having thirteen men crammed into a space meant for eleven at most, and he couldn't exactly sit down. He was halfway wedged between Hank Brannigan, Bianco, and the door. And there was no way he was going to be able to get his weapon into action if they got hit.

But better to be moving than stuck on foot when the noose tightened.

***

Brannigan was silently cursing the Russian engineers who had designed the UAZ, even though he was trying to put it through paces it had never been designed to meet. He got it moving, though, rolling toward the T-intersection ahead without stalling the engine. Unfortunately, it looked like the gas gauge was broken; it was showing empty when the vehicle clearly still had fuel.

How much was the question, and it could very well turn out to be a question with life-or-death consequences.

He took the turn as fast as he could. The UAZ was designed for offroad use, so it had a high center of gravity, and with thirteen men crammed into it, it tipped dangerously to one side as he went around the corner. He widened the turn just enough to keep them from rolling over, and then he was rumbling down the dirt road through the trees. There was enough weight in the van that the bouncing from the rugged surface of the road wasn't nearly as noticeable as it might have been.

The road was still all but clear. Only a few other vehicles were on it, shadowed by the trees, and the police hadn't worked their way that far south yet. It was only a matter of time, but he started to let himself hope that they'd slipped the net.

The road south was clear as he turned onto it and shifted back up through the gears, accelerating through the fields and toward the mountains to the south. They weren't going to go very fast in this thing, but as long as they were out of the city, they were already going to be harder to find.

But not impossible. "We need to ditch this thing and get alternate transport," he told Krivov. "*Somebody*'s going to put out a BOLO for a blue UAZ minibus full of men crammed in like sardines."

Krivov looked a little confused. "Bolo?" he asked.

"Be On the Look Out," Brannigan explained. "Even if they don't have aerial assets, they'll have people looking for a stolen blue UAZ."

Krivov nodded as he got it. "I will call." He pulled his mobile phone out and dialed hastily, putting it to his ear.

Brannigan ignored him, concentrating on the road. The palatial Quba Rixos Hotel loomed on the hill ahead, and if he remembered the map right, they were going to have to go right or left.

Somebody must have answered, because Krivov started talking fast, a stream of Russian that Brannigan couldn't hope to make out. And asking Javakhishvili to translate would have been difficult, since their medic was crammed into the back of the van, and it wouldn't exactly have been politic, either.

"Go right," Krivov said suddenly, pointing. They were almost to the intersection, and Brannigan was already slowing down. Fortunately, he hadn't already started to turn the other way, though he'd been thinking about it. After all, if the Azerbaijanis were going to look for them heading for Russia, then right would have been the logical direction.

He'd been at this mercenary business long enough to know that sometimes figuring out which way the enemy expected you to jump, and then going the other way, could just be the hair-thin margin upon which survival rested.

But Krivov had their backup on the phone, so he'd have to play along for now.

He turned off the dirt road and onto the paved highway skirting the base of the hill where the Rixos was perched. He wouldn't have been surprised if the Azerbaijani police conscripted the hotel's security to help with the chase, but the entrance was around on the east side of the hill. They still had time, and that was even assuming that their route had been observed.

"There is a logging road up ahead. At the next intersection, turn left into the trees." The stress seemed to be making Krivov's accent more pronounced.

Brannigan just nodded that he understood. He had to concentrate on the road. It was paved, and in better shape than the dirt road they'd taken through the fields, but that wasn't saying much in Azerbaijan.

Coming up on a hairpin turn, he had to slow, watching the trees ahead even as he craned his neck to scan the sky for helicopters. He didn't think that the Azerbaijani National Police had many, particularly not in that neck of the woods, but with their connection with INTERPOL, it was possible. And a firefight in the middle of a city was bound to attract more attention. This wasn't one of the breakaway republics like Nakhchivan or Nagorno-Kharabakh.

But the sky remained clear. For the moment.

They followed the winding highway for another mile and a half, driving as fast as he dared with the top-heavy, overloaded vehicle, before Krivov started pointing. "It should be here."

Another paved road met the highway on the right, but Brannigan couldn't see any other road going into the trees on the left. He slowed more, dividing his attention between the road, the forest, and the sky. He could barely see behind them; the side mirrors were small, and there were too many bodies blocking the central rear-view mirror.

There. He wasn't going to let Krivov see that he'd had a hard time finding it, but he finally spotted the opening in the trees, the narrow logging road winding back into the shadows. He slowed further; it was going to be a tight turn, and the UAZ didn't exactly have the smallest turning radius.

"Vehicle from behind." Burgess's voice was slightly muffled by the crowding in the back. But those words still put a jolt of adrenaline through Brannigan, and he glanced at the mirrors. He'd already started the turn, though, and saw only trees and fields.

He craned his neck to see as he dropped his hand to the Kalashnikov that had been passed up to him; he didn't want to get closed in or pursued by the police, but he didn't want to get them T-boned, either, and he was all too familiar with how people drove in Eastern Europe and Central Asia.

Fortunately, he'd slowed and almost stopped before making the turn. The white Audi sedan tore past the UAZ van, honking loudly. A moment later it had disappeared around the bend, leaving a faint cloud of dust behind.

Brannigan let out a sigh, taking his hand off the AK-103 and accelerating into the turn. *Just some jackass out driving too fast. Nothing to do with us.* He'd been in the Third World enough not to expect that every driver acting erratically was necessarily part of the security forces, or willing to talk to them. Given the Azerbaijani police's reputation for extortion, the locals probably weren't going to be particularly eager to call on them, unless there was an immediate threat to their safety.

Or they saw a chance to use the police to screw someone else over. He'd seen that firsthand, too. Hell, he'd been the intended instrument, more than once.

In moments, they were on the logging road, rocking and trundling beneath the trees, the shadows closing in around the vehicle.

"There should be turnoff on left, about half a kilometer ahead," Krivov said. "Anatoly's contact will meet us there."

"Anatoly's our lifeline out of here?" Brannigan was momentarily proud that he hadn't slipped and started to say "Dmitri." "Great."

"He has been reliable," Krivov said flatly.

"Maybe to you," Brannigan muttered under his breath.

"What?" Krivov asked, over the growl of the engine and the creaks and bangs of the battered suspension.

"Nothing," Brannigan said. "Just clearing my throat."

Krivov looked at him for a moment, as if trying to figure out whether he was lying or not, but he didn't comment.

Covering that last half klick seemed to take forever, but Brannigan finally spotted the turn. The next leg fed into an even narrower dirt track that disappeared into the thicker forest, angling uphill. The branches almost completely overshadowed the road, providing a decent amount of overhead concealment, which made him feel a little better. If the Azeris got a chopper overhead, they'd have a hard time spotting the van.

When he looked back in the tiny rear-view mirrors, he couldn't see the road they'd come in on, so he put the van in neutral and set the brake. "Everybody out."

It took a minute. Brannigan and Krivov were the first ones on the ground, Brannigan hauling his rifle out and scanning the woods before turning back to see what was taking so long.

Santelli had just gotten the door open, and spilled out as Brannigan looked back. "Fuckin' sardine can," the squat, former Sgt Major grumbled. He stumbled a little as he backed out of the doorway, though he compensated quickly and kept his AK-103 pointed up and away from anyone else even as he recovered.

The rest of the Blackhearts extricated themselves painfully. They had endured most of the very bumpy hour crushed either in or against the seats. Now they spread out, stretching and straightening their limbs as they took up security in a loose perimeter around the treeline.

Curtis handed Brannigan his chest rig, and he started shouldering into it. "How far out is Anatoly's contact?" Flanagan asked Krivov as he pulled Akbarov out of the van. Abu Mokhtar's Azeri contact looked bleary, and there were red marks on the side of his face, as if he'd been shoved onto a seat and then sat on.

"About thirty minutes," Krivov said, his eyes on Akbarov.

"All right, then," Brannigan said. "Carlo, get security set. Joe, start getting the van camouflaged; if we can get it off the road and into the trees, even better." He looked at Krivov. "I guess we need to decide what to do with Akbarov."

Krivov had already walked around to where Wade was holding Akbarov by the shoulder, his fingers visibly digging into the gap under the man's collarbone. Akbarov seemed to have given up on resisting, but he was cringing and trying to flinch away from Wade's grip. Krivov grabbed him roughly by the opposite arm. "I will question him."

Brannigan raised an eyebrow. "Here? Now?"

"There is little time," Krivov said, pulling slightly on Akbarov, though Wade still hadn't released him. "With the disturbance in Quba, and his disappearance, the opposition will soon take steps. The more quickly we get the information from him, the better."

Brannigan suspected that the Russian already had a plan in mind to get the information "quickly." And he further suspected that it wasn't going to be something that he could just sit by and watch.

*But do we really have a choice in the matter? Is my objection going to be anything more than a toothless protest? We're still operating on Russian sufferance, here.*

"What exactly do you have in mind, Krivov?" he asked quietly.

The Major smiled coldly. "Do not insult my intelligence by 'playing dumb,' Colonel. With little time, I cannot well try to establish rapport with him. And do you really think that it is truly possible with these black-asses?"

*Unfortunately, he's got a point.* It didn't make Brannigan particularly eager to watch Krivov working Akbarov over. If the kid was a real true believer, it could get ugly, really fast.

Wade still hadn't let go of Akbarov's shoulder. His face was blank, and Brannigan could see this coming to a head faster than he'd realized. Wade, he knew, didn't really give a damn about Akbarov getting worked over. He'd probably volunteer to do it himself under different circumstances. But he was also a stubborn bastard, and he wasn't going to just meekly hand the prisoner over simply because the Russian insisted.

"And that time's going to be wasted if he screams and brings somebody down on us," Brannigan pointed out. "We're not *that* far from the city. If they start sending patrols out, just in case, do you really want to risk compromise because we couldn't spare a couple extra hours?"

Krivov frowned, but he looked around at the trees and back toward the road they'd left not all that far behind. The Russian didn't want to admit it, but Brannigan knew he'd scored a point.

"Very well," he said grudgingly. "We will wait until we are away from here."

Brannigan nodded. He'd won this one. He doubted he was going to win again when they got back to Dagestan. But that was a fight for another time. He looked at Wade. "Keep him quiet."

Wade just nodded, with that icy hint of a smile. "Sure thing, boss." Akbarov flinched again as the big man tightened his grip.

Brannigan turned his attention to the rest of their position. Most of the Blackhearts were now out on the perimeter, except for Curtis and Bianco, whom Flanagan had pressed into pushing the van into the trees.

Flanagan and Santelli were standing not far away, hands on weapon firing controls, watching and listening. They'd been ready to intervene if Krivov had pressed things too far.

He nodded once. Both men returned it, then turned to their assigned tasks.

Brannigan glanced up at the sky again, what little he could see through the boughs overhead. Still no helicopters or drones, but he could hear vehicles on the highway down the hill.

It was going to be a long half hour.

***

Thirty minutes came and went. There was still no sign of Anatoly's contact. Brannigan pulled out the map he'd snagged in Dagestan and started studying it, despite all the labels being in Russian, trying to plan a foot route. They'd have to commandeer transportation somewhere eventually, if they were going to get out of Azerbaijan, but they really needed to get some distance from Quba first.

The other side of the mountains seemed to be all small villages, though. They'd be insular and clannish, wary of strangers and especially watchful when outsiders showed up. Finding and acquiring transport without a fight would be difficult. If not impossible.

The growl of a diesel engine and a hissed warning broke his train of thought. Stuffing the map back into his chest rig, he snatched up his AK-103 and stood, getting behind a tree and scanning their perimeter.

The van was most of the way off the road, and Flanagan, Curtis, and Bianco had broken off several branches so that they hung down over the back. It wouldn't shield it from close observation, but hopefully it would prevent a cursory glance from picking it up.

The Blackhearts themselves, while dressed in civilian clothes instead of cammies, had faded into the woods, using the trees and the leaves the best they could. He could catch a glimpse of a sleeve here, a pantleg there, but for the most part, they were using what concealment was available to its best effect.

The truck rumbled into view. It was an ancient, rust spotted Zil, its rounded hood bouncing a little since one of the catches seemed to be broken. The branches overhead rasped over the filthy tarp tied down over the back.

Dmitri was driving.

He stuck his head out of the side window when Brannigan stepped out onto the narrow dirt road, his rifle in his hands. "Get in," the Russian mobster said cheerfully. "We have a long way to go."

# CHAPTER 14

Brannigan was the last one into the truck, waiting at the back with rifle in hand until the last of the Blackhearts had clambered into the bed, Santelli flipping the back of the tarp down with a puff of dust. Only then did he move up to the cab, pulling the door open.

Krivov was already in the passenger seat, looking down at him. Brannigan stared at the man for a moment before he smiled, the expression never reaching his eyes.

"Move over." He didn't say it, but the implication was impossible to miss. *Before I move you*

*If you think I'm going to leave you and Dmitri in front while I sit in the back, blind and deaf, you've got another think coming, Boris.*

Krivov waited just long enough to make it clear that he wasn't just going to jump when Brannigan glared at him, then shifted toward the middle of the cab. Brannigan kept his expression bland as he reached up and hauled himself inside, keeping his rifle pointed down at the floorboards as he pulled the door shut. *I really,* really *hate these joint ops, with 'friends' who may as well be enemies.*

It reminded him too much of so many of the political games played in the officer corps. Not everyone played them, but the majority of those who got promoted and ladder-climbed toward stars were better at playing the political games than they were at war.

And he included Mark Van Zandt on that list, too.

It was a delicate dance of ego and appearance that he detested, especially when real lives were hanging in the balance. Only it was even more pronounced here and now. He was sure that the Russians were looking for any sign of weakness, any chink in the Blackhearts' armor that they could exploit. They might have a common enemy for the moment, but he didn't forget that Russia had been treating the US as an enemy for decades, even after '91, and while Krivov might not know about it, Brannigan was remembering the Russian bodies they'd left in the snow in Romania.

*Never should have agreed to this mission. Should have let Abernathy's people handle it*. But it was far, far too late for second thoughts now.

"Let us go, then, hey?" Dmitri acted as if he hadn't noticed any of the silent byplay between the two commanders. Brannigan was pretty sure he'd taken it all in, though, and was calculating how to turn it to his advantage even then. For all his affable exterior, Dmitri was a very dangerous man. And Brannigan hadn't even needed to see the example of the other mobster's missing eye to know that.

Grinding the Zil's gears, Dmitri got them moving with a bang and a lurch, barely scraping past the rear of the UAZ van and back down toward the logging road.

***

Sitting across from Santelli, Flanagan braced himself against the swaying and occasional jarring bumps as the Zil negotiated the very unimproved road and put his eye to the slight gap beside the rear flap. He couldn't see anything except trees and a short stretch of the empty dirt road behind them.

"See anything?" Curtis asked.

Flanagan straightened just as the truck hit a particularly nasty bump, narrowly avoiding hitting his head on the metal frame that held the tarp up. "We're still on the logging road. Nothing much to see."

While it was dark under the tarp, Flanagan could still make out Curtis fidgeting. "Relax, Kev. Nothing we can do right now except keep an eye out."

"While letting that fucking Russki drive," Curtis muttered. "We know what happened the last time we trusted that fucker."

"What did happen?" Bianco asked. "It's pretty obvious you guys recognize this guy, but I don't."

Santelli snorted, but kept his own counsel. Flanagan looked around the back of the truck, realizing that he, Curtis, Santelli, and Brannigan were the only ones left from the Khadarkh mission. Villareal had been killed in Burma. Aziz had gone down on the Tourmaline-Delta. Hancock had been killed in Argentina. And Childress was a wreck of a man, still trying to recover from two traumatic wounds, neither of which would ever completely heal.

"Dmitri—yeah, that's the name he gave us in Dubai; it's probably as fake as 'Anatoly'—was the facilitator who got us the weapons and the insert platform onto Khadarkh. Thing was, he was supposed to pick us up after we got back out to sea." He spat out the back, suddenly overcome by distaste for the current situation. "He never showed up. We had to go back and fight our way onto the *Oceana Metropolis*, holding it with what ammo we had left until Captain Ortiz could get the engines started and get us underway." He glanced toward the front. "When we saw him again, just a couple days ago now, he spun us a story about how one of his subordinates didn't wake him up in time. Maybe it's even true." The bitterness in his voice belied his words.

"And somehow, this guy just so happens to be the *Spetsnaz* contact with the Azerbaijani mob?" Wade was openly skeptical.

"Just so happens," Santelli said dryly.

"I think he's a spook," Flanagan said, as he peered out from behind the back flap again. Still only forest and pitted, rutted dirt road. The boughs overhead were still thick enough to make aerial interdiction difficult. "Intel types have been using organized crime as proxies for forever. Were I a betting man, I'd say that our friend is either MGB, or he used to be."

"Could be he's only officially 'former,'" Wade said. "I've seen that before."

"So, this is all just one big Russian intel op, and we're helping out?" Bianco asked. "How fucked is that?"

"About as fucked up as some of those furries we saw at Max-Con, Vinnie," Wade replied. "But it is what it is. At least we're still armed."

Flanagan couldn't help but wonder just how much comfort that really was, having an AK with a handful of magazines, so far away from any genuinely friendly support.

But, he mused as he watched the road stretch behind them, vanishing into the trees as they went around another curve, Wade was right. It was what it was. They'd just have to cope as best they could and be ready to fight or run when the time came.

***

The cab stayed uncomfortably silent, except for the engine's rumble—and occasional rattle—for a long time. Dmitri, fortunately, didn't seem to feel like his affable persona really required a great deal of chatter. He was focused on the road, in any case.

They trundled along the ridge for about a half a klick before the road started to descend toward a narrow valley ahead.

Shortly thereafter, Brannigan could see they were coming up on the outskirts of a village hugging the valley floor and creeping up the hillsides to either side. Most of the houses, aside from the big, red-roofed school, were nestled amid small fields.

They didn't even get a second glance from the locals as they passed through. They were just one more beat-up, rusting rattletrap of an old Soviet farm truck, passing through the countryside. Brannigan wasn't falling for the illusion; many such people were highly observant, especially when it came to strangers. They noticed the unfamiliar truck, as well as the three men in the cab. They just weren't showing it.

Whether they'd answer the security services when questioned was another matter. Not knowing the village's predominant culture, it wasn't a question that Brannigan could answer. But he knew that it was still a question, and that it wasn't one they could dismiss lightly.

He wondered just how many more villages they were going to be leaving breadcrumb trails through before they got to the border.

***

The afternoon dragged on. The Zil hadn't exactly been the most powerful of trucks when it had been new, and it was far from new. The suspension was shot, and Dmitri had to slow to a crawl in many spots as they crawled up into the mountains.

For a long way, they were able to stick to mostly logging roads that threaded their way through the woods and backroads that wove through the little fields. But as they got closer to a village that he was pretty sure was the same one the map was calling Qirizhdehne, they were definitely descending into the valley.

"Aren't we going to try to stay off the main road?" he asked.

"There is no way to from here," Dmitri said, his eyes still locked on the road ahead. "We must go up a narrow canyon ahead.

There are no roads to the sides. It is the only main road from Qirizhdehne on, I am afraid."

Brannigan said nothing more. There was nothing more to be said. It was just one of those things. Sometimes you had no other options. He'd be perfectly willing to hoof it over the mountains, but getting Akbarov over the border on foot would be difficult at best. He'd slow them down and could cause all sorts of other problems. Yelling and screaming where somebody might hear him wasn't the least of those problems. Moving prisoners on foot was always difficult.

And on top of that, he had to admit that Krivov had had a point. As soon as they'd grabbed Akbarov, Abu Mokhtar's people had to have known that something was up. Akbarov's information had an expiration date, and it was coming up fast. They probably couldn't afford the time it would take to hike out.

That was, of course, assuming that Akbarov was who the Russians insisted he was, and this wasn't all just a wild goose chase.

He keyed his radio. "Woodsrunner, Kodiak. We're going to be getting back on the main road, so make sure everybody's on alert and our little buddy is staying quiet."

"Roger," was Flanagan's reply. Brannigan didn't need to worry beyond that. If Akbarov started kicking up a fuss as they passed through Qirizhdehne, Wade would probably choke him out in a heartbeat.

*And he'd enjoy every second of it.*

They rolled into Qirizhdehne just as the sun was nearing the mountains to the west. The village was even more spread out than the first village they'd passed through. Small, stone and brick houses with peaked roofs huddled behind roughhewn stone and brick compound walls, spread out over the slopes to the north.

The first thing he noticed was that they were almost completely alone on the road. He could see a few trucks and ancient, beat-up SUVs parked near or in some of the compounds, but only a few. This part of Azerbaijan was clearly dirt-poor, and even their ancient, battered Zil was going to stand out a little bit. He kept his hand on his AK, even while making sure it was thrust far enough below the line of sight of the window that if anyone was going to see it, they would have to climb on the running board and peer in the window.

They were getting looks from the few people he saw out and about. The village—at least, the part he could see from the road—didn't look exactly busy. But then, he had seen an awful lot of Third World villages that were just like it. He knew they were being watched, but these people weren't going to draw attention to themselves unless they felt threatened.

It took only a few minutes to pass through the village. The locals seemed to fade away in front of them. Then they were heading uphill and back into the trees, the massive rocky cliffs of the mountains looming overhead on either side, blocking out what remained of the sunlight.

The rock walls closed in as they kept going. As the sky turned a deeper blue overhead and everything started to fade into shades of gray, Brannigan watched the canyon walls get closer and closer, until they were passing between rocky cliffs so close that it felt like they were going to rip the side mirrors off.

He wasn't given to claustrophobia, but the knowledge that a single, well-placed charge would bury them forever meant he didn't breathe easily until they were out of that slot and the valley was opening up just a little.

Massive, barren peaks still loomed black against the darkening sky. The road was a faintly pale line twisting up and between them. He was really starting to wish that he'd insisted on night vision, even if it was going to be shitty Russian night vision. As it was, they were limited to what could be seen in the wan cones of light from the Zil's headlights.

They continued winding up into the mountains, the road climbing up out of the valley, though the peaks to the south still rose steeply above them on the left. He couldn't see much to the right as the gloom deepened in the shadows of the mountains, but he was pretty sure the valley fell off steeply below the road. The gray of the dirt and gravel track in the headlights vanished sharply into blackness beyond the headlights.

The mountains got darker and darker; they weren't moving fast. The old Zil rattled and groaned as Dmitri kept it inching up the mountains, rocking on the wheels while the suspension creaked and popped alarmingly.

He glanced at his watch as they went around a hairpin turn and down toward a bridge across the slender river that ran down the bottom of the narrow valley. They were moving more slowly than he'd hoped; it was later than he'd thought.

A few lights gleamed on the other side of the bridge. He hadn't seen any power lines going up into the mountains, and given the general level of poverty he'd seen the farther they'd gotten from the city, he suspected that any lights in the village ahead were either generator-powered or straight-up oil lights.

The Zil was making too much noise as they passed over the bridge and trundled past the village to make out the generators' rumble, but he was sure it was there. Somewhat to his surprise, though he might have heard dogs barking, the village stayed quiescent. There was no reaction to their passage in the dead of night.

He still kept his hand on his AK as they threaded between the houses and continued uphill, straining his eyes to scan the darkness beyond the headlights.

***

It was getting close to midnight. Despite himself and despite the ride's discomfort—the cab wasn't exactly spacious, there was a broken spring digging into his right buttock, and the constant rocking and bouncing had knocked him against the frame more than once—Brannigan found that his eyes were getting heavy. It had been a long and stressful day. And without the exertion of a foot movement, it was easy for the body to start to shut down.

But he forced his eyes open, hoping that neither Krivov nor Dmitri could see how much he was struggling. It was never a good time to show weakness in front of Russians.

Dmitri started to look a bit distracted, leaning over the wheel and squinting into the dark. He was slowing down, glancing down at the map on his lap.

Brannigan frowned, dropping his hand from the AK's dustguard to the pistol grip. "Something wrong, Anatoly?" he asked, almost unable to suppress the unconscious and slightly sarcastic accent on the man's alias.

Dmitri didn't answer but slowed even more, only rolling ahead another hundred or so yards before he stopped altogether, putting the truck in neutral and setting the brake.

He just sat there, staring into the darkness for a long moment before he reached down to open the door and stepped out.

Brannigan did the same, but Dmitri looked over at him and shook his head. "No, wait here. I will be back soon."

Brannigan ignored the gangster's admonition as thoroughly as Dmitri had ignored his question, dropping to the ground with his AK in one hand and stepping back to the tailgate. He could faintly hear Dmitri cursing in Russian over the rattle of the idling engine, but he knocked on the tailgate anyway. "Give me three," he said quietly.

Flanagan, Santelli, and Wade piled out. "Set up security," he said. "I think we might be at Dmitri's rendezvous. Either that, or we've reached our pre-arranged ambush."

The others didn't comment much; they were all at least as tired as he was, though the back had to be exponentially less comfortable than the cab. Instead, they just spread out, Santelli taking the rear while Wade and Flanagan accompanied Brannigan toward the front, fanning out on the uphill flank as best they could given the steep and rocky ground.

The Blackhearts were pros. They knew what to do in hostile territory. None of them needed to have their hands held.

Dmitri was still standing near the front of the truck, just outside the direct cone of light from the driver's side headlight, looking back toward them, his frown almost more visible in his body language than in what they could see of his facial expression. Shaking his head, muttering in Russian again, he turned back toward the front, apparently giving up on trying to get the Americans to let him do his thing without overwatch.

He walked out into the headlights, his hands in his pockets. He moved up about fifty yards ahead of the truck, almost past the light, and stopped.

Brannigan wished again for night vision, or even just some magnified optics on his Kalashnikov. But wishing wasn't going to make it so, so he strained his eyes and his ears, peering into the blackness beyond the headlights for any sign of the enemy.

There. It was only the faintest flicker, but he'd definitely seen the glow of the headlights momentarily reflected out in the dark. A moment later, the faint *bang* of a vehicle door being closed reached his ears.

He took a knee behind a boulder on the hillside, as much to brace himself to keep from sliding downhill as anything, and settled down to listen.

After a few moments, he heard a faint voice out of the dark. After shielding his eyes from the headlights for a moment, he thought he could make out three or four silhouettes standing on the hillside just above Dmitri, and what might have been a truck just beyond them. He couldn't see well enough to tell if they were armed, but under the circumstances, he thought it was probably wise to assume that they were.

It was not going to be an easy shot with an AK if this went south.

He was still considering whether to move up some more when Dmitri answered the query from above.

While they were too far away for Brannigan to make out words even if he'd been able to understand the language, Dmitri didn't sound stressed at all; he sounded like he was greeting old friends. Unfortunately, that didn't make Brannigan feel any better; the mobster was obviously practiced at the act. He hadn't been trustworthy when they'd first crossed paths in Dubai, and Brannigan was even less inclined to trust him now.

Not that he was going to trust Krivov, either, but Dmitri had a history of stabbing them in the back. Krivov hadn't had as many opportunities yet.

After a short exchange of words, two of the four men came down to join Dmitri, while the other two climbed back up toward the vehicle. Dmitri led the first two back to the Zil.

"Everything is fine, my friends," Dmitri called. "These are my associates. They will take us the rest of the way to our rendezvous."

The two men were revealed as Dmitri walked back into the light. Brannigan was pretty sure they weren't *Spetsnaz*, or even Russians. They were both wearing dark jackets and dark slacks, and one was pretty pudgy. His best guess was that they were Azeri mobsters.

Dmitri halted at the front fender and waved. "Come, come, it is late, and we still have far to go. These are friends."

Brannigan heaved himself to his feet. There weren't a lot of options. They had to get moving, and this hadn't blown up *yet*. "Come on," he murmured, as he led the way back down toward the road, keeping an eye up toward the vehicle up ahead, even though he could barely see it, and that only when he didn't look directly at it.

"This is Yusif, and this is Elnur." Dmitri pointed first to the pudgy one, then the smaller. "They are going to get us past the border guards." He looked almost apologetic. "They will need to be in front. Everyone else must ride in back. Otherwise, we will have to explain why two Russians and a large American are trying to cross out of Azerbaijan."

Brannigan glanced at Wade, who was standing right at the edge of the light, his rifle clenched in both hands, staring at Dmitri. Wade met his gaze momentarily with a look of disgust. He didn't like it, either.

*But, again, what can we do?* "All right. We'll ride in the back. With all the guns." He was watching Dmitri carefully as he said it.

*Mark's going to have to pony up some extra after this. Even if I have to wait until the next job to hit him with the rate increase.*

Dmitri just spread his hands, as if to say, "What else can I do?" The two Azeri mobsters were watching impassively, their hands in their pockets. They both looked slightly nervous at the openly displayed rifles, as well they might.

"Let's go, then." Brannigan waved the other Blackhearts back toward the back. When Krivov grudgingly climbed out, Brannigan pointed him toward the tailgate as well. "After you."

The Russian didn't look any happier about this than Brannigan felt, which was almost a relief.

Brannigan and Dmitri waited until the Azeris had climbed into the cab and the last of the Blackhearts was in the bed. "I'll be right behind you," Brannigan said, before turning toward the rear. "In case anything happens."

It had more than one meaning, and he was sure that Dmitri understood that.

***

A few minutes later, the Zil lurched into motion with a grinding, rattling roar. Brannigan braced himself against the back of the cab, his rifle pointed at the tarp overhead, and held on.

If it had been dark up front, it was pitch black in the bed. There was no way to tell what was happening except by sound, and the creaking, banging, and rattling of the suspension on top of the growl of the engine meant that there weren't many audible cues, either.

The trip turned into a fog of darkness, noise, and jolting movement. He started to lose track of time, just as he'd lost track of exactly where they were.

From the fidgeting and muttered Russian cursing, he suspected that Krivov wasn't any happier about it.

They slowed and stopped. A door banged. Brannigan lifted his AK to the ready, even though he couldn't see anything. Voices murmured in the night outside. They didn't sound urgent or hostile, but if this was a setup, he wouldn't have expected them to. Everything would stay nice and friendly right up until gunfire ripped through the canvas and sheet metal around them.

But the door banged shut, the engine roared, and then they were moving again with another painful lurch. Nobody had fired a shot. Whatever had been the reason for the stop, it hadn't ended in violence, at least.

Of course, that didn't mean that everything was good. They could be rolling toward an Azerbaijani prison or diverted to another ambush, for all he knew.

The sleepiness that had plagued him up in the cab was gone, replaced by a white-knuckled tension as he waited in the blackness, helpless to do anything but wait and try to prepare to go out shooting if and when they were betrayed.

The ride after that seemed to stretch on to eternity. None of the Blackhearts talked, except for Javakhishvili, once. Akbarov had started whimpering again, and the Georgian had cut him off with a curt, "*Zatknis.*"

Once again, he felt the truck slow and stop. This time, the engine shut off with another rattling cough. He wondered if it would even start again. The ancient diesel had been sounding more and more unhealthy as they'd climbed.

A door slammed. Footsteps crunched outside. Then the back flap rose, and a head appeared above the tailgate. In the sudden slight illumination from outside, Brannigan could see that more than one AK-103 was pointed at it.

"Come." Dmitri seemed completely unfazed by the rifles pointed at him. "We are here."

Santelli and Flanagan flipped the flap the rest of the way open and let down the tailgate before dropping out and hooking around the corners. Neither man started shooting, so that was a good sign.

The rest of the Blackhearts followed. Krivov tried to take Akbarov in hand, but Javakhishvili already had him. He almost threw the Azeri facilitator off the back of the truck, dropping off right behind him and cranking his arm up between his shoulder blades before he could try to move.

Brannigan was the last one off, somewhat to his chagrin. He was usually the first one on the ground, but the rest had moved too fast. He suspected they'd done it on purpose, too.

The starlit night seemed brilliant after the unremitting darkness in the back of the truck. The moon was rising over the eastern peaks, casting a faint, silvery glow over the scene.

They were parked in a shallow valley, with a rise immediately to the left. A huge massif bulked black against the sky to the right.

Dark figures stood up on the rise above them.

He watched them carefully. Nobody had opened fire yet. And Dmitri didn't seem to be concerned. Neither did Krivov, for that matter.

Krivov was on the radio. After listening to the faint, tinny reply, he motioned to the Blackhearts to follow him. "They are Russians. The helicopter is incoming."

Brannigan cocked his head at that. Sure enough, he could hear the faint, distant beat of rotor blades.

The question was, who was going to get on the helicopter?

With Gomez taking point, they started up the rise, Javakhishvili shoving Akbarov ahead of him. The Blackhearts spread out into a wedge, facing the Russians up above. They were outnumbered, but if this turned out to be a trap, they'd be ready.

As they got closer, the figures resolved themselves into men wearing what looked an awful lot like what US Army Rangers might wear. *Holy crap, that is a lot of Western gear.* If not for the decidedly Russian weapons and the strange NVGs, they might have been part of just about any unit he'd worked with before retirement.

He was still watching them carefully, even as Gomez slowed a few yards away, and Krivov stepped forward, quietly greeting one of the Russians. They held a short conversation, and the man in full gear pointed to the north, where Brannigan thought he could just make out the dark dot of a helicopter moving against the stars.

Krivov came back down to join him. "Everything is all right," he said. "The helicopter is an Mi-17; there will be plenty of room for all of us." He stepped closer. "We are in Russia, my friend. There is nothing to worry about, now."

"Right," Brannigan said dryly, as the massive Hip helicopter swung around above them and began to descend toward the landing zone the *Spetsnaz* had laid out, whipping dust and grit at them as the rotors beat the air to slow the bird's descent. "Nothing to worry about at all."

# CHAPTER 15

It was still dark when the Mi-17 touched down back at Makhachkala. It had been a long, loud, brutal trip, and Brannigan felt like he'd been shaken half to pieces along the way. He and the rest of the Blackhearts got off the ancient Russian helicopter—that Brannigan suspected had been built when Russia had still been the Soviet Union—with considerable relief.

The bird had touched down not far from the small compound where they'd planned and prepped. A half-dozen kitted-out *Spetsnaz* were waiting just off the HLZ, their A-545 rifles slung but ready. Brannigan felt a jolt of adrenaline as he saw them, and looking around the inside of the helo, as dark as it was, he could see that the rest of the Blackhearts—except for Jenkins, who'd apparently fallen asleep—were also up and ready, facing the rear of the bird, though Santelli was still watching Krivov and Dmitri up by the cockpit.

But the Russians stayed where they were, waiting, looking fairly relaxed. Almost bored.

*Of course, they don't* have *to storm the bird if they want to take us. We're on their turf.*

He was probably being paranoid, but under the circumstances he couldn't imagine approaching the situation any other way. True, there was little reason to turn on them at this point in the game, but they'd grabbed Akbarov, and he could well see that being the extent of their usefulness to the Russians.

They'd have to be on their toes every step of the way.

Krivov stood and grabbed Akbarov off the jump seat, where he'd been sitting blindfolded and flex-cuffed for the entire flight. Even in the dark of the inside of the fuselage, Brannigan could see that the Azeri gangster was shaking, and he caught a sharp whiff of urine as Krivov frog-marched the man off the ramp.

"You want me to go with them, Colonel?" Javakhishvili didn't sound especially eager, but he was also keeping his voice low so the Russians wouldn't overhear as the high-pitched whine of the engines spooled down.

He didn't really want to ask it. Javakhishvili's antipathy for the Russians wasn't just random prejudice. He had a history, if one somewhat more removed by circumstance than some of his countrymen. If any of them had a reason to distrust Russians, it was Herc.

But they needed to learn everything about this situation they could, and he didn't exactly trust Krivov or Pichugin to pass any intel they got. At least not all of it.

"If you can stay awake." They were all hurting; they'd been up for over twenty-four hours at that point, and none of them except Hank were especially young men anymore. "If Krivov gives you static, I'll step in as best I can." It wasn't as if they had a *lot* of leverage, but he'd do what he could.

Javakhishvili chuckled. "That won't be a problem. I brought plenty of 'uppers.'" At Brannigan's frown, more felt than seen in the dim light coming in the scratched and pitted Plexiglas windows, he waved any objections away. "No meth or anything like that. Mostly caffeine pills. But they'll do the job." The fact that Javakhishvili didn't have some particularly sarcastic comment to add told Brannigan plenty about how strung out the man was, and not just because of physical exhaustion.

"I wouldn't ask you to, but if you're up to the task, go for it." Brannigan started down the ramp. "We can use all the intel we can get."

The Russians at the base of the ramp watched them as they got off, each man ducking carefully and turning aside early to avoid the tail rotor. Brannigan had seen a Marine getting off a CH-53 who hadn't paid enough attention, many years before. The man hadn't died. His helmet had saved his life. But the helmet had been destroyed and he'd been rather severely concussed.

The Blackhearts, with Wade leading the way, moved out from under the still-spinning rotors and gathered off to one side of the bird, still watching the Russians. For their part, the geared-up Russkies appeared to be generally ignoring them.

Brannigan didn't know whether to take that as a good sign or not.

He waved Santelli, Flanagan, and the rest back toward the tent where they'd stayed before. Flanagan gave him a nod, with a significant glance at Dmitri and Krivov, who had just led Akbarov past the line of Russian shooters. Brannigan returned the nod and turned back to Javakhishvili. "You need to go to the tent first?"

"Nah, I got what I need right here." The Georgian tapped his pack. "I don't want to give them too much of a head start."

Brannigan stayed by Javakhishvili's side as he started to follow Krivov and Dmitri. One of the Russians stepped forward, holding out a hand to forestall them, saying something in Russian. Javakhishvili countered it, pointing toward the Quonset hut where Krivov and Dmitri had taken Akbarov.

The Russian looked uncertain, holding up a hand for them to wait, and turned to his radio. He spoke quietly in Russian, frowning as he listened to the reply.

Brannigan and Javakhishvili waited. Brannigan could *feel* Javakhishvili's growing impatience. But as long as the other man kept a lid on it, Brannigan kept himself calm and his expression blank.

They were starting to hear raised voices from inside the hut, but nothing more than that, yet. Brannigan's eyes narrowed. They *were* dealing with Russians, after all. The odds that they were going to be gentle in an interrogation—particularly when the detainee was involved with the Chechens—were slim to none.

It felt like a very long time before Krivov came out of the Quonset hut. "What do you want?"

Brannigan bit back the snarl in response. He was tired and strung out from stress. But antagonizing the Russians more than absolutely necessary would be a recipe for disaster for all of them. After all, they were there because they were deniable. Van Zandt's people might be standing by in Georgia, but Georgia was a long way away.

He inclined his head toward Javakhishvili. "If this is going to be a joint thing, I want Herc here to sit in on the interrogation. He speaks Russian, so he won't need an interpreter."

To Krivov's credit, he didn't simply say no right away. He looked a little uncertain, in fact, and glanced toward the main compound. "I do not know if *Polkovnik* Pichugin would agree with that."

"Then, where is he?" Brannigan took a step forward. "I'll talk to him."

If anything, that seemed to make Krivov even more uncomfortable. "I think he is not available." Something about the way he said it made Brannigan think that "not available" probably meant "dead drunk on his cot."

Brannigan raised an eyebrow. "Then I guess you get to make a decision. Your people asked *us* to be here. We can help a lot more if we've got some first-hand intel."

Krivov didn't answer right away. He fished in his pocket and brought out a cigarette. He lit it, the pungent smoke almost making Brannigan cough even from a few feet away. Apparently,

Russian cigarettes were still Russian cigarettes. It smelled worse than Pichugin's Sobranie Black Russian had.

The Russian officer took a deep drag, blowing the smoke toward the sky. Finally, grudgingly, he nodded, and waved at Javakhishvili as he turned back toward the Quonset hut. Javakhishvili looked at Brannigan, took a deep breath, and followed.

The shouting from inside started up again as Brannigan turned away and walked back toward their tent.

***

The tent was dark and quiet; most of the Blackhearts were already snoring. Santelli and Wade were still up, still wearing their kit and with AK-103s kept close. Wade stood near the back flap, while Santelli was sitting on a cot near the front, leaning on his knees, staring at the floor, his chin on his fists.

Santelli looked up as Brannigan came in. It was too dark to make out his expression, even in the glow of the sodium lights on the airstrip behind him, but he looked almost like he wanted to say something, then subsided.

Brannigan paused for a moment, every fiber of his being wanting nothing more than to lie down and stare at the backs of his eyelids for a few hours. Or a few days. But something made him sit down next to Santelli.

"Everything good?" He honestly wasn't sure if he was talking about the security situation or Santelli himself. His old Sergeant Major hadn't been his usual self this trip, and it was starting to worry him. On top of all the other worries this job had come with.

"We got the watch set." Santelli sounded distracted, but an adult life laden with such responsibilities had translated into an ability to accomplish the needed tasks despite internal distractions. Not everyone was capable of that kind of compartmentalization, but Santelli had a gift for focusing on the here and now when something needed to be done.

He was still human, though, and Brannigan wondered if the human side of Carlo Santelli had started to tell. Especially after Roger Hancock's death.

"The Russkies acted confused. Like they didn't understand why we were still setting security." Santelli managed a half-hearted chuckle. "Wasn't that great an act, either."

Brannigan nodded in the dark. He hadn't worried too much about security being set; he trusted Santelli. And Wade. And Flanagan. The Blackhearts were all there because they wanted to be. They all knew the score—well, except for Hank, but he'd either learn or he'd be out—and there wasn't a shirker amongst them. Even Jenkins tended to step up when it was time.

"So, what's eating you?" He was too tired to beat around the bush, and Santelli wasn't going to get bent out of shape if he was blunt. Santelli was as blunt as they came.

He didn't get an answer right off. The squat, balding Sergeant Major didn't look at him, but stared down at his own hands for a long moment.

"I don't know, John." Santelli still didn't look at him. It was dark as pitch, the two of them were little more than slightly darker shadows in the tent. "Something about all of this is still bugging the shit out of me. There are too many questions. I still don't get what exactly we're doing out here." He seemed to turn to face Brannigan at last. "I mean, are there even any nukes for real? Seems like the only thing we're really worried about is this gold cache, when it would make a lot more sense to kill two birds with one stone, find out where the transfer's going, and hit this Abu Mokhtar asshole while scooping up the nukes. Instead we're trying to pull a heist on a terrorist bank? Makes no sense to me."

Brannigan didn't really have an answer because he had a lot of the same suspicions. This all felt a lot like a wild goose chase, though now the question was weighing on his mind: *Just what are we here for, anyway?* The search for answers to that question was occupying his mind far more than any terrorist gold.

He knew there had to be more to this than met the eye, even though the Russians hadn't let anything slip yet.

But he had to give Santelli an answer, if only to draw him out. They'd all talked about their worries surrounding the mission. Something else was bugging Santelli.

"If the mission doesn't make sense, there are always two options. The first is that whoever passed down the mission parameters is an idiot, and worth about the attention you'd give a drunken monkey. I think we've both dealt with a few of those over the years." Santelli chuckled bitterly at that, staring down at his hands again.

"The second possibility is that we're here for a reason that *does* make sense, but we haven't been told, either because the employer is afraid of it leaking... or because we're *really* not going to like what it is."

"You think we're in the middle of option two?" From the tone of his voice, Santelli wasn't asking for an answer so much as a confirmation.

"I think it's more than likely." Brannigan glanced at the faint crack of light at the tent flap. They were too far away to hear anything from the Quonset hut—even if the generator hadn't been rumbling next door. "And I think that Van Zandt and Abernathy think so, too. They want to know what it is as much as I do."

"So, what? We're really here to spy, but we're just supposed to figure that out on our own?" Santelli was starting to sound pissed.

"I think so. And believe me, Mark and I are going to have *words* about it when we get back." He clenched his fists. It wouldn't be the first time he'd been thrown into a situation without all the information, not only all the intel, but all the actual commander's intent. And there had been a time when he would have expected that kind of thing from the sort of officer Mark Van Zandt had been.

But that had been years ago. And he'd thought that he and Van Zandt had moved beyond some of the bad blood that had stood between them in the aftermath of East Africa. They didn't quite *like* each other, but they'd developed a sort of professional respect, as Brannigan had found a new purpose through the Blackhearts, and Van Zandt had developed a new way of thinking as he'd plunged into the murkier world where the mercenaries operated.

He wondered. Had Van Zandt adapted to the shadowy world of covert, deniable operations to the point where he'd use Brannigan and the Blackhearts as expendable pawns in a bigger game?

*Or is Mark just a pawn, himself? Who is Abernathy, and what exactly is his game?*

"We'll find out what's going on, Carlo. That's why we're still here." *Well, that, and the fact that disentangling ourselves is going to take some more work and preparation. Which we should be already farther along with than we are.* "It's got to be something big, or Mark and Abernathy wouldn't have brought us the job."

"Maybe." Santelli didn't sound especially convinced, but he wasn't going to contradict Brannigan. That was just his way.

The two of them sat in the dark in silence for a while. Brannigan wasn't the greatest of counselors, and he'd never had to try to play one with Santelli. The other man was blunt and open; he wasn't given to deviousness, but he was also one of the most stoic men Brannigan had ever served with. He didn't necessarily *appear* that way—his loud, brash, very Italian manner and thick Boston accent didn't usually get associated with "stoicism." But he was an old-school Marine veteran, and talking about his feelings wasn't something he was prone to.

Normally, Brannigan would have been glad to let it lie. He wasn't big on talking, much less talking about feelings. But if something was getting under Santelli's skin, he needed to know.

They were way out in the cold, regardless of the Russians' assurances of friendship and cooperation. Every man had to be on the cutting edge, or they could all go down.

"We've talked about the mission already, Carlo. Something else is bugging you. Is it something I need to worry about?"

Santelli rubbed his hands together nervously. Brannigan's eyes had adjusted to the dark enough that he could see the other man hang his head and stare at the floor.

"I don't know exactly how to put it." He sighed. "Something's been bugging me since Roger was killed. At first, I thought that it was just that I didn't want to be the second in command. I didn't want that kind of responsibility. Leadership I can do. Command? I don't know.

"But now I'm not so sure. I'm still worried. I still wake up dreading what comes next." He looked up at Brannigan. "I keep thinking about what Melissa's going to think if I never come back. I don't expect the Russians to send proper condolences to our families if we just disappear out here. And what's going to happen to Carlo Jr. if he has to grow up without a dad because I vanished into the Caucasus somewhere, and neither he nor his mother know where, when, or why?"

He looked back down at the floor. "I think maybe I'm losing my nerve, John."

Brannigan held his peace as he thought for a long moment. This he could deal with. Kind of. He'd had to steel young men's hearts for combat a lot over his many years of service.

Except that Santelli wasn't a young man anymore. And even Brannigan knew that there came a time when every man had to hang it up.

"The odds were every bit as long on Khadarkh and in Burma. What was different then?"

Santelli rubbed his hands together. "I don't know. Maybe I still thought I could run with the big dogs. Thought I was still a young buck, full of piss and vinegar. Then I got so wrapped up in the team that I couldn't back out. I didn't *want* to back out. I still don't want to back out. But I'm scared, John. Scared about what's going to happen to my family if I buy it like Roger did. Or Doc. Or Aziz. Or…"

Brannigan cut him off before he could go through the litany of their dead. It was painful enough to think on as it was.

"We're all scared, Carlo. Hell, my *boy*'s here with us. I'm regretting saying 'yes' to him every step of the way. But we're committed for now, so we've got to find that little cave where we stuff all our fears and worries until the job's done, and seal it up until we're on the bird back to the World. I *know* you can do that; I've watched you do it for twenty years.

"When we get back—*when* we get back—then we'll talk. I've told Marines for twenty years not to make big, life-altering decisions while downrange. I know you've done the same. So, now I'm telling you. Stick it out, put it out of your mind, and don't let it drag you down when we need you sharp and on your toes, Carlo. If you decide that this is the last go-round, then I'll stand by you. You know that. But we can't make that call in the middle of the mission. See it through, then we'll see."

Santelli sighed and nodded. "Like you said, sir. We're committed.

"I'll see it through."

# CHAPTER 16

Javakhishvili watched Krivov work with decidedly mixed feelings.

On the one hand, he had no sympathy for a gangster who worked with Chechen terrorists. He'd seen enough in his wanderings overseas to have nothing but a burning hatred for jihadis of all stripes. He'd seen men, women, and children tortured, horrifically murdered, or manipulated or blackmailed into making themselves *shahid*, "martyrs" who killed innocent people while immolating themselves in the process. Jihadis were monsters fueled by nothing but hatred, and they left nothing but horror and grief in their wake.

On the other hand, he didn't have a much higher opinion of Russians.

Akbarov was tied to a chair in the center of the room, which had been partitioned off with sheets so that he saw nothing but his interrogators. Krivov had been joined by a wiry, swarthy man who might have been a Kazakh. That one seemed to be the one doing most of the working over, while Krivov asked the questions.

"We know that you have handled many of Abu Mokhtar's financial arrangements. We know that you have set up his shell companies. If it involves his money, you have had a part in it. So, where is the gold?"

Akbarov was already bruised and bleeding, his head hanging on his chest. He shook his head, and the Kazakh interrogator stepped in and hit him. The punch knocked his head halfway around, and he spat blood.

Javakhishvili watched dispassionately. *At least they're not bringing out the car battery and the sponges yet. Though I'm sure they've got them squirrelled away somewhere.*

He wondered just how much it would really bother him if they got that hardcore. Javakhishvili considered himself a faithful Eastern Orthodox Christian, but he had a hard time getting stirred up over a terrorist getting the heat put on him. He'd never bought into the idea that Christians were supposed to be pacifists—he never would have entered his chosen profession if he had. Torture seemed like a bit of a gray area to him; he knew that there were arguments against it, but he had always kind of figured that if it was okay to kill someone under certain circumstances, then it was okay to hurt them, too.

As for the arguments that it simply didn't work, he'd seen the lie put to that, too.

But when it was Russians doing the torture, he suddenly found himself getting a lot more squeamish. It bothered him, on a purely intellectual level. He always started to wonder if he wasn't being a bit of a hypocrite, objecting to the brutality just because it was Russians doing it.

Maybe he was. The Russians were still thugs, and he couldn't trust them as far as he could throw them. He was sure that on some level, this wasn't about getting the truth for them; he instinctively believed that all Russians were sadists, and that they were beating the hell out of Akbarov mostly for kicks.

Some of that probably had something to do with the fact that he didn't entirely believe anything they'd been told about this op in the first place.

The crudity of the whole interrogation struck him as well, as the Kazakh interrogator hit Akbarov a few more times, leaving him gasping and coughing blood in the chair while Krivov watched, his arms folded, his face impassive. He'd expected the Russians to be more sophisticated about this; he'd grown up on stories of just how viciously inventive and cunning the KGB interrogators could be. Of course, it was possible that Krivov and his men simply hadn't had that training, being *Spetsnaz* instead of MGB, but somehow that didn't fit, either.

Krivov must have sensed him watching, because he looked up and returned Javakhishvili's scrutiny, his face still blank. The Russian major raised an eyebrow slightly, then tilted his head toward the prisoner with what might have been a questioning look.

*Oh, is that it? You let me in here so* I *could play 'good cop?' Fuck you, you Russian dog.*

Javakhishvili played dumb, acting like he hadn't noticed. He would let the Russians do their thing, while he watched and listened. In part, he was just being the stubborn Georgian who didn't want to help the Russians any more than he had to. But he was also being careful; none of the Blackhearts knew for sure what the game was, and he didn't want to put the rest of the team into a compromised position because he played into Krivov's hands.

*I wish we had just taken a quick smash-and-grab job somewhere, without all these intrigues and complications.*

Not that they'd ever had a job without intrigues and complications. It seemed to be part and parcel of their new career as deniable mercenaries.

Krivov waved the Kazakh off, and the smaller man stepped away, rubbing his bloodied knuckles. He hadn't actually hit Akbarov in the face that much; he'd concentrated on the midsection, but he'd rattled Akbarov's skull a couple times, if only to make it clear just how serious they were. But gut punches hurt almost as much with considerably less risk that they'd kill him. Javakhishvili could kind of appreciate that. He'd seen a couple of men die of a cerebral hemorrhage after being punched in the head.

Krivov let the man gasp and moan for a few moments, before crouching down in front of him, looking up at Akbarov's battered features. "Why do you keep their secrets, Etibar? I know what you have done, what you buy and sell. You are no true believer. So why not talk?"

Akbarov's initial response was so mumbled and muted by spit and blood that Javakhishvili couldn't make it out. When Krivov cupped a hand to his ear, the Azeri gangster spoke louder. "They will kill me."

Krivov laughed quietly. "You are not in the Americans' hands, Etibar. You are in Russian hands. We are not so soft-hearted as they. Think about that."

He stood and stepped back, folding his arms and watching Akbarov, who didn't move. He just sat there, staring at the floor.

Finally, Krivov nodded to the Kazakh, who stepped back in, pulling Akbarov's head back up by his hair.

Javakhishvili watched as they went back to work, wrestling with his conscience the entire time.

***

It took several more hours, and the caffeine had worn off some time ago. But Akbarov finally broke.

Javakhishvili almost missed it; his emotions deadened by hours of brutality and the exhaustion of coming off an op and going right into interrogation, he was starting to nod. So, when Akbarov started mumbling, he almost didn't hear it. Only when Krivov pulled the Kazakh interrogator back and started taking notes did he sit up and start paying more attention.

He listened closely, making sure he got as much as he could. Brannigan would want to hear this, especially so that he could compare what Javakhishvili passed on to what the Russians told them.

***

The sun was coming up when Burgess heard footsteps outside, approaching the tent. The rest of the Blackhearts, except for Bianco, were all asleep, snoring fit to wake the dead. Burgess was a bit of a light sleeper; he was glad he'd gotten to sleep before some of them had started up. He was also glad that he had the last watch; he wouldn't have to try to get back to sleep while a human sawmill went to town in the tent.

He moved to the tent flap, his AK in his hands, and peered out. He let out a sigh of relief. It was Javakhishvili, looking worn down to the bone but otherwise healthy and unhurt. He pulled the flap open and ushered the other man inside.

"Thanks, brother." Javakhishvili and Burgess had worked together on contract several years before either of them had ever heard of the Blackhearts. They had a history, which was why Javakhishvili had recruited Burgess in the first place.

Javakhishvili ran a hand over his face. "Damn, I'm tired. I really just want to sleep for a week, but John needs to hear this."

Burgess pointed him toward a cot just inside the flap. "He's right there."

Brannigan was already sitting up. "That you, Herc? Did he talk, or did you just get tired of watching the Russians work him over?"

"He talked." Javakhishvili found an empty cot and sank down onto it. He forced himself to stay upright, no matter how much he really wanted to just go flat and close his eyes. "And yeah, I'm pretty sure it was legit info, too. He wasn't just telling us what he thought we wanted to hear."

"And?"

"He said he doesn't know where the cache is. But he knows where the drop site is, and he insisted that he thought we can find the cache from there. He says the shipments get dropped with the Chechens in Khalatala, and then they leave to the north." Javakhishvili looked a little ambivalent for a moment. "Krivov wasn't buying it, so he pressed. Turns out he *wasn't* telling the whole truth. The Azeri mobsters were supposed to have left by the time the Chechens departed, but they *are* mobsters. They stuck around and followed the trucks. They went to Mazimchay."

Brannigan frowned. "Shipments, huh? I thought this was a cache we were trying to find, not shut down a pipeline."

"Oh, that's where it gets interesting. It seems that the Turks are bringing gold bullion out of Syria and Libya and shipping it to the Azeri mob while the Azerbaijani government looks the other way. Then the mob passes it along to the Chechens and Dagestanis." Javakhishvili rubbed his hands together. "Sounds to me that the Turks are pissed at the Russians, and so they're helping out their jihadi friends who are also pissed at the Russkies."

"Hell." Burgess rubbed his chin. Brannigan had brought the map out and found Mazimchay, and both of them were looking down at it and frowning. It lay right on the Georgian border. "Is he sure the cache is in Mazimchay? The Pankisi Gorge is less than sixty miles from the border, and the Chechens have supposedly been using that as a support and infiltration route for decades."

"He thinks it is, but he's never actually seen it." Javakhishvili stuck his thumbs in his eyes. He was awfully tired. "He said that they saw about ten to fifteen Chechen fighters there in the village, and it's not a big village. Mazimchay would be the logical conclusion, if they haven't built another fortress higher up in the mountains."

Brannigan pulled out a map, flipping on his red lens headlamp after fishing it out of his gear. "That would make sense. Assuming it's not just a red herring, and the cache is actually in Georgia." He stroked his mustache, then glanced up at Javakhishvili. "Did they say anything about the nukes?"

Javakhishvili shook his head. "Not a word. Never came up."

"Hmm." Brannigan stared at the map again. "Well, if it is in Mazimchay, then that makes things simpler for us if we have to run for it. Georgia's right there. I can call Abernathy's contact and let him know." He grimaced. "*After* we go over plans with Krivov and Pichugin. I'm sure they'll find a way to make this harder than it needs to be." He looked up. "Get some sleep, Herc. We'll wake you up if we need you."

***

To Brannigan's complete lack of surprise, the Russians didn't come to talk until mid-afternoon.

Not that any of the Blackhearts were especially put out about it. It had been a long day, and for Javakhishvili, a longer night. The watch schedule, with so few of them, had limited the rest they'd been able to get, so they weren't really up and about until mid-morning at the earliest.

When Krivov finally showed up, he had a PSD of still-armed *Spetsnaz* with him. He didn't comment on their presence or look especially disturbed, but they were still there in the background, looming. It seemed that the Russians weren't all that comfortable with the Blackhearts keeping weapons on their base.

*Tough shit. Should have hired your own guys, then.*

That thought brought a lot of questions back to the forefront, but Brannigan wasn't so naïve as to think that Krivov would answer them, if he even knew the answers himself.

"So, did he finally break?" Brannigan knew the answer, and Krivov had to know that he knew, but since Krivov was just standing there, it seemed like the thing to say.

"Yes, he talked." Krivov seemed to be going along with this dumb little game, so Brannigan just kept his face blank. "*Polkovnik* Pichugin wants to see us."

Brannigan heaved himself to his feet, slinging his AK-103. "Let's go talk to the man, then."

Krivov led the way over to the main compound, where Pichugin was waiting in his tiny office, leaning on the desk. It was a field desk that looked like Marshall Zhukov might have used it in World War II.

"We have place of gold cache." Pichugin's accent seemed to have gotten even thicker. "Cache we believe is in Mazimchay, but it will require reconnaissance to be certain."

When Pichugin seemed to just be leaving it at that, Brannigan decided to keep things rolling. "So, what's the plan? Are we going in? Are we going in with the *Spetsnaz*? How are we getting there, and what's the execute criteria if we *do* find a cache there?"

"You will fly to Balakan with *Mayor* Krivov. From there, you will proceed to Mazimchay and attempt to locate cache." The overweight *Polkovnik* paused to breathe. Brannigan could smell the rancid Russian cigarettes from across the desk. "Once cache is located, contact *Mayor* Krivov and we will coordinate extraction of gold from site."

"Just like that?" *That's not a plan, that's a mission statement.*

"You may need to secure cache on site first. We can provide some air cover, but you will need to find trucks to get gold to Balakan airstrip for loading." Pichugin looked supremely unconcerned as Brannigan glared at him in some disbelief.

"I've got eleven men. You want me to secure a cache, steal multiple trucks, load the gold, and then drive out with only eleven men?"

"Akbarov only ever saw five to ten men at their rendezvous." Pichugin was already changing the story from the interrogation. Javakhishvili had said that Akbarov had counted ten to fifteen. "They will rely on secrecy, I think. It should not be too hard. If reconnaissance shows too many opposition, then fall back to Balakan and replan. But Americans wanted part of this mission. This is your part." Pichugin looked slightly surly at Brannigan's question. He was in charge, and Brannigan was questioning him.

*That's because this is supposed to be a* joint *op, Ivan.*

“In other words, if this goes south, then you don’t have to worry about anyone finding Russian bodies on Azerbaijani soil.” It might not have been the most politic thing to say, but he was beyond caring right then. The Russians were jerking them around, and he was getting more and more suspicious about this entire op.

The fact that neither Pichugin nor Krivov said anything in reply was answer enough.

# CHAPTER 17

The next day was taken up with mission prep. The Russians were stonewalling most of their requests, apparently out of sheer bloody-mindedness, but they were getting geared up and ready to go fairly quickly.

Wade had disappeared for a while, but had stuck his head in the tent flap after about an hour. "Hey, I need a body."

"We're fresh out. But it's a Russian base, so they've probably got a mass grave around somewhere." Curtis had clearly gotten a little *too* much sleep.

"Funny." Wade stabbed a finger at him. "You're it. Thanks for volunteering."

"I didn't volunteer for shit." But Curtis was already getting up off his cot. "Thought I got away from this sort of stuff when I got out."

"Quit your bitching." Wade held the flap open. "You knew how this worked before you opened your big mouth."

"I will have you know that I serve a vital role for this team. Who else would keep morale up? Y'all gloomy bunch of humorless bastards. Joe's been rubbing off on too many of you." Curtis ducked through the flap. "What did I get railroaded into? Because I did *not* 'volunteer.'"

Wade jerked a thumb over his shoulder. "I got us a couple of UAZs and some more weapons. I need another driver."

"Oh, that's easy."

"*And* somebody to help me strap 'em down in the Antonov." Wade grinned as Curtis's shoulders slumped. "Oh, no, you ain't getting off that easy."

"What kind of weapons?" Curtis suddenly brightened. "PKPs?"

When Wade shook his head, the shorter man's face fell again. "Still no belt-feds. They seem to be weirdly reluctant to give us that kind of firepower."

"Man, we're doing *their* dirty work." Curtis kicked at the ground as he groused. "They want it done right, why won't they give us machineguns?"

"These will be more useful than machineguns where we're going." Wade led the way toward the back of the *Spetsnaz* compound. "Though I'm not entirely sure that they really *do* want it done right." A bit of the anger Wade was justly famous for within the Blackhearts leaked out as he snarled.

"I fail to see what could be more useful than a proper belt fed." Curtis was a machinegunner first and foremost, and he didn't tend to like anything that didn't default to full auto. When the fact that the AK-103's selector lever went to "auto" *first* had been pointed out to him, he'd just shrugged and said that it didn't really count.

Wade didn't answer at first, but led the way toward a pair of ancient-looking UAZ-469s. Effectively the Russian answer to the Jeep, they looked more like poor man's G-wagons. In this case, the poor man was *very* poor. Both vehicles had clearly seen better days.

"Those are our vehicles?" Curtis almost moaned. "Do they even start?"

"They start." Wade tossed him a set of keys. "They actually run a lot better than they look. And they shouldn't stand out much in northern Azerbaijan. I think they look the way they do for just that reason."

"Oh." Curtis got in the left-hand vehicle. "You think these are *Spetsnaz* Trojan Horse vics?"

"I suspect so." Wade got in the other and started it up. "Probably seen some use here in Dagestan."

Wade led the way back to the tent, parking the vehicle by the front flap between the tent and the airstrip itself before hopping out. Curtis followed suit, and then joined the Blackhearts as they gathered around the two UAZs.

"These should do the trick for transport." Wade was opening the fabric back on his vehicle. "And they were a little bitchy about parting with these, but I was able to get Krivov to sign off on it, given how close we're going to be to the border." He reached in and pulled out a weapons case, laying it on the hood and opening it to reveal a stubby weapon with a thick integral suppressor shrouding the entire barrel. A Russian red dot sight was mounted on the rail bolted to the side of the receiver.

"AS Vals." There was an appreciative grin on Burgess's face as he picked it up. "I didn't even know these were still in service."

"Still in service, and they've got enough of them that they agreed to loan us a few." He pointed at the second vehicle. "Got two VSS Vintorezes for our sharpshooters. I figured that if we've got Azerbaijani and Georgian border guards that close, some suppressed weapons would be a better choice than the AKs."

"Good call." Brannigan had looked in the back, and was pulling one of the VSS rifles out, a similarly stubby, integrally suppressed, 9x39mm marksman rifle. The VSS was an older design, and had been phased out in most cases in favor of the modernized VSS-M, but it was apparent that many units were still keeping the older ones around. "How'd you get them to part with these?"

Wade grinned. "Cigarettes and movies." His grin got even wider. "I made sure I brought some trade goods this time around."

Brannigan nodded appreciatively. Wade might have come across as a blunt instrument a lot of the time, but he was a lot smarter and more cunning than his bull in a china shop personality might have suggested.

"All right, then. Flanagan and Gomez get the Vintorezes, everybody else, grab a Val. We'll see if we can find somewhere to test fire and zero these things, then we need to start getting that An-12 loaded up."

***

The UAZs were strapped down in the Antonov's hold, most of the gear was set, and Flanagan and Santelli were going over their last-minute checks. The Russians seemed to be dragging their feet; Krivov was nowhere to be found at the moment, and they had to wait on him.

Brannigan slipped back into the tent and pulled the satellite phone out of his pack. He wasn't sure that the Russians *didn't* know he had it, but he had been careful not to show it around Krivov or any of the rest. It was a bit of a hole card, and given the fact that he was pretty sure the Russians were keeping them in the dark about some vital elements of this op, he figured it was only fair if he returned the favor.

The phone rang for almost a minute before it connected. "What have you got, John?" It sounded like Abernathy himself.

"I've got a lot of questions, a lot of sketchy operational decisions, and not a lot of support." He might not know exactly who Abernathy was, but he was an independent contractor, and wasn't going to beat around the bush, especially when he was the one on the ground. Though he frowned as he thought he picked up some strange noises in the background as Abernathy listened.

The older man grunted. "Sounds familiar. Lay it out for me."

Brannigan outlined what they'd found out and where they were headed. Abernathy listened in silence, not interrupting.

In the pause after he finished speaking, Brannigan could swear that he heard radio chatter in the background, and a voice raised that might have been announcing someone coming in. Was Abernathy in a TOC somewhere?

"Well if you're operating right on the Georgian border, that should work out well. Write this number down." Abernathy rattled off a sat phone number. "That should get you in touch with my guys in Telavi. If things go sideways, run for the border and call them. They'll have the phone on all the time, and they'll be waiting for it."

*I've heard that before*. But so far, Abernathy hadn't given them any reason not to trust him. In fact, as generally unreadable as the old man was, Brannigan had been inclined to trust his no-bullshit manner a lot more than Van Zandt's secret squirrel business.

"Got it." Brannigan read the number back just to be sure. "We'll be wheels up in the next couple of hours."

"Roger that. My boys will be waiting. Now, if you'll excuse me, we've got some things happening here." More voices were raised in the background, though Brannigan couldn't make out what they were saying. "Call Faireborn in Telavi if you need anything else." With that, he hung up.

***

The UAZs were strapped down securely in the An-12's hold—Wade and Santelli had done most of the work themselves, and had double-checked it after the Antonov's loadmaster had gone over it—the rest of the gear was in the backs of the vehicles, and the Blackhearts were all aboard. The props were already starting to turn, and there was still no sign of Krivov.

"Where the hell is he?" Flanagan was getting pissed, which was a little different. Usually it would be Wade getting spun up, but Wade was sitting next to the rear UAZ, his head back and his eyes closed, and the normally quiet Flanagan was checking his watch with his teeth clenched.

"He'll be here." Brannigan was leaning back against the vibrating aluminum wall behind him. "Trust me; I don't think that the Russians want us running around without a minder. Even if this is just a heist, they'll want their cut. They don't want to take the chance that we'll just run. Whatever the game is, they want us to play our part."

He'd barely finished speaking when Krivov came up the ramp, dressed in jeans and a plain green jacket, a large duffel slung over his shoulder. The bag looked just the right size to carry a set of combat gear and another AS Val.

"You are ready?" Krivov raised his voice enough to be heard, but still managed to look and sound bored. Brannigan's eyes narrowed as he looked up at the Russian major.

*Right, act like you've been waiting on us, and not the other way around. Jackass.*

"Waiting on you."

Krivov nodded and headed up toward the cockpit, threading past the two vehicles and stepping carefully over the cargo straps and the Blackhearts' boots as he went. The duffel looked heavy; he must have come loaded for bear.

Of course, so had the Blackhearts.

Krivov disappeared into the cockpit, and a moment later, the ramp started to rise. It cut off the dappled Makhachkala sunlight, and a few minutes later, the throb of the engines rose to a scream, and they started to taxi.

A few minutes later, they were pulling for the sky. Next stop, Azerbaijan.

***

The Balakan airstrip wasn't anything fancy. The tiny terminal building sat next to an orchard, and the entire single asphalt runway was surrounded by a high hedge. The An-12 landed easily; the strip was far longer than the short takeoff cargo plane needed. The engines' howl subsided to a roar as they slowed and taxied toward the terminal in the dying glow of post-sunset twilight, the ramp already starting to lower.

The bird stopped as the ramp touched the asphalt. The loadmaster was already starting to undo the cargo straps on the UAZs, and the Blackhearts set in to help. They had a limited amount of time on the ground. The Azerbaijanis apparently didn't have a lot of security forces in the Balakan area, but it wasn't the Azeris that Brannigan was most worried about.

Wade and Bianco were already in the vehicles, and started them as the last of the cargo straps came off. Wade was already rolling the moment he got a thumbs up from Santelli, and Bianco was close behind.

The rest of the Blackhearts followed the vehicles off the plane, and Brannigan looked around for Krivov, only to see their Russian minder just then coming out of the cockpit. He pointed toward the vehicles—it was still far too loud aboard the plane to talk much—and then turned and started down, climbing into the passenger seat beside Wade.

They had to wait a moment to make sure everyone was up. It was a tight fit; the UAZs hadn't exactly been designed to carry six men with weapons and gear in any sort of comfort. Of course, being Russian vehicles, Brannigan hadn't exactly expected comfort in the first place.

Finally, he got a thumbs up from Flanagan in the second vehicle, and he pointed toward the exit, a small gate in the hedge on the far side of the terminal building. Fortunately, it was open; he'd half expected it to be secured. There didn't even appear to be a guard posted.

The two UAZs roared out through the gate. So far, so good.

But their luck didn't last. Even as the An-12 revved up, the rumble of the engines turning to a roar behind them, a set of headlights came around a corner behind them and raced toward the two vehicles.

"Who's this?" Wade peered through the rear-view mirrors. "Somebody think they missed their flight?"

Brannigan twisted around in his seat to take a look, but all he could see was the glare of the headlights. "Might be nothing. Might just be somebody driving home. It's still pretty early in the evening."

"Maybe. But this isn't a direct route to anywhere." Wade kept glancing at the mirrors as he led the way toward the M5 Yevlakh-Zaqatala-Georgia Highway. "And the timing seems awfully weird."

"Just drive. We'll see if we can lose them before we get up into the hills." Brannigan didn't need to look at Wade to see what the big man thought of that. He was of a similar mind, himself. There weren't a lot of places to try to lose a tail between the Balakan airstrip and the Georgian border. It was all fields, orchards, woods, and villages. They didn't have much room to work with, and not enough cover in the room they did have.

"Turn off here. We're not heading straight for the target while this guy's still behind us." Brannigan pointed to the left as they came to an intersection just past the orchard. He glanced at his watch, feeling Krivov's eyes on the back of his head. They had a hard time to hit; the An-12 would return at 0300 the next morning, and despite Pichugin's words about replanning if things didn't proceed as anticipated, Brannigan suspected that it probably wouldn't be coming back to pick them up if they weren't on the strip with the gold at that time.

Wade took the turn, with Bianco close behind.

The headlights followed.

It didn't necessarily mean anything. They were heading toward another small village if Brannigan was remembering the map right. They might have just ended up in front of an

Azerbaijani farmer heading home after going into town and the bazaar.

But somehow, he didn't think so.

"Pull over." He didn't want to risk running into a cul-de-sac or a dead end with possible enemies on their tail. "Let him go past."

Wade looked a little skeptical, but he complied. A few moments later, Bianco did the same behind them.

The headlights behind them also pulled over, about a hundred yards back.

"Oh, I don't like this." Santelli was all the way in the back, facing the rear flap on the canvas top.

"Nothing much to like." Brannigan peered in the side mirror. The headlights were still back there, still unmoving. He turned to Krivov. "Did your people try to find out if the Chechens had lookouts on the airstrip before they decided to use it?"

Krivov shrugged. "I do not know."

"Brilliant." Burgess was hauling his AS Val out of its case. "What do you want to do, boss?"

Brannigan thought for a moment. "Give it another minute or two and see if they move. If they don't, we'll pull a U-turn and get a better look as we go by them."

"Is that a good idea?" Krivov sounded uncertain for the first time. Maybe it had really sunk in that he didn't have that much control now, being the sole Russian surrounded by American mercenaries.

"Not especially, but we're running out of options. If I'm reading the map right, we can't get through this way; we passed the last turn that would take us back toward the airport and the town about a hundred yards back. Coincidentally, right where that vehicle's sitting." The tone of Brannigan's voice said just how coincidental he thought that placement was, but he didn't know how finely tuned Krivov's sarcasm detector was. "If they're nobody, we just roll on past. If they're a threat…" He keyed his radio, one of the few bits of gear that they'd managed to get through Customs. "Woodsrunner, Kodiak."

"Send it." Flanagan sounded as calm and collected as ever.

"We're going to double back. If something happens when we roll past that car behind you, be prepared to pull up and ventilate anyone in it." He really didn't want to start the shooting yet, but if they were already burned…

"Roger that."

Arguing had never been one of Flanagan's faults.

"Take us around, Wade." He started pulling his own suppressed rifle out, and the others in the back did the same, even Krivov, who had one of the newer ASM Vals. The Blackhearts had gotten the older pieces, that had probably been retired from Krivov's unit.

Wade had to make a three-point turn to get turned around; the road was narrow and hemmed in by hedgerows. Once he was facing back the way they'd come, he put the UAZ in gear and started to slowly head back toward the intersection.

The headlights stayed where they were. The bad guys—if that was who they were—weren't spooking.

Wade pulled his Val up onto his lap. "Might want to get ready to engage, boys. If they are Chechens, they might be trying to do the same thing to us that we're planning on doing to them."

Brannigan hoped not. It was only about three miles to Mazimchay, but he'd rather not have the vehicles shot to shit before they even got properly started.

Not to mention the fact that the UAZ wasn't armored, and if the Chechens started shooting at them at point-blank range, they were probably going to lose somebody.

They rolled toward the headlights, weapons ready.

# CHAPTER 18

They came alongside the battered Mitsubishi Pajero and Brannigan watched the windows, his hands on the AS Val in his lap.

He couldn't get a good look until they'd passed the cone of the other vehicle's headlights. Once they did, though, he saw that there was only one man in the cab. He couldn't make out his face—it was still too dark—but he was obviously on a phone.

"Hold your fire." The man wasn't an immediate threat. All the same, he was watching the UAZs closely as he talked, his head turning to follow them as they drove past.

"Spotter." There wasn't any question in Wade's voice. "So, they know we're here and they know we're coming." He looked in the rear-view mirror as they put the Pajero behind them.

"Maybe." Brannigan honestly didn't think Wade was wrong. His impression was only strengthened a couple minutes later, as the Pajero flipped a U-turn and came after them. "But they haven't opened hostilities yet, and I'd rather not start shooting before we're in position to hit the cache, if we can help it."

"If he sticks to us, we're going to have to dump him at some point." Wade was nothing if not pragmatic about such things. “Can’t have him following us all the way to our drop point.”

“Let’s see if we can’t make it look like an accident.” As soon as he’d said it, he knew how Wade was going to take it, and sure enough, the other man smiled that madman’s grin of his. “Not that way, Wade.”

“What?” It was hard to tell if Wade was being defensive or joking. “We can’t just leave him back there to report on us all the way in.”

The problem was that Brannigan knew he was right. There wasn’t a great way out of this. Rural terrain was not ideal for losing a tail, short of ambushing him and killing him, and that risked even greater compromise. The Vals might be very quiet, but a suppressed gunshot is still a gunshot.

Not only that, but once you killed someone on an infiltration, you had to consider your cover blown, because *somebody* was going to be looking for the dead man. And for all they knew, the Chechens might immediately know that their spotter had been taken off the board as soon as he went silent.

Assuming that this was a Chechen spotter, and not an Azerbaijani security service officer, whose duty it was to keep an eye on the airstrip. Which might or might not be worse.

“Head south, take us around the airport, and then head into town.” It wasn’t a great solution, but it was better than opening the ball in the middle of the countryside. “We’ll try to lose him in town then head up into the hills.” He hoped that there was still enough traffic on the roads in Balakan at that hour to facilitate the plan.

“We could put him in the ditch.” Wade took the next turn, accelerating down the dirt road toward the southeast.

“That risks wrecking one of these vehicles, and we don’t exactly have a backup at this point in the plan. Plus, we’re already getting into the villages. We’d attract a lot more attention, getting into a wreck here.” They were passing houses, windows glowing between the darkened trees, and more traffic was starting to show up, two cars and a truck passing the other direction in the last couple of minutes.

"We should not go far into town." Krivov didn't sound *scared*, exactly, but he didn't sound comfortable, either. "We cannot be stopped by Azerbaijani police."

Under different circumstances, Brannigan might have said something sarcastic in reply. After all, the beef between the Azerbaijanis and the Russians was a lot closer and nastier than anything the Azerbaijanis might have against Americans—and Brannigan was under no illusions that the Azeris harbored a lot of love for Americans, either, given their partnership with the Turks—but with the amount of firepower and explosives they were carrying, not to mention having a Russian in the car, it was better not to take chances.

Brannigan watched the headlights behind them in the side mirror for a moment, then keyed his radio. "Woodsrunner, Kodiak. Let's split up. We'll head north, you head south. Rendezvous at the north end of the highway bridge over the river."

"Roger that. Breaking off." A moment later, the second UAZ took a sharp right turn and disappeared around the corner, its own headlights flickering for a moment between the trees and hedges before being eclipsed altogether by the nearest house.

The Pajero's driver seemed to hesitate a moment, then followed the second vehicle.

"North?" Wade didn't sound all that certain if they should head for the rendezvous or loiter to support the second vehicle.

"North. But slow roll so that we don't have far to go if they do need help."

***

"And he's following us." Bianco was watching the side mirror as they took the turn. The back was too crowded for the main rear-view mirror to be worth much, even if the plastic on the back flap hadn't been scratched to near opacity. "Great."

Flanagan was studying the map with his red lens flashlight. "Turn left up here, then take the first left, go around the curve, and then a right, left, and a left onto the main drag." He squinted at the map, trying to make out the Cyrillic, silently cursing the fact that all the Russians had were Russian maps. "There might be a market there, hopefully there's enough traffic to lose this guy."

"Provided he ain't a better driver than me." Bianco went around the turn as quickly as he could without flipping the vehicle, and Flanagan had to brace himself. "I *really* don't like driving in tight, crowded Third World streets."

"Slow down." Flanagan glanced at the traffic behind them. Their tail was still the only one back there. "This ain't *Bullitt* yet."

"Key word being 'yet.'" Bianco was sweating, even though it wasn't a warm night. "I really wish I'd let somebody else drive."

"You'll be fine." Flanagan still held onto the dash as Bianco took the next turn a little too sharply.

The Pajero was accelerating, trying to catch up. If there had been any doubt that they were being followed, that would certainly have clinched it.

"Joe…" Bianco was looking in the rear-view mirror. "I think that speed is our only way to lose this guy."

"I don't think we're going to outrun a Pajero in a UAZ." But Flanagan was watching the oncoming headlights in the side mirror. "Let alone a UAZ loaded down with six dudes." He turned his attention back to the map. "Keep going. I think we can lose him if we get into thick enough traffic, and it's a Thursday."

"What does Thursday have to do with anything?" Jenkins craning his neck to watch the headlights.

"This is Azerbaijan. Which is majority Muslim. Friday being the Muslim version of Sunday, most Muslims head in for a night on the town on Thursday night. Which means that traffic is going to be a bastard, but that might give us the opportunity we're looking for, if our tail back there isn't as good at negotiating the traffic." Flanagan pointed. "Turn in here."

The local traffic as they turned toward the bazaar was getting thicker. It wasn't at a standstill yet, but it was going to significantly slow them down. Bianco's knuckles were turning white on the steering wheel as he hesitated at the intersection.

"Take it, Vinnie. They're not going to stop to let you in, and we can't afford to be polite right now." Flanagan glanced over his shoulder. Their tail was right on them, and the traffic wasn't getting any lighter. "You're going to have to take advantage of every opening you can find, even if it doesn't look like the vic will fit."

Bianco winced, but started forward. He stopped with a lurch as an old Lada nearly collided with the front quarter panel, the driver leaning on his horn. Bianco almost started to back up, but Flanagan snapped at him. "Keep going. This is the way they drive. Just got to reach down, grab hold, and go with it."

With his knuckles still white and his teeth gritted, Bianco surged out into traffic, cranking the wheel over hard as he got into the somewhat widening gap as the Lada driver kept honking. The Lada was right on their back bumper as Bianco moved into traffic, cutting the Pajero off.

"Good." Flanagan watched the frustrated spotter as best he could, wishing that he had jumped in behind the wheel instead of Bianco. He'd done some time contracting in the Middle East, and the Azeri traffic looked almost identical in its chaos. "Keep looking for openings and see if we can widen the gap." He pointed. "There. Get in front of that guy."

Bianco complied, though he was still hesitant and jerky, wincing at each honk of a horn, although there were a *lot* of drivers honking at just about everyone. It was familiar enough to Flanagan.

"Relax, Vinnie. This is business as usual." Javakhishvili was in the back, watching their six with his AS Val across his knees. "Trust me; I've seen a lot worse than this."

"That's not exactly all that comforting at the moment." Bianco eased between an overloaded truck and a surprisingly new-looking Chevy Malibu, advancing by fits and starts, struggling with the gears and obviously sweating the possibility that he was going to stall them out in the middle of traffic.

But the UAZ didn't stall, though Bianco ground the gears a couple of times as he shifted to avoid it. After weaving through traffic for a few more minutes and almost half a mile, he started to relax a little. Flanagan breathed a little easier, seeing that Bianco wasn't about to freak out, and glanced over his shoulder.

The spotter in the Pajero was trying to catch up with them, but he was getting tangled in the traffic. He thought he could see the other vehicle about fifty yards back, hemmed in between a van and a bus. They hadn't lost him yet, and if the driver was familiar enough with the local area, it was still going to be difficult. But they were opening the gap.

"Keep going. Bang a left up here on the main road." That would be easy enough; most of the traffic was going that way.

Having managed to get that far without a collision, Bianco was getting more confident, and they made the turn smoothly. The main road looked like it should have been two lanes, but functionally it was more like three or four.

"Push as hard as you can." Flanagan was hoping to encourage Bianco a little, as well as widening the gap. "Get as many cars and trucks between us and him as possible."

With Flanagan pointing out openings—that Bianco might not have seen otherwise—they wove through the twin—or sometimes triple—strands of traffic heading into town. Flanagan lost track of the Pajero in the mass of headlights behind them, but he was pretty sure that it was still stuck at least half a dozen vehicles back.

"Take this next right."

"Won't that look out of place?" Bianco braked hard to avoid slamming into the vehicle right in front of him as it stopped abruptly. "Everybody else is going into town."

"Don't care. We're not that worried about everyone else right now; I just want to get some distance from that jackass in the Pajero." Flanagan searched the traffic behind them again, but still couldn't pick out their tail. "As long as he's tied up in here, we might be able to get a few turns on him and get away. That's our only goal right at the moment."

Bianco nodded, his lips pressed tightly together, his attention otherwise entirely on the traffic around him. It was still tight; there were inches between the UAZ and the cars and trucks in front, behind, and to the left.

They inched forward, a car length at a time, until it looked like he finally had enough space to make the turn. "Go for it."

Bianco gunned the engine, bouncing onto the shoulder as he cut the turn as tight as he could. He almost slammed into an oncoming truck that wasn't paying attention to lanes, but he swerved aside, almost scraping the market compound's outer wall to the right as he squeezed past.

Then the road ahead was clear, and he breathed a deep sigh of relief as he accelerated away from the road, putting ever more distance between them and their tail. Flanagan clapped him on the shoulder.

"Good work, Vinnie. We'll make a Third World driver of you yet."

"I hope not." Bianco took the next left as Flanagan pointed that way. "Now what?"

Flanagan hunched forward to peer through the side mirror again. "Looks like we're still clear. Let's put a couple more turns behind us, then head for the rendezvous."

***

Krivov was fidgeting in the back. Brannigan looked over his shoulder at him. "They'll be here."

The Russian went still, as if just then realizing how impatient and nervous he seemed. "We have a short timeline. If we are not at the airstrip on schedule, the aircraft will not be able to come back for us anytime soon."

*And then you get stuck E&Eing to Georgia with the Americans. Can't be a winning proposition for a Russian.* Aside from the Chechen population in eastern Georgia, the Georgians themselves had no great love for Russians, *especially* not after the '08 war. And some of that antipathy went back to the Soviet days.

"We planned in flex time. We're still within our parameters." He wasn't going to admit to the *Spetsnaz* officer that they were getting awfully close to their abort time. If they hit it, he was scrapping the rest of the mission and going looking for Flanagan and the other five Blackhearts.

"Kodiak, Woodsrunner." Brannigan sighed in relief and grabbed his radio.

"Send it, Woodsrunner."

"We're about two minutes out. Contact broken." Flanagan made it sound like it hadn't been any great task, but that was Flanagan. He'd *had* to be unflappable, with a best friend like Curtis.

"Roger that. We're on a turnout on the left side of the road, just below the bridge." Brannigan looked back at Krivov. "See? I told you they'd make it."

Even in the dark, Krivov didn't look impressed. Brannigan's lip curled a little under his mustache as he turned back toward the front. He wasn't really all that interested in impressing the Russian, but the man's attitude was pissing him off.

A couple minutes later, headlights shone on the road above and ahead of them, and another UAZ turned down the unimproved strip of road that led down to the river. Wade blinked their own headlights and got a responding blink from the other vehicle. "It's them."

Brannigan got out as the other UAZ stopped and killed its headlights. Flanagan stepped out of the passenger side and came down to join him.

"Everything good?"

"Yeah." Flanagan nodded in the dark and pointed toward the town to the south. "We lost the tail in traffic down by the bazaar. Took enough turns on the way here to be sure we had him shaken off."

"Good to go." Brannigan clapped him on the shoulder. "Load up. We're burning darkness. Let's get up there and do the job before something else goes sideways."

***

They didn't get that far before something else did, indeed, go sideways.

Only about a mile down the road, Wade slowed, squinting into the dark beyond the headlights. A small café squatted next to the road ahead, a single, sputtering electric light above the door illuminating it. "Is it just me, or are those trucks waiting for something?"

Brannigan struggled to make out what Wade was talking about; the headlights hadn't been conducive to night adjustment, and the light over the café's door didn't shed a lot of illumination.

But the three trucks parked outside were all facing the road, and while their lights were off, there was movement around them. Someone *was* there, waiting. Waiting for what? Or who?

"Do we want to take the chance?" Wade was watching the café narrowly, slowly letting the vehicle roll forward but keeping his foot off the gas.

"What is happening?" Krivov craned his neck to see out the windshield.

"It might be nothing." Brannigan frowned. "Then again, it might be a snap checkpoint or an out-and-out ambush." He checked his watch, then pulled out the map again, shielding the red lens light as best he could as he studied it.

"Pull over." He pointed off between the trees. A narrow unimproved road led back toward several more houses in the fields and woods at the foot of the mountains that rose black against the night sky to their right. "We'll push up into the woods, stash the vehicles, and proceed on foot. If the Chechens—or the Azeris—think that they spotted hostiles coming in, then they might have put more security out, and that looks a lot like more security."

"There are not supposed to be more than ten or fifteen men on the cache." Krivov's impatience was starting to get on Brannigan's nerves. "We cannot afford to waste time."

Brannigan turned an icy eye on him. "If you're all that eager to say hello, then we'll let you out here. You can walk over there and see what they want."

Krivov didn't have an answer. Brannigan decided he'd leave it at that.

Wade took the turn, and a moment later they were trundling up between the dark rows of trees. A few lights glimmered around them from the surrounding farmhouses, but they appeared to be the only vehicles on that road. Their headlights would stand out somewhat, but without NVGs—which the Russians had not provided, no matter how bitterly Wade had bitched about it—they didn't have a lot of choice.

Brannigan kept an eye behind them as best he could, but the café was hidden behind the trees. There was no sign of pursuit, though.

Finally, as the woods got thicker around them, Brannigan decided they'd gone as far as they dared. "Pull off into the trees here. We'll conceal the vehicles and proceed on foot." He checked his watch, the hands still glowing faintly. "We've got about three and a half miles to go, and that's over two ridges. We'd better step it out."

# CHAPTER 19

Flanagan and Gomez slipped through the woods as quietly as they could. Given the fact that both men were rivals for the title of best fieldcraft man in the Blackhearts, that meant that they moved like ghosts, hardly making a sound.

Gomez had worked his way slightly ahead of Flanagan. The two of them were about two hundred yards ahead of the rest, having pushed up to scout ahead. Each man cradled a VSS Vintorez sniper rifle in his hands; as the scout element, Brannigan had decided that they were also going to be their overwatch.

It was dark as hell under the trees, but both men had had nearly an hour for their eyes to adjust. Flanagan found it a lot like camping when he'd been a kid; they hadn't had NVGs back then, either, and he had been one of the Scouts who'd refused to use a flashlight unless absolutely necessary. He'd developed some impressive night eyes at the time, and while he was quite a bit older now, he was slightly amazed at how much of that dark adaptation came back when there was no artificial light to spoil it.

After an hour, the world was a stark mix of gray and black. Unfortunately, the trees were thick enough that there was a *lot* of black under their branches, and they were still having to make their way more by feel than sight. It had slowed them down.

That might have worked to their advantage when it came to being quiet, except that Flanagan could still hear the assault element behind them. The rest weren't nearly as good at this as he and Gomez were.

Childress had been the other contender. As focused on the mission as he was, Flanagan still missed the gawky backwoodsman.

It had been a long, grueling movement already, over one wooded ridge, down into the valley, across a stream, and back up this slope. He'd hiked over harder terrain—compared to the Altiplano, this was nothing. But with time ticking away, they'd had to push, and climbing a hill in the dark is still difficult, even at a lower altitude and without a seventy-pound ruck on your back.

The two of them had to stay relatively close together; otherwise they'd lose each other in the dark. They both had a pretty good idea where they were going, though they were having to draw on old skillsets to navigate; the woods at night were the realm of compass headings and pace counts. Flanagan was glad that they'd thought of that during the train-up, and he and Gomez, at least, had been careful to record and memorize their pace counts on different terrain.

Still, the woods were tough. There weren't as many fallen trees in those woods as he might have expected, but there were enough. They'd already had to go around blowdowns twice, losing more time with each detour.

Gomez knelt next to a tree, and Flanagan barely saw the movement, straining his eyes in the pitch black under the forest canopy. He picked his way through the undergrowth and the trees, carefully placing his feet to keep from crunching leaves under his boots, and sank down to a knee next to Gomez.

"What's up?" He scanned what little he could see of the crest above through the woods, though most of what he could make out was simply little strips of sky through the slight gaps in the trees. He strained his ears, but aside from the occasional broken branch or rustle of movement down the slope behind them—which made him wince every time—he couldn't hear anything out of place, either.

Gomez's whisper was nearly inaudible. "You smell that?"

Flanagan drew in the night air. It was cool and redolent of the earthy smells of the forest. But there was something else…

"I smell woodsmoke."

"That's it." Gomez was still staring up toward the crest of the mountain, his presence almost more felt than seen in the dark.

"Could be farmers. This is Azerbaijan. People are poor up here." But Flanagan knew why Gomez had stopped, and he couldn't say he disagreed with the call. Complacency kills, and advancing to contact, this far away from friendlies—he didn't count the Russians as friendlies—made it even worse. They *had* to treat every anomaly as a threat.

"Could be. Or it could be sentries."

Flanagan tried to remember what he could about Chechen tactics and strategy. There wasn't much; he'd seen a few books and articles on the subject, going back to the Chechen wars in the '90s, but he hadn't read any of them. Even after Chechens had been spotted in the wars in the Middle East and Central Asia, the Soviet-Afghan War had always been the go-to example for enemy tactics. He was regretting that oversight now.

"Let's move up and see what's going on." He hesitated, but finally reached down and keyed his radio, practically subvocalizing into the mic. "Kodiak, Woodsrunner. We smell woodsmoke up here, and we're going to move up to the crest and see if we can spot where it's coming from. Hold what you've got until we can confirm that we're not about to stumble onto some sentries."

"Roger." Brannigan's reply was a faint, scratchy murmur, almost impossible to hear.

Flanagan was glad they'd thought to bring headsets.

He tapped Gomez, and the two of them got up, moving carefully up the slope. Flanagan was smelling and listening as much if not more than he was looking for the enemy.

While most of the movement so far, while cautious, had been relatively straightforward, now they climbed the mountain with even greater care. Each man moved in turn, slipping from tree to tree, staying deep in the shadows under their branches. Where possible, they avoided even the faint bands of starlight that filtered down through the forest canopy. Shadow on shadow was hard to see, even on NVGs.

And they had to assume that the enemy had night vision, even if they didn't. A lot of night vision devices had started to get into jihadi hands—some from American supply to local forces, some on the black market, some on the regular civilian market. The night wasn't any one side's exclusive domain anymore.

Step by step, feeling out the ground with each footfall before putting weight on it, they crept up the slope. The smell of woodsmoke was getting sharper and stronger. If Flanagan had had his suspicions that it might simply be coming from one of the farmhouses, or from Mazimchay itself, on the other side of the ridge, then those suspicions were being laid to rest. The fire was much closer than that.

He paused under an oak, searching the crest above him. Was that the faint orange flicker of firelight he'd just seen?

The two of them stayed put for a long moment, listening and searching the shadows. All that Flanagan could see was blackness above them, though he might have heard low voices. It was hard to tell; if they were there, the two Blackhearts were still too far away to make them out over the whisper of a faint breeze in the treetops overhead.

Finally, Flanagan decided that they had to move. The night wasn't getting any longer, and if he *had* seen or heard something, it wasn't close enough that they were going to stumble on it immediately.

At least, he hoped it wasn't.

Putting his toes down first, shuffling them carefully to get under any branches or leaves on the ground, he started up toward the crest again.

He got about twenty yards, still moving from tree to tree, before he froze.

They were close enough to the top of the ridge that he could see over the crest itself through some of the gaps in the trees. And a figure had just stepped into one of those gaps.

Flanagan sank to a knee behind the tree trunk, carefully easing one eye out to watch the man standing there, silhouetted against the night sky. He was still far enough away that Flanagan couldn't make out a lot of detail, but he didn't appear to be wearing a helmet or NVGs. He was faintly lit by a flickering glow from off to his right; there had to be either a fire or a lantern there.

He was pretty sure that was an AK in the man's hands.

He keyed his radio three times. He was still far enough away that he didn't think a subvocalized call would be heard, but he didn't want to take chances. The triple squelch break would tell Brannigan that it wasn't safe, and they needed to halt until he and Gomez had dealt with the situation.

One way or another.

The higher they crept, the more obvious the voices got. He still couldn't make out words, but he didn't speak Chechen, anyway, so that wouldn't have gotten him far. More importantly, they knew that there was an outpost up on the ridge. At least, he assumed that was what it was. He doubted these were teenagers from Mazimchay up in the woods having a bonfire.

Though he'd certainly seen stranger things in warzones over the years.

But as they got closer to the top, he could see the man standing in the gap in the trees more clearly. And he was no teenager out for a night of fun in the woods.

The man was dressed in camouflage fatigues and the kufi hat that was popular with Chechen fighters. Flanagan's early impression from a distance was also confirmed; the man was armed.

He started to circle around to the right, trying to keep to the thicker trees, putting more of the trunks between himself and the Chechen, keeping as deep in the shadows as he could. It might have been an overabundance of caution; the Chechen wasn't wearing NVGs. But it paid not to get sloppy.

Gomez was still close, but he was a silent shadow underneath the nearest tree. He was no more likely to be seen from there than Flanagan was.

Halting for a moment, Flanagan raised his VSS, peering through the optic. The Russian scope wasn't the best glass he'd ever used, especially in the dark. It took a moment to find his target, but the faint light of the fire helped.

The Chechen wasn't looking out at the woods. He was staring at the fire and talking. He looked so close through the scope, as dim as the image was, that it seemed as if Flanagan could have reached out and touched him.

*Good news and bad news*. The good news was, there was no way that guy was going to spot the two of them so long as they kept to the shadows and stayed quiet. Staring at the fire was a rookie mistake; he'd have no night eyes at all.

The bad news was that they couldn't get over the ridge that way.

He turned to the right and started up, moving higher up the ridgeline toward the bulk of the mountains above Mazimchay. Maybe this was the only listening post. Maybe there was a way around higher up.

But after a few minutes, he started to doubt that this was going to work. The woods were getting thicker, and the lay of the terrain was increasingly forcing them back down toward the draw below. He stopped after another hundred yards, crouched under a fallen tree, and turned back as Gomez joined him.

"This way ain't gonna work, man." His whisper was so low he could barely hear it himself. "We're getting pushed back downhill."

Gomez didn't answer at first. He just looked up and down the mountain, as if reading the forest and the terrain, though Flanagan was pretty sure that even the gimlet-eyed half-Apache couldn't see in the dark any better than he could. No, Gomez was thinking.

"You want to try downhill from the LP/OP?" Even with Gomez's mouth barely a couple inches from his ear, Flanagan still had to strain to hear him.

He thought for a long moment. It made some sense, but then they'd have bad guys right on their flank as soon as all hell broke loose.

*Which is the same problem we'd have if we moved higher up. Not to mention having bad guys between us and the rest of the team. Shit.*

"Maybe. But we're going to have to deal with these guys if we're going to set in overwatch up here."

"Agreed." Gomez, as always, was taciturn to the point of making Flanagan feel like he was being chatty.

"What are you thinking?" Flanagan looked back toward where they'd seen the sentry, but the woods were too thick; he could see no trace of the firelight or the man who'd been standing out in the open.

"I think we go back and move up on the LP/OP. Get eyes on, count who's there. Get into position and wait for the assault element to hit the town." Gomez's eyes might have glinted faintly in the dark. "These VSSes are pretty quiet."

"And if we miss one, we're screwed." But Flanagan had to admit that he wasn't entirely opposed to the idea.

"We better not miss, then." It was a typical Gomez answer.

Flanagan didn't have an answer to it, though. So, he just got up and started back the way they'd come.

He didn't entirely retrace their steps, though. Instead, he moved higher, heading for the crest of the ridge where it snaked down toward the valley and the villages of Balakan District. If they were going to sweep through the LP/OP and occupy it, he wanted the advantage of attacking from high ground.

It was slightly crazy, the more he thought about it; two of them were going to try to take on what had to amount to a fire team at least. But then, if they'd been entirely sane, they probably wouldn't have been Blackhearts, and wouldn't have been out here in the first place.

They were closer to the crest than he'd thought, and he turned back to the southwest just before going over it. The trees stayed thick all the way over, and he had to adjust his route a little, as the woods were too dense to follow the military crest—just below the actual top of the ridge—as closely as he might have wanted.

Woodsmoke stung his nostrils. The wind was coming up the ridge and blowing the smoke—if gently—toward them. Voices came with it, echoing faintly through the forest. The fire popped and crackled.

Flanagan slowed his advance to a crawl. He took a step. Paused. Looked and listened. Took another step. Rinse and repeat.

He was very glad he had done that after a moment. He froze and peered hard through the blackness under the boughs. Had he seen movement?

There. Only the fact that he hadn't seen an artificial light source for most of the last two hours allowed him to just barely make out the silhouette in front of him. A man was sitting against a tree, facing a small clearing that stretched down the hillside in front of him. And he was wearing NVGs.

Flanagan slipped behind the nearest tree, crouching under the low branches next to the thick, gnarled trunk. He barely dared to breathe. If that guy heard something and looked their way…

It might not be the end of it. It was very dark, and those might be early generation NVGs, that needed quite a bit of ambient light to work properly. And even the most advanced NVGs couldn't see through tree trunks.

But the slightest noise might give them away.

The man said something in Chechen. At least, Flanagan thought it was Chechen. He got a derisive answer back, and spat what sounded an awful lot like a curse in reply.

Flanagan listened carefully. The second voice had sounded like it had come from near the fire. If he had gauged his location right, that meant there were at least three.

He had to assume there were more. But with that one sentry there with the NVGs, he was practically pinned in place.

Lifting the Vintorez sniper rifle very slowly, he put his eye to the scope. At first, he could see nothing but blackness, and wished that they'd gotten red dots like the AS Vals had. But a slight bit of movement drew his eye, and a moment later he could just make out the slightly darker silhouette of the sentry against the faintly lighter gray of the tree behind him.

Easing the selector lever down ever so slowly and carefully, he felt it click into position. He let out his breath as his finger rested lightly on the trigger.

# CHAPTER 20

Krivov was getting antsy. "We need to move."

Brannigan looked back at him. "We move when my boys are ready for us to move." He kept his voice pitched low, but there was enough steel in his tone to even shut the Russian up. For the moment.

But as time stretched out without the double squelch break that would tell him that the overwatch was in position, even he started to get impatient. No, not impatient. Worried about the timeline. They really did only have so many hours of darkness to work with, and they were still most of a mile from their objective.

Finally, he moved to join Wade where he was kneeling next to a tree, scanning the darkness around them. "We need to get into position so that we can move as soon as those boys are set. Can you take us farther down and around the shoulder of the ridge, so we can cross over the crest and come at Mazimchay from the west?"

"Sure." Wade jerked a thumb over his shoulder. "But a couple of those thunderfooted morons back there better be a lot more careful. The whole point of having Joe and Mario out front was so they could pick out any outposts before the rest of us stumbled on 'em. If we're going to push ahead without them in front of us, we're going to have to move a lot more carefully." He spat. "*And* we need to let them know."

"Agreed." Brannigan looked up, then pointed to the northwest, about forty-five degrees offset from their previous course. "Let's go. I'll call Joe and fill him in."

Wade got up and started moving, as Brannigan looked back at Jenkins and motioned him to his feet. Then he keyed his radio. "Woodsrunner, Kodiak. Don't respond if you can't. We're moving around to the west side. Boris is getting antsy. Get in your overwatch position and stand by."

He didn't get a reply, but he had hardly been expecting one. If Flanagan and Gomez had been in the clear, they'd have already made contact.

The ten of them had been waiting down in a draw that threaded its way down the side of the ridge, and Wade started up the shallow slope of the finger to their left as he pushed uphill.

The rest of them spread out as they followed, falling into a Ranger file as they worked their way through the trees. Brannigan followed Wade, wincing slightly as he heard Jenkins and Krivov crunching through the leaves. Somewhere back there, a branch snapped, the *crack* achingly loud in the forest quiet.

Wade stopped, looking back. Brannigan moved up to him. "Keep going. I'll handle it."

He stayed where he was as Wade and Jenkins moved up the slope. He was actually a little impressed with Jenkins. The former SEAL was usually the low man on the fieldcraft and skills ladder, but he was moving quietly enough this time.

*So, who's making noise?*

Krivov shuffled past him, and he had his first culprit. He grabbed the Russian by the load bearing gear.

"If you don't watch where you put your feet and stop making a platoon's worth of noise, I'm going to slit your throat and leave you here for the Chechens to find." His voice was a low, ferocious hiss. "And I'll have a plenty believable story for your boss Pichugin when we get out of here, too."

Krivov tried to jerk away from him, but his grip was like a vise. "Some fucking *Spetsnaz* who can't walk through the woods without announcing his fucking presence to everybody for half a mile." He shoved the Russian forward. If it hadn't been almost pitch black under the trees, he was sure that he would have seen Krivov shooting a venomous glare at him.

It didn't bother him. Right then, he was half tempted to follow through with the threat rather than give Krivov a chance to stab them in the back.

He wouldn't; he had his own code of honor. But that didn't mean he wouldn't end the Russian with a quickness the moment that betrayal started to manifest itself.

At least, he would if one of the other Blackhearts didn't kill Krivov first.

Trust was not in great supply on that mountain.

Regardless of who wanted to sink a knife into who, they kept moving, and Krivov started moving more carefully. He wasn't making as much noise. And Brannigan couldn't help but notice that once Krivov got quieter, no one else was making as much noise as he'd been hearing before.

It had all been the Russian, which he found interesting.

He stretched out his legs, taking longer steps but still placing his feet carefully to avoid making noise, and got back to his position right behind Wade.

Wade stayed down in the draw as it led the way up toward the crest of the main ridge. In many places, Brannigan would have expected tougher going down in the low ground; the vegetation tended to be a lot thicker down there, where there was more water and less wind. But that particular part of the Caucasus foothills apparently didn't see that much extreme weather; the forest floor was every bit as thick on top of the finger as it was down in the draw.

It didn't take quite as long to get to the top as he had expected. Wade found a decently sheltered route through the oaks and hornbeams; terrain didn't seem to make that big a difference right there. But he started to move off to the left and downhill some more as they started to see the handful of glimmering lights from Mazimchay below them. Brannigan saw why a moment later; a clear-cut field had been carved out of the woods only a few dozen yards in front of them.

He paused, searching through the trees, trying not to lose too much night vision from looking at the lights, small and scattered as they were. A generator chugged down there somewhere; this was a poor part of the country, and grid power was presumably spotty where it existed at all.

A moment later he stopped, sinking to a knee even as Wade saw the same thing he'd just picked out, the big former Ranger lifting a fist to tell the rest to freeze. Brannigan belatedly passed the signal back, watching the men moving around in the faint glow of a fire barrel, just off the main road.

Two big, ancient-looking GAZ trucks were parked on the edge of the field, and a knot of men in camouflage fatigues and carrying AKs were gathered around a couple of fire barrels under the trees. It looked like almost a platoon's worth of fighters. Brannigan shot Krivov a glare that he probably couldn't see in the dark.

They weren't even on the objective, and they'd already seen more fighters than the Russians had insisted were in the village in total.

It was enough to give him pause. Did they dare try to continue, or did they need to back off and get the Russians to offer more support?

The decision was taken out of his hands a moment later, as a burst of gunfire rattled through the night from somewhere uphill.

***

Flanagan let his breath out as his finger tightened. Then he let the pressure off and came off the scope as he sank toward the ground behind the tree.

A branch cracked nearby, entirely too close and somewhere off to his right. There was someone else out there, even closer than his target.

He sank down to the prone, getting flat behind the tree and trying to spot the interloper through the darkness, trying not to make a sound that might give him away. If he was close enough to hear the other man moving, then he was close enough for the other man to hear him.

The leaves crunched ever so slightly under him as he eased himself down. But the oncoming footsteps were louder; the other man wasn't acting like he expected any trouble, even though he was out on sentry duty.

One of the Chechens called out, and the man to his right answered, getting a coarse laugh in response. Flanagan started to tense up even more; the man was walking toward his tree.

*Damn it, go somewhere else.*

But his desperate thought brought no effect. No Jedi mind tricks out here. The man was coming around the side of the tree, probably to relieve himself.

And if he came much farther, he was going to step right on Flanagan's leg.

It was possible that he might just be able to hold still and pretend his leg was a tree branch or a root. But anyone remotely sober—and if the Chechens were good Muslims, they wouldn't be drunk, at least not around each other—would be able to tell the difference between a tree root and a leg. At the very least, the man might turn a light on to see what he'd stepped on.

There was nothing for it. He couldn't even warn Gomez.

He rolled to his side as the Chechen, his AK slung across his back, already unbuttoning his fly, stepped around the treetrunk. It was dark enough that the man was as much a dark silhouette as the tree itself, but Flanagan's eyes were adjusted enough that he could still see him. And at that distance, he didn't need to use the scope. He just pointed the VSS and squeezed the trigger three times.

The VSS Vintorez's integral suppressor was a very good one, which was a little surprising since it was Russian. It made little more noise than the *click* of the action cycling. The 9x39mm bullets were subsonic, but they tore through the man's torso with little *thwacks* that Flanagan could actually hear from that close.

The man grunted as his knees gave way and he fell on his face, a faint gurgle coming from his throat. He hit hard, the AK knocking against the tree with a faint *clack*. Flanagan winced, then rolled back over and turned his VSS toward the rest of the sentries.

"Dukvakha?"

Flanagan cursed silently. One of them had heard the man fall. Maybe they'd heard the suppressed weapons fire, too, but hadn't quite known what it was. Either way, they knew something had happened out there in the dark, and when Dukvakha didn't answer…

Sure enough, the man he'd been about to shoot first was getting up, peering toward him. "Dukvakha?"

Flanagan put his eye to the scope, searching through the dim glass for the sentry's silhouette. But Gomez beat him to it.

Another three shots *click*ed off to his left. The three bullets slammed into the sentry, one of them tearing out his throat. He collapsed, hitting the tree he'd just been sitting against, and slid down toward the ground.

Then one of the others opened fire into the woods.

Flanagan was already flat on his stomach, but he buried his face in the leaves for a moment as bullets *crack*ed and *snap*ped overhead, slamming into tree trunks and ripping through limbs. Shredded leaves fell down onto the forest floor.

He was pretty sure the Chechen was shooting blind; there was no way he could have seen the Vintorez's muzzle blast in the dark. The integral suppressor ran the entire length of the barrel, and it would have retained any of the muzzle's flash. But blind fire can still be dangerous when it's aimed in your general direction.

He shimmied behind the tree, hoping that Gomez had already gone prone and gotten some cover. He was no longer confident that he had any idea how many Chechens were up here on the listening post.

The gunfire stopped, either because the Chechen realized he had no idea where the enemy was, or because he'd run his magazine dry. Flanagan suspected it was the latter. But without the incoming to keep his head down, he shoved himself to his feet and moved, stepping around Dukvakha's body and circling to the right. He had to watch his angles and make sure that he didn't move around too far, to the point that he and Gomez were aiming at each other, but if they stayed on the opposite slopes, they could shoot up at the bad guys without risking friendly fire, even if they were directly across from each other.

Another figure loomed out of the dark. He just barely registered that this man had a helmet and NVGs on before the Chechen raised his rifle. Flanagan ducked behind a hoary tree just as the Chechen's AK spat fire and knocked bark and splinters off the trunk right next to his head.

Flanagan was in a bad spot. The Chechen was too far away to point shoot, and using the scope was going to be difficult. But he took a deep breath, dropped prone, and rolled out just on the other side of the trunk, after making sure that most of his body was still behind cover.

The Chechen wasn't quite where he'd expected. He was moving, maneuvering on the tree, though he was moving uphill, and Flanagan had gone over the crest as he'd circled around. He had to drag the muzzle back, sweating even in the evening chill as he tried to find his enemy in the scope. The sight picture was a mass of blacks and dark grays that just kind of blended together.

He was glad he'd thought to turn the illuminated reticle on as soon as they'd left the vehicles. It wasn't perfect, but it was something.

The Chechen got four more rounds, though Flanagan was pretty sure that the first two missed. The third and fourth hit, though, spinning the man halfway around and eliciting a wail of pain.

Another burst of gunfire rattled out in the dark, closer to the fire, but was cut short. Flanagan couldn't be sure, but he had a feeling that Gomez had just struck again.

Someone down by the fire—which he could see faintly through the trees now—was yelling into a radio. If they hadn't been blown before, they sure were now.

Getting back up, he started to work his way, tree-to-tree, toward the fire. He was careful not to look at the flames themselves, though he had already decided that he was going to grab that pair of NVGs if he could.

He might have heard the rapid *clicks* of more suppressed 9x39 fire off to the left. The yelling in Chechen got even more high-pitched. Which had the added advantage of giving him a better sense of where the man was.

Rolling his feet into every step, he stalked his prey, scanning his surroundings as best he could. The fire was getting brighter. He might have even cast a slight shadow behind him as he moved to the next tree.

There. A young man with the wispy beginnings of a beard on his chin and a kofi hat on his head was screaming into the radio as he tried to back away from the fire. He was clearly about half a second away from bolting.

Flanagan put the faintly glowing chevron of the PSO-1 scope's reticle on the young man's chest and squeezed the trigger.

The first round was slightly deflected as it punched through the young man's thumb and glanced off the radio. He sat down hard, staring in shock at the mangled meat that had been his thumb, hardly noticing the bullet that had to have torn into his chest somewhere around his ribs.

Flanagan's second and third shots were more effective. They tore through the young man's heart and lungs before he could scream. He just sat there for a second, struggling to breathe as dark froth sputtered from his mouth and nose, then fell over backward.

The hillside went quiet, except for the sputter of the fire and the increasingly agitated yells in Chechen coming over the radio.

***

Brannigan cursed. Every eye at the little encampment was turned up toward the ridge, and one of the Chechens was on the radio, even as more gunfire echoed down the slope.

He got low, signaling the rest to do the same. Wade was already aimed in, just off to his left, and to his irritation, Krivov moved up to join him.

The rest of the Blackhearts spread out along the treeline, getting down in the prone behind their rifles. Santelli was moving from tree to tree, up and down the line, making sure that they weren't getting so focused on the bad guys down on the field that they abandoned rear security. Finally, the squat, thickset former Sergeant Major dropped down next to Brannigan, almost shoving Krivov out of the way.

But Brannigan had been watching the Chechens. One of them was yelling into a radio, in between directing the other gunmen to either get into the trucks or start moving on foot. He already had about ten starting across the field and up the slope, toward the sound of the gunfire.

Unfortunately, another six were moving straight toward the treeline where the Blackhearts were waiting.

# CHAPTER 21

Flanagan knelt just outside the circle of firelight, though if there was anyone else out there with NVGs, he'd probably still be visible. He hadn't drawn fire yet, though.

That squawking radio worried him. The Chechen on the other end was getting louder, and so far, unless there was another Chechen sentry somewhere out in the trees, there was no one left alive on the outpost to answer. Which meant that the bad guys were going to be responding soon.

He keyed his radio again. "Kodiak, Woodsrunner. Just got walked on, had to go loud. We are definitely made; suggest you fall back and go firm for a few minutes while we draw the bad guys off up the mountain."

There was no response at first. Finally, just as he was about to try the call again, he heard Brannigan's low murmur over the radio, faintly distorted by static. "Copy all. Bad guys are moving down here; bad time to try to move."

*Hell.* That meant that the Chechens were too close to the assault element, which meant that he and Gomez were too far away. They'd blown the approach—if he was being honest, that had been an unavoidable chance contact, but it still *felt* like they'd blown the approach—but unless they did something drastic quickly, all they would have accomplished would be to put the entire assault on the back foot.

A moment later, Brannigan clarified. "You've got about ten coming your way, but we've got another half a dozen moving toward our position. If you can, break contact and find another overwatch spot."

That put things in a slightly different light. Flanagan chewed on it for a moment, before he slipped back through the trees, searching for the second man he'd killed. He was changing the plan in his head.

He and Gomez could conceivably draw off more of the Chechens, opening the way for the assault element to get into Mazimchay and pull off the heist. But would the two of them manage to draw enough of them far enough away without getting horribly murdered along the way?

And was the heist even worth it anymore, given the obvious disparity in numbers? He knew that Brannigan had to be asking the same question. The Russians' intel had been crap.

The other possibility was that it had been a deliberate lie. He couldn't help but notice that Krivov was the only Russian on the ground with them. Even Dmitri hadn't come along. In fact, the gangster had been nowhere to be seen during the final preparation phase.

He found the corpse as Gomez caught up with him. The other man was ahead of him, already wearing a high-cut helmet and mounted monocular NVGs. He must have taken them off another of the dead Chechens.

"Hope you didn't hit that guy in the head," Flanagan whispered as he unclipped the chin strap and started pulling the helmet off the dead man's head.

"Nah." Gomez didn't elucidate further; he didn't really need to, and if anything, Gomez was a man of fewer words than Flanagan. And Flanagan took some pride in being called "taciturn."

It took a little adjustment to get the helmet to fit; the Chechen had had a bigger head. It wasn't a ballistic helmet, either. It was too light, and he could feel the vent holes in the top; it was just a lightweight bump helmet, used more to mount the night vision than for any sort of real protection.

That was fine with him; he had no desire to go hiking around the mountains in a full ballistic helmet.

The NVGs were old but serviceable PVS-14s. He twisted the knob and the forested hillside in front of him sprang to life in shades of green and black in front of his left eye.

"We've got company coming. Let's go say hello." He wasn't sure how well he was going to be able to aim with the PSO scope and the NVGs, but it wouldn't be the first time he'd had to adjust. He'd just have to shoot with his right.

The VSS rifles didn't have laser sights, but with the Chechens using night vision, shining IR lasers around wouldn't have been a good idea, anyway.

He got up and started moving, easing his way down the slope to get closer to the town, Gomez falling in beside him. They'd circle around and try to come at the Chechen reinforcements from the flank and rear, hopefully catching them from an angle they wouldn't expect.

It was what he'd hoped to do with the outpost, but that had gone badly.

They hadn't gone far when he froze, lifting a fist and listening, hard.

He hadn't imagined it. He scanned the sky, looking for the small black dots in the sky that would be the helicopters he had just started to hear in the distance.

***

Brannigan cocked an ear. Was that helicopter rotors he heard? Were the Azeris responding that quickly?

It was possible. The border outpost was less than a mile away; they had to have heard the gunfire. And while the relations between Georgia and Azerbaijan were *generally* cordial, there were still some border disputes. The border guards weren't likely to be too sanguine about a firefight right next to their post.

But Krivov tugged at his sleeve. "Those are our Mi-38s and Ka-52s. That is our diversion; Anatoly's contacts will be calling their underworld contacts soon to warn them that a Russian raid is coming from over the Georgia border. This should divert their attention."

Brannigan shot a glare at him. "Why is this the first I'm hearing about this?"

Krivov shrugged. "This was part of plan all along."

*That we were conveniently left out of. Naturally. What else haven't we been told?*

But with the Chechens already halfway across the field, this was neither the time nor the place to debate the issue. *If* they made it out alive, then there'd be words. Strong words.

He watched the oncoming Chechens as they stopped in their tracks and turned to look toward the northeast and the helicopters coming down over the mountains. Brannigan still couldn't see them; it was too dark, and they were running blacked out.

That alone made him hesitate. He didn't trust the Russians not to open fire on any movement they saw on the ground. They were Russians, after all, and target discrimination was *not* their strong suit.

And that was assuming that they were actually there to help in the first place.

The Chechens were too close to warn the rest of the team. He could only hunker down and hope that Jenkins, Javakhishvili, or Wade didn't do something impulsive if the Chechens got any closer.

***

Wade lay in the leaves under an oak, his AS Val pointed toward the faint silhouettes moving across the field. The moon was finally coming up over the eastern horizon, but it was still less than half full, and while the illumination was welcome after the deep black darkness under the trees with only starlight and the faint glow from Balakan to light their way, it still wasn't nearly enough.

He could hear the helicopters, but he couldn't see them, even though he took his cheek off the rifle to scan the sky. Not for the first time, he cursed this entire mission bitterly. It wasn't that he was all that averse to risk, especially if the rewards were commensurate. He wasn't even particularly opposed to working with the Russians, if it meant getting paid and killing some jihadis. Wade didn't consider himself an ideological man, but he hated those savages with every fiber of his being.

But this mission had been a cluster from the get-go. The Russians were keeping them in the dark, the gear was crap—though he could appreciate the Vals—and they were now outnumbered, outgunned, and outclassed by the Chechens.

He wasn't impressed with the PK-AS red dots that he'd scraped up for the Vals, but he supposed that they were better than nothing. The glass wasn't quite as dark as the PSO-1s that Flanagan and Gomez had, but they still cut down the amount of light getting through, and the reticle was brighter and fuzzier in the dark than he would have liked. He also wasn't all that sure about just how well it was zeroed.

At least he wasn't trying to see the iron sights against black silhouettes in the dark.

His finger slipped inside the trigger guard and rested on the trigger. He would ordinarily let Brannigan open the ball, but if they got too close…

The helicopters' growl was getting louder. And the Chechens knew what that sound was and didn't want to be out in the open.

They hesitated at first. At least, most of them did. They must have been the younger, more inexperienced fighters. Two of them immediately turned and dashed for the treeline back by the fire barrels, desperately trying to get out of the open before the helos were on top of them.

That, at least, told him that the incoming birds probably weren't Azerbaijani support for the Chechens, unless the bad guys just hadn't gotten the word yet.

He eased his finger off the trigger and crept backward, deeper into the shadows under the trees, hoping that the branches overhead would conceal him if the helicopters above had thermal sights.

Then they could only wait as the situation developed, and Brannigan decided what to do next.

***

Flanagan kept working his way along the mountain slope above Mazimchay, careful to move from tree to tree and avoid exposing himself to the sky above. He trusted the Russians' target discrimination about as much as any of the other Blackhearts, which was to say he didn't.

Gomez was a ghost behind him; he only knew the other man was there when he turned and looked back to see him. He was extremely glad for the NVGs; at least now they were on the same rough footing as the Chechens.

He could see the helicopters now. Four of them were circling over the mountains just to the northeast. He actually thought that they were still in Georgian airspace—not that they had to be very far to the north to stay out of Azerbaijan.

He watched the quartet as they circled, his eyes narrowing behind the NVG monocular. They weren't moving in; they were flying racetracks just on the other side of the border.

*They're not coming over here. They're not a strike force; the Russians don't want their fingerprints on this any more than necessary. The birds are just there to draw eyes.* His lip curled as he remembered hearing Pichugin talk about air support. Apparently, "support" had just meant "diversion."

He wasn't sure if that was a good thing or a bad thing. They weren't going to get Russian help on the ground, but that might actually increase their chances of survival.

Gomez moved up on his flank. Flanagan followed. Gomez was right. They were still in the fight, and sooner or later the Chechens were going to figure out what he just had—that the Russians were just putting on a show.

They got past the fire, putting the glow well behind them as they got deeper under the shadows of the trees. Flanagan paused again under a lone fir, even as the Russian helicopters turned back to the northeast and climbed back over the mountains, apparently having decided their diversion was done.

There was a lot of movement down in Mazimchay. Headlights were swinging out onto the single main road. The response to the attack was gathering steam. They had to keep moving and keep the enemy guessing.

Gomez had moved up another couple of trees, but he had just stopped and dropped to a knee. Flanagan followed the line of the other man's weapon, but couldn't see what he'd seen, so he moved higher, careful to make sure he had enough trees between him and the fire farther up the ridge, so as not to be silhouetted against the glow.

There. He saw two of them right away, working their way up the slope, moving fast but with their heads up and their AKs ready. These weren't the untrained, *Insh'Allah* sort of fighters that they'd encountered in other jihadi groups. These were Chechens. They knew how to fight. The only jihadis who might rival them were the Pashtuns in Afghanistan.

He dropped back behind a tree, moving more slowly than his instincts urged him to. The Chechens were still far enough away to make it unlikely that they'd see him, but rapid movement draws the eye, and he was pretty sure that at least the one in the lead had night vision on.

Aiming was actually somewhat more difficult with the NVGs on. He eased around the trunk of the tree, keeping the NVG tube to one side of the scope, and put his right eye, which was still night-adjusted, to the scope. It took some searching to find his target. If he could see the oncoming Chechen through his NVGs, then the reticle was off, and vice versa. He concentrated on the PSO-1's reticle, finally finding the advancing silhouette.

It was still a tricky shot. He fired three times, the rapid *click click click* the only sound above the whisper of the breeze in the treetops and the faint buzz of the helos in the distance.

The first round hit the man in the stomach. The next two walked up his torso, and he fell backward, his head snapping back as the last round went through his teeth.

It was better shooting than Flanagan had expected to manage. The Chechen crashed down on his back and didn't move.

More *click click click* sounds rapped off to his left, and the second man back fell on his face. Gomez had claimed his scalp, too.

He could see movement behind the fallen Chechens, but only a little bit. They knew that their pointmen had just gone down, but because of the suppressors on the VSS rifles, they didn't know where their enemy was.

They probably didn't even know for sure what had happened. And the longer they stayed put and didn't advance further, the more Flanagan was convinced that they had no idea what exactly had just occurred. They'd hunkered down and were trying to figure out why the two men up front were dead.

This wasn't working the way he'd planned. But Flanagan was nothing if not flexible. He stalked forward, still moving from cover to cover, circling downhill and around onto the flank.

If he couldn't get them to chase him, then he'd just have to hunt them.

# CHAPTER 22

As the helicopters receded into the distance, Wade watched the Chechens through his sights.

His finger hovered near the trigger. The shooting up higher on the ridge had died down, and he didn't know if that meant that Flanagan and Gomez had broken contact or had been killed. If these bastards didn't move soon, he was going to have to assume the latter.

If Joe and Mario were dead, Wade was killing all of the Chechens in front of him. That was just the way it was.

He could faintly hear what sounded like the squawk of a radio. One of the Chechens had moved closer to the fire barrel, and Wade could see him more clearly as he talked with someone farther down in the village. Or higher up the mountain.

A moment later, the man was pointing up the mountainside, rapping out quick, terse orders. Three more of the Chechens shouldered their rifles and started to cross the field again, this time heading more to the northeast, toward where the gunfire had sounded.

That told Wade that Flanagan and Gomez were still in the fight. Good.

He didn't take his eyes off the men who had stayed near the trucks and the fires. If it were up to him, he'd hit them now, wipe them out and then move in. But it wasn't up to him. He could take matters into his own hands in a heartbeat if he just squeezed the trigger, but while some of his compatriots might question his moral compass, Wade was a highly disciplined man. He might agree that he was something close to a functional sociopath, but he was one with very strict boundaries he wouldn't cross. And he'd been a professional soldier for over two decades. He knew the absolute necessity of unity of command at a time like this. Brannigan was the team leader. It was Brannigan's call.

Wade might disagree with the team leader's call, but he'd never deliberately disobey it.

He just watched as the Chechen react force trudged up toward the woods. Unless he was seeing things, most of them had helmets and NVGs in addition to their AK-74s and AK-203s. He silently and viciously cursed the Russian stinginess that had left them at a disadvantage against the Chechens.

Presuming that it was stinginess and not a deliberate handicap. Wade might not quite share Javakhishvili's hatred for Russians, but he didn't exactly trust them, either.

Not that there were many people Wade trusted in the first place. Most of them were on this mountainside.

He heard a faint rustle behind him, and a hissed voice, barely audible. "Friendly."

Brannigan took a knee behind the tree that formed most of Wade's cover. "As soon as that bunch is out of sight, we need to dump these guys and move."

"Roger that." It was music to Wade's ears. He settled down better behind his rifle, already picking his target.

They watched as the Chechens started arguing. The man with the radio was obviously in charge, but it looked like the rest weren't happy to be staying behind while their buddies went after the intruders. Wade just watched, his finger back alongside the trigger, breathing evenly, waiting for Brannigan to open the ball.

But the situation was changing even as they watched. The Chechen with the radio appeared to be losing the argument. One of the others, a younger man with a hatchet face and sunken cheeks that were deeply shadowed in the flickering firelight, was jabbing a finger up the mountain, his expression intense and angry.

A moment later, another burst of gunfire sounded up above. The angry young man got more insistent. The older man with the radio said something into it and waited for a reply.

Wade was starting to get impatient. They couldn't wait all night. He kept his cool, though. He was as aware as Flanagan that they had to be the hunters tonight. If they slipped up, they were all dead.

The younger man was getting the better of the argument. As another rattling burst—that somehow sounded more than a little desperate, as it went on and on, as if someone was mag-dumping into the trees—echoed from above, the chief with the radio nodded, and gestured toward the mountainside. The rest of the Chechen fighters left their post and hustled across the field, after their comrades.

"Well, that was easy." Brannigan tapped Wade. "Into the trees. Stay out of the firelight."

Wade hardly needed to be reminded, but he held his peace. He got up slowly, careful not to make any unnecessary noise, and circled around behind the tree, heading almost due north, around the field.

If this worked, they'd be inside the enemy's perimeter before another shot was fired.

***

Hank Brannigan wasn't sure what he was doing.

If he'd thought he was out of his element during training, now he was seriously doubting the sanity of the decision to even attempt to join his father's team, let alone come along on this expedition. They were eleven men against who knows how many, hundreds of miles away from support. If he'd proposed this mission to his superiors in the Marine Corps, he would have been laughed at until they'd figured out he was serious, after which he would have been shuffled off to the deepest, darkest hole of an S-shop they could find, where he couldn't cause any more trouble.

Now here he was. Underequipped, outnumbered, outgunned, and well aware that he and everyone with him would simply disappear and be disowned if any of this went badly.

To say that he was starting to regret every decision in his life that had brought him here would be putting it mildly.

He was so wrapped up in his thoughts that he almost didn't notice Curtis getting up next to him and starting to move away. Only when the short, loudmouthed little man glanced back and noticed that Hank wasn't with him did he backtrack.

"Hey, kid." Curtis' whisper was a low hiss that couldn't have carried more than a few feet. Hank was momentarily surprised, after what he'd seen of Curtis so far, that the man could be that quiet. "We're moving. On your feet."

More gunfire thundered under the trees above them. Hank glanced that way. "Shouldn't we go up and back those guys up?"

He couldn't see Curtis's reaction in the dark, but he didn't move. A moment later, he heard a faint tinny voice, and realized that his earpiece had fallen out. *No wonder you don't know what's going on, dumbass*. He shoved it in just in time to hear the end of Curtis's transmission.

"…And I think he's right. Woodsrunner and Pancho Villa need some backup. Requesting permission to take Noob and go up to link up with them."

"Go." Brannigan didn't say anything more. There wasn't time.

All the same, Hank kind of wished that he had. He wasn't ready to go into the woods with no night vision, against most of a squad, with only himself and Curtis. Well, and Flanagan and Gomez, but they had to link up with them. Again, without NVGs or IR.

*You wanted to prove yourself to the old man. He's giving you a chance. Don't get wrapped up in the fact that you're his son. You can't expect your dad to give you extra slack on the battlefield.* He hadn't really expected his father to give him any extra slack in the first place, or so he'd told himself. The reality of being the low man on the totem pole was a bit sobering, though.

"Let's go, Junior." Hank was momentarily grateful that Curtis hadn't called him "Noob" again, though he suspected it was going to take a long time to get rid of that callsign.

He followed Curtis as the shorter man started up the mountain, sticking to the trees and trying to get glimpses of the Chechens who were climbing toward Gomez and Flanagan.

***

Flanagan paused just before reaching the next tree. He didn't know what had just rung an alarm bell in his head, but he'd spent enough time in the woods to know that when something instinctively warned him to freeze, he needed to listen.

Staying stock still, he scanned the shadows under the trees around him. He could still hear some movement and low voices ahead, as the Chechens debated whether to go forward or wait on reinforcements. They still weren't sure where the shots that had downed their lead scouts had come from, and as fanatical as they might be, they weren't in a huge hurry to go charging in to die for no good reason.

Most of the time, in Flanagan's experience, the fanatics were only interested in dying if they could take a lot of the infidels with them. Dying alone and silently, in the dark, didn't appeal.

But the Chechens who were hunting them weren't what had alerted him. He was still trying to figure out what it was.

There. Lights were moving down in the village below, and while the men moving into the trees weren't carrying them, the lights backlit them enough for Flanagan to get a few glimpses. The Chechens knew they were under attack, and they were mustering everyone they could from the village to counter it.

*We're about to get dogpiled.*

In a way, it was a good thing, if he and Gomez could just maintain contact without getting pinned, flanked, or otherwise run down. The more he saw, the more he was convinced that there were well over fifty Chechen fighters in Mazimchay, and that would make an assault on the cache site damned near suicidal. Unless they managed to draw most of the fighters off.

*Which means that we need to get loud. Preferably without actually giving our position away.*

He had an idea how to do that, but it was going to require some careful maneuvering. And probably going back and looting the dead bodies near the fire again.

The Russians had provided a few explosives, but only two frag grenades. This was supposed to be a stealthy heist, after all. There were only supposed to be a dozen or so fighters on the ground. Abu Mokhtar's primary fortress was somewhere in Chechnya itself, reportedly in the mountains near Mount Tebulosmta. The cache was supposed to be just that: a cache.

But with the intel proving bad, they had to adjust a bit. And Flanagan wanted more grenades.

He turned back and got Gomez's attention, then pointed back uphill toward the remains of the outpost. Gomez didn't hesitate or ask questions. He just signaled an affirmative.

Then Flanagan heard Curtis over the radio, calling for Brannigan's permission to head up the mountain to join him and Gomez. That would help, provided they could link up quietly, but the fact of the matter was, if he was picturing the terrain and their dispersal correctly, the group of Chechens in front of him was between them and the rest of the Blackhearts.

A branch snapped, and he looked up. The Chechens had spread out into a line and were advancing along the ridgeline, facing the two of them, now only about a hundred yards away. They were about to run out of time.

He'd been hoping to hold onto his one grenade until he could get some more and set up a better ambush. But you don't always get to be picky in combat.

Quietly swinging the Vintorez on its sling to his side, he pulled his single RGO grenade out of his gear and pulled the pin. He catfooted his way to the next tree, holding the spoon down, as the Chechen skirmish line got closer and closer.

The grenade weighed a little over a pound, and if he remembered right, its kill radius was somewhere around six meters. It also had an impact fuse which meant he needed to be very careful not to bounce it off a nearby tree.

He waited, listening to the oncoming Chechens past the thumping of his own heartbeat. Wait too long and they'd be on top of him. Throw too soon, and the frag would fall short.

It was now or never. He hooked the grenade around the trunk, aiming for the ground between two of the advancing Chechens, neither of whom were looking right at him as he threw.

The little ball of metal and explosive sailed through the air with a faint *ping* as the spoon flew free. Flanagan dropped flat, getting as much of his body behind the tree as he could. He didn't see it land. He didn't see if the Chechens reacted, or even if they heard it before it detonated.

The explosion was deafening in the quiet of the night. The flash lasted for a fraction of a second, but the *boom* shook the ground and echoed across the valley. Fragmentation lashed the trees, stripping leaves from the nearest and scoring their bark.

When Flanagan rolled out from behind the trunk, he saw that at least two of the Chechens were down, having been just close enough to be killed or incapacitated. The others had either run for cover or were staring, frozen in shock, at where the explosion had ripped through their midst.

One of them was smashed off his feet as a series of rapid *click click click* reports sounded off to Flanagan's left. Gomez wasn't wasting time.

Flanagan found a target almost as quickly, dumping the man with a fast pair of shots. Then he was falling back, sprinting as lightly as he could back to the next tree back, bent almost double.

The fact that they weren't taking any return fire yet told him that the survivors still weren't sure what was going on. Which had been the whole point of hitting them with a grenade in the first place. It made a lot of noise, and it would hopefully draw the bad guys from down in the village, but without giving away their position.

Now they just had to link up with Curtis and Junior before they got cut off.

# CHAPTER 23

Wade moved through the woods as fast as he could without making a lot of noise. He was a little pissed, in a way, that the Chechens had fucked off and gone after Flanagan and Gomez; he'd been ready and willing to plunder the NVGs off their bodies. He was getting older, and his night eyes weren't quite what they'd once been. He could see, and the red dot on his Val helped, but he really, *really* wanted some NVGs.

He'd circled around the trucks and the fire barrels, passing into the relatively small patch of woods between the open field and the edge of the village below as the *boom* of an explosion rolled across the valley.

He froze at the sound, scanning the woods around him. That sounded some distance away, so he didn't *think* one of his teammates had set off a mine or an IED. At least, not any of the ones down here.

"Keep pushing." Brannigan was next to him, his voice just below a whisper. The Colonel was as cool and calm as ever, despite the fact that his son was up on the mountain, somewhere near that explosion.

It didn't affect Wade that much; he would be the first one to admit that his emotions were fairly detached from most things he did. Some said that made him broken; he tended to reply that it made him effective in situations that would have other people losing their minds.

He kept moving, though Burgess had moved up next to him during the pause. He still hadn't gotten to know the older former SEAL well, but while Burgess hadn't made a big deal about it, it was becoming obvious that he was damned near Flanagan's equal in the bush.

He also had eyes like a cat. He suddenly shot out a hand and grabbed Wade's sleeve after only a few more strides.

Wade strained his eyes to see what had brought Burgess up short. They had moved a good dozen yards away from the fire barrels, and the edge of the woodline was barely another couple dozen yards away. Beyond lay a squat, darkened house with a peaked roof, surrounded by trees and bushes. The moving lights appeared to be higher up, off to the northeast. If the Chechens had people around that house, they were staying quiet and keeping the lights off, which didn't fit the rest of the activity they were seeing.

But Burgess pointed, drawing Wade closer so that he could follow his pointing finger. He shook his head after a moment of staring hard. "I can't see shit."

Burgess bent down, and Wade followed, as the quiet man reached out and seemed to snag something with his fingers, though his touch was very light. "Tripwire." He traced it carefully to the base of a tree. "I think it's a directional mine. It doesn't feel like an IED. Either a Claymore or a MON 50."

Wade felt the wire then, letting out a long breath of a sigh. That could have been bad, though he'd never have known what had happened.

"They've got the fucking woods mined with their own people moving around in 'em?" He couldn't quite believe that even jihadi booger-eaters would be that stupid.

"They've probably got the safe zones marked out somehow." Burgess stayed in a crouch, looking around carefully, but the shadows under the trees stayed a nearly impenetrable black.

Another explosion thundered up on the mountainside. Wade thought he could hear yelling somewhere up to the northeast, near the lights. "That's going to slow us down when we really can't afford to slow down."

"What is it?" Brannigan had joined them.

"Mines." Burgess was tracing the tripwire, very carefully. He was moving down toward the treeline as he went. Finally, he stopped at a tree near the edge of the field, then retraced his way back to where Brannigan and Wade were on a knee, hardly daring to move in case there were more mines.

"I think they've got the flanks mined, aimed back at the road." Burgess only paused to say that before he moved back the way they'd come a little bit, checking for more tripwires. He found another one, about five yards farther up the mountain, and traced it. When he rejoined the two of them again, he was even more certain.

"It looks like they've got tripwires and mines aimed back toward the mouth of the valley, in the woods. It would keep an attacking force canalized on the road. But I think I can thread us through it." He looked at Wade, though Wade couldn't see anything more of his face than a silhouette barely visible against the deeper blackness of the trees around them. "If that's fine with you."

Wade wasn't going to let his pride get them killed. "It's all yours. I didn't even see that shit."

Burgess started moving, carefully threading through the gap between tripwires. Wade followed, while Brannigan stayed back to make sure that Jenkins and Bianco knew where to go.

Higher up, engines revved, and Wade could hear shouting. They'd kicked the hornet's nest, all right.

*Now we've just got to avoid getting blown up before we can get to the objective.*

***

Hank flinched at the explosion uphill from where he and Curtis were working their way up through the woods. This was getting real.

Curtis hadn't even blinked, as far as he could tell. If Hank hadn't been so focused on getting through the night in one piece, he might have wondered just what the Blackhearts had seen, if that deafening announcement that things had gone loud didn't faze him.

Curtis slowed and stopped, lowering himself to a knee behind a tree, and Hank moved up to a supporting position just above him. He couldn't see what had prompted Curtis to stop. After a tense few seconds, he was about to ask in a low whisper, but then he didn't have to.

Three Chechens were hustling into the treeline just ahead of them, visible as little more than dark shapes in the gloom.

He wasn't sure what to do. He *thought* they were bad guys, but he couldn't see a whole lot of detail. And he wasn't sure if his father wanted them to engage before linking up with Flanagan and Gomez…

Curtis didn't hesitate. He shouldered his Val and proceeded to hose the three closely packed Chechens with half the magazine.

The Val's suppressor was a lot quieter than Hank had been expecting; his Marine Corps experience had mostly been with the Surefire suppressors and supersonic 5.56, so he was used to suppressed gunfire still sounding like harsh *crack*s that couldn't be disguised as anything but gunshots. The subsonic 9x39 combined with suppressors that were a lot better than he'd been led to believe that Russian suppressors could be was almost *silent*. Curtis's fire sounded more like a distant sewing machine, a rapid series of *clicks* that he couldn't be sure even sounded like gunshots.

Two of the Chechens stumbled and fell. The third one dashed behind a tree, spraying return fire, flame spitting from the muzzle along with the much, much louder rattle of AK fire. Hank plunged toward the forest floor as bullets *snap*ped overhead, a few of them glancing off the trees and ricocheting away with harsh, whining buzzes. Bark and shredded leaves fell around him like rain as he damn near hugged the tree for cover.

Then Curtis slammed two more shots at the Chechen and the AK went silent, even as the thunderous reports echoed off the mountains.

"Let's move, Junior." Curtis, who ordinarily seemed to Hank to be the happy-go-lucky joker of the team, was deadly serious, his voice a low, venomous hiss. "What the fuck did you wait so long for?"

"I..." He didn't have an answer. He didn't know. *Was I really waiting for permission to engage? What the hell did I think was going on?*

He knew the truth, even as Curtis grunted and started up the hill again, reaching for his radio at the same time.

*I'm not used to the lack of structure, the loose chain of command and, frankly, the near-total "initiative-based tactics" these guys have made second nature. I suppose that it's inevitable, working out here on the jagged edge with only a handful of dudes, but fuck me. I'm going to have to learn a whole new way of thinking if I'm going to stick it out with this team.*

*Provided we survive this insane mission in the first place, of course.*

Curtis was murmuring into his radio. Hank could hear his voice more clearly in the headset than he could with his unaided ear. "Woodsrunner, Gambler. Just smoked three more coming to join your pals up there, and we are coming to you. Where do you want to link up?"

There was no immediate reply, but another explosion up above might explain why. A moment later, Flanagan's voice answered. "There are bad guys between you and us. Push due east, over the crest of the ridge, and then push another hundred yards up the ridgeline. I'll contact you and walk you in when we get clear of this bunch."

Curtis looked over his shoulder as he answered. "Roger." Hank followed what he thought was the line of his gaze, and he saw that Curtis was looking at the bodies. A moment later, the shorter man led the way down toward the cooling corpses of the men he'd just killed.

"Cover me." He scrambled down to the nearest body and crouched over it. Hank found a tree nearby, facing the village, and barricaded himself on the trunk, getting down on a knee and pointing his rifle around the tree toward Mazimchay itself.

He could hear more shouts, though the lights weren't moving out of the village. Pretty soon, though, he could just make out movement in the open fields between the trees. More fighters were coming from somewhere down there, pushing up the side of the ridge.

While he kept his attention mostly focused on the oncoming enemy fighters, he could hear Curtis rummaging around behind him. A moment later, Curtis tapped him on the shoulder. "Here. Put this on. Shouldn't be too much blood on it."

Hank looked down. Curtis was holding out a high-cut helmet with what appeared to be a PVS-14 night vision monocular mounted on it. Hank hesitated. He really didn't want to put something that a jihadi had been wearing on his head. It had nothing to do with any kind of superstition or fear of something a dead man had worn; he was more concerned about what he might catch. The jihadis he'd faced had never been the most hygienic.

But under the circumstances... He saw that Curtis already had a helmet and PVS-14 on his own head. He let the Val hang and pulled the helmet on. It was a tight fit, and he had to fiddle with the chinstrap and the NVG mount to get it to sit right. Even so, the headache from the too-tight, hard pads started immediately.

But he could see better. Which made it much easier to make out what looked very much like over a dozen men coming out of the village and heading up into the hills, already in a skirmish line, their weapons up and searching the shadows for the Blackhearts.

"Come on." Curtis tugged him uphill, deeper into the woods. "We'll be able to do more once we link up with Joe and Mario."

***

Flanagan and Gomez had fallen back toward the outpost they'd slaughtered earlier, once they'd stopped the advancing react force in its tracks. The fire in the barrel had died down a little without the Chechens feeding it, though the glow around it still seemed blindingly bright in the green shades of the PVS-14's tubes. Which would be bad if the enemy got close enough, but under the circumstances, it worked to their advantage. It was easier to spot the bodies that had grenades.

A new plan had been forming in Flanagan's mind as it had become evident that the enemy was present in Mazimchay in far greater numbers than the Russians had suggested. If they could cause enough ruckus up on the mountainside, they might draw the majority of the Chechen fighters away from the cache, opening the way for the assault element to get in, grab the gold, and get out.

Except they still had to keep the bad guys occupied for quite a while. No one imagined that getting millions of dollars—Flanagan still didn't believe that the number figure that had been attached to the cache was remotely feasible—worth of gold out was going to be easy. They were going to have to steal vehicles and convoy the hell out. Which meant time.

Which meant that he and Gomez, with Curtis and Hank Brannigan to back them up, had to keep a dozen or more bloodthirsty Chechen jihadis occupied long enough for the assault element to get out.

Flanagan wanted every grenade he could get his hands on.

The first man had three, which was promising. He was the greediest, though, because none of the other two he searched had any. Gomez, crouched by another body up on the crest of the ridge, held up one. So, they had five. Gomez should still have his one the Russians had provided.

A branch cracked out in the dark. Flanagan stayed low, making sure he was still in the shadows, even under NVGs. He had a large oak or something similar between him and the fire barrel; he was out of the glow. Gomez had to move quickly, but he slid into the dark like a ghost. He had a talent for that.

More footsteps crunched in the leaves. A voice called out for one of the outpost watchers.

*Amateur hour. Some of these boys must not have fought at night in a while, if ever.*

He was about to dig out one of his seized grenades, but Gomez beat him to it. He heard the spoon fly free with a faint *ping* as it sailed through the air, and he made himself as small as he could behind the tree.

The grenade went off with a *thud* that shook the ground and the tree above him. The report rolled out like thunder over the valley again. Only after the echoes died down a little could he hear the faint moans out in the woods. Gomez had gotten somebody.

Flanagan was already moving, heading uphill and up the ridgeline. They could *not* afford to get pinned down to one spot. They had to keep moving like sharks, circling their prey and drawing them off, picking them off one or two at a time. It was tricky, especially since the only advantage they had was their silenced weapons. The enemy could see just as well as they could.

Then he heard the familiar rattle of an AK on full automatic down the hill, and knew that things had just gotten more complicated.

***

Brannigan heard the gunfire, too. And he'd heard the radio transmissions. He was forming a better mental image of what was going on, but it was still maddeningly incomplete. He wanted to hit "Pause" and get full data dumps, but he knew all that would do would be get his boys killed. They were professionals. And with Joe up there on the ridgeline, he was pretty sure that their diversionary attack was well in hand.

Until it wasn't. He just hoped that one of those four called for help before things went completely pear-shaped.

But whatever Flanagan was doing up there, it seemed to be working. The houses between them and the lights that shone through the trees about three hundred yards away were dark and quiet, and while a single vehicle had just roared past on the main road, heading down toward the highway, there was no other movement. Even the dogs had stopped barking after the first bursts of gunfire.

Burgess and Wade were ahead of him, moving from tree to bush to hedge, working their way toward the lights. They didn't know for absolute certain, but that seemed to be ground zero for the Chechen presence in Mazimchay. If the cache was in the village, it was probably there.

He looked back to find Krivov. The Russian was there, still with them, still sticking close behind him. So, he hadn't run off and left them in the lurch. Yet.

They closed in on their objective, as another explosion *boom*ed up on the side of the ridge.

# CHAPTER 24

Two Chechens still stood guard on the house, the two barns, and the rest of the enclosure, such as it was. It looked like the place had been a small farm, and there were still goats tied up next to the wall, even though the wall didn't stretch all the way around the land. The Blackhearts were approaching from the stand of trees immediately to the southwest. Mazimchay was a lot easier to hide in than Quba had been. Only some of the woods had been cleared, most of the houses secluded from each other by stands of trees, hedges, and patches of forest.

Of course, it had still been slow going, especially since there were still traps set throughout a lot of those stands of trees. Burgess had stopped and either disarmed or steered them around IEDs or mines several times already. Brannigan was glad for the other man's acute night vision. It was certainly better than his own.

Now that they were on the objective, they spread out carefully, feeling their way through the trees, each man carefully checking for tripwires as he went. Brannigan could still hear shooting up above them, and that was definitely the focus of attention for the two guards he could see from the shadows, as well. The pair of them were obviously positioned where they were supposed to be watching the back, but they were talking and looking up toward the ridgeline.

So much the better.

Brannigan tried to avoid looking at the lamps outside the house. Looking directly at any one of them would completely destroy his night adaptation.

Of course, once things went loud and they went inside, that was probably going to happen anyway. He didn't want to be fumbling around inside a building in the dark without NVGs.

He brought his Val to his shoulder, putting the red dot on one of the guards' chest. Still, he waited, letting the rest of the assault element get into position.

But he wasn't going to wait forever. Not when Flanagan and the others were engaged up on the ridgeline. He pushed down the selector lever and his finger slipped into the trigger guard.

Three 259 grain bullets smashed the left-hand guard off his feet. A moment later, another trio of *clicks* announced the second man's death, even as he spun around at the sound of his buddy's demise. He took two to the side and the third hit him in the head, snapping it over to one side as he collapsed.

Then they were moving, without any other commands or instructions. The Blackhearts closed in on the back door, weapons up and ready.

A curious call came from around the corner, answered by a pair of faint *click*s. Then Brannigan, Wade, and Krivov were at the door.

There was no window; the door was a solid panel door set into the plastered wall. Krivov flattened himself against the wall, his muzzle pointed up at the sky, while Wade moved on the door itself, and Brannigan got into the stack behind him. Brannigan reached around Wade and tested the door handle.

It was unlocked. It also opened outward, strangely. He yanked it open and dropped his muzzle level as he hooked through and into the house.

The back door opened on what appeared to be a kitchen. It was currently deserted, though the light—a single bare light bulb in a fixture bolted to the ceiling—was on. It was too small for them to spread out much to clear it, but there was nowhere for anyone to hide.

The kitchen opened up onto a main room ahead, and Brannigan could already hear voices and what sounded like a radio. So, someone had stayed back to coordinate. And probably call for reinforcements.

There weren't any side halls to worry about. He took the plunge, clearing a good chunk of the room through the door before he even reached the threshold, pausing only a fraction of a second before he stepped through and into the room.

The room had once been a living room from the looks of it. Most of the furniture had been shoved against the walls, and a small field table had been set up in the middle, in front of the fireplace. The lights were on, both one on the ceiling and two lamps in the corners. The windows had been covered with ponchos.

The two men were both in camouflage fatigues, wearing tactical vests and the same kofi caps the Chechens liked to wear. A pair of AK-203s were leaning against the table, and a full Russian military radio set was squawking on top.

Both turned as the Blackhearts flooded through the door. The one with the red beard and no mustache goggled for a moment, but the hard-eyed, clean-shaven man with longish hair immediately grabbed for his Kalashnikov.

Brannigan and Krivov both opened fire, cutting him down with a dozen rounds between the two of them. Wade finished the red-haired man with a Mozambique drill, thumping two rounds into his chest and finishing him off with a third through the eye before he'd even started to fall.

The two Chechen fighters crumpled with a pair of meaty *thuds*, both rifles clattering to the plank floor beside them.

Brannigan scanned the room. There was another radio, a computer, and probably a dozen cell phones sitting on the table or the couch. Several ammo crates were stacked in a corner. But there was no sign of the cache.

Not that he'd exactly expected them to keep it in a farmhouse. It was probably in the barn outside.

At least, he hoped it was. If they'd dispersed it throughout the village, there was no way they were ever going to get it all out.

Unfortunately, the two Chechens were far past interrogation.

He turned toward the short hallway off to the left that led to two more rooms, but Jenkins and Javakhishvili were already coming out, their weapons hanging from their slings. Javakhishvili shook his head. No one and nothing.

Burgess, Santelli, and Bianco had stayed outside. Brannigan keyed his radio. "Guido, Kodiak. Any movement?"

"Not around here." Santelli's Boston accent sounded even thicker over the radio, somehow. "Looks like some of their buddies from down the road might be coming this way, though." A distant *thud* announced the fact that Flanagan and Gomez were still in the fight. "Or they're heading uphill. Too early to tell yet. We're set in and waiting."

"Roger. House is clear; we're moving to the barn to continue the search for the cache." He pointed toward the back door they'd entered through, and Wade was already moving. He'd rather exit on the side that Santelli and Bianco were covering than on the far side. They might be exposed to enemy fighters they weren't prepared for if they went that way. Especially since they'd been inside, with the lights on. Their night vision would be shot for the next hour, at least.

There was no sign of the three men on outside security when they slipped out into the yard. That just meant that they were doing what they were good at. Even if they'd been dumb enough to hang out in the open and the light in hostile territory, Santelli would have gone high and right on them the minute they did.

With Wade in the lead, they quickly crossed the yard, passing the disinterested goats that hadn't even reacted to the killings outside the house. They paused at the barn doors, which were built to slide open. Wade hesitated, one hand on the door handle. Given what they'd seen in the house, Wade was probably expecting—just like Brannigan—that that door was going to creak like crazy as soon as he pulled on it. The other Blackhearts—and Krivov—leveled their weapons and waited on Wade.

He hauled the door open with a surprisingly low groan. The tracks resisted the movement, but the doors weren't rusted all the way shut.

The interior was dark and quiet. With Brannigan in the lead, the three Blackhearts and the Russian flowed inside, weapons up and searching. There was enough light coming from the farmhouse that they could see, if imperfectly.

If they'd been expecting a regular working barn, or even a warehouse disguised as a barn, that wasn't what they found. There were no pallets, no crates, no boxes on the floor.

Instead, there were just four big cargo trucks, lined up two by two, facing the door. The two in the lead were GAZ-66s with canvas-covered beds. A Matra M22 and a Mercedes box truck squatted behind them in the dark.

The four of them carefully moved around the vehicles, checking the dead spaces between, around, behind, and under them, just in case. It appeared that the Chechens didn't have anyone on guard with the trucks, however; there was no one else in the barn.

Brannigan decided to risk a light, pulling a small handheld flashlight out of his gear and playing it over the trucks. There were no out-of-place wires, and nothing underneath that looked like it might be a bomb.

"Jenkins, hop up there and see what's in the back." He handed the younger man the light. He had a hunch, and he hoped it was true. *Can it really be that easy, though?*

*"Easy?" Four trucks full of gold—if that's what we're looking at—is* way *more than that Antonov is going to be able to carry. Which just made this far, far more complicated.*

Jenkins had unlaced the cover at the back of one of the GAZ-66s, and he was hauling himself up to peer over the tailgate. "Holy shit. There's got to be... Damn, I don't know how much. But there's a *lot* of gold bars back here."

"Jackpot." Wade's voice was low and not nearly as celebratory as it might have been. He was clearly thinking along the same lines Brannigan was.

"Check the others." He looked at Krivov, but the Russian was in the shadows, his facial expression hidden in the dark. "This might take more than one lift."

"That might not be possible." Krivov's voice was as readable as his face.

"Then what's the plan? Are we supposed to *drive* these across Georgia and into...where? Ingushetia? I don't recall you being all that popular there, either."

"There is a backup plan with Anatoly." He sounded downright dismissive.

"Oh, really?" *Go figure, the fucking gangster has his fingers in the pot again.* "When were we going to be told about this 'backup plan?'"

"When it became necessary." Krivov was clearly not going to say anything more than that. "They will meet us at the airfield. If we do not need them, they will not show themselves."

Brannigan didn't have time for recriminations, but this fit the rest of this damned op. *If we get out of this alive, Van Zandt's coughing up a bonus. A* big *one.*

He was about to say something more when the radio crackled in his earpiece. "Kodiak, Woodsrunner. You might want to speed things up. The bad guys know the game is up, and they are coming your way."

***

Flanagan moved along the ridge, following a route that would take them up toward the crest of the Caucasus up to the northeast. He was getting farther away from the rest of the Blackhearts, but there was no other way. He had to draw as many of the Chechen fighters off as possible and get them as far from Mazimchay as he could before they realized what he and Gomez were doing.

They were still whittling them down. He and Gomez had killed two more since he'd fragged the first group. If he was counting right, there were still about six coming after them. They were moving more slowly and carefully now, but they were still coming on.

He looked back over his shoulder, up at the crest of the ridge. Still no sign of Curtis or the younger Brannigan. They hadn't called for help, and he hadn't heard any more shooting from down their way since they'd made contact and called up, so he assumed they were still in the fight.

It was weirdly quiet. The bad guys had gotten a lot more cautious after several of their own had been blown up or shot without seeing their enemy. He could hear them talking on the radio, and they weren't nearly as good as either he or Gomez at moving silently in the woods, but the lack of gunfire in the middle of what amounted to a battle for survival was eerie.

He spotted Gomez, crouched behind a massive, ancient tree, peering through his scope. The other man was holding his position, which gave Flanagan pause. He found some cover and looked for their adversaries.

The Chechens were a couple hundred yards down the slope, halted in a stand of trees. He could hear the radio clearly from that close, even though he couldn't make out the words.

He couldn't tell what they were talking about, but since they'd stopped, he had to assume that Brannigan and the others had hit the objective, and someone down below was calling for help.

*That means it's time to up the ante again.* That sounded an awful lot like something Curtis would say, but he dismissed the thought as he pulled out another frag, slung his Vintorez, and started to creep down the hill.

He was about halfway there when he heard Curtis's whispered voice in his ear. "Woodsrunner, Gambler. Where are you?"

He couldn't answer. The Chechens were far too close. They were close enough that he half imagined that they could have heard Curtis's voice in his earpiece.

"Gambler, Pancho Villa." Gomez's voice was low, nearly inaudible even over the radio. "Stand by."

Flanagan paused behind a fallen tree, slipping his finger through the ring to pull the pin. He could just see the Chechens ahead, crouched or squatting among the trees, softly arguing. The radio had gone silent.

He yanked the pin even as they started to stand up and turn back toward Mazimchay. With a heave, he tossed the grenade as hard as he could. They were a bit far for a grenade toss, but the slope would help.

The frag sailed through the air toward the knot of Chechen fighters as they started to move away, hustling toward the village below. One of them might have looked back at the faint *ping* of the spoon flying free.

But Flanagan's aim had been ever so far off, though it had been a good throw. The grenade hit a tree trunk just above the group, and after the fuse had been armed long enough for the impact fuse to activate.

It detonated with a flash and another harsh *thud*, followed by a *crack* as the lower branches were snapped off by the combination of the explosion and the frag. A long limb groaned and broke off, hitting the forest floor with a *whump*.

One of the Chechens screamed; they hadn't been quite far enough ahead of the tree to avoid all the shrapnel. But the frag had detonated too far away—and on the wrong side of the tree—to kill any of them outright.

Another Chechen opened fire, spraying a long burst up the slope. Flanagan shrunk back behind his tree, though he was fairly certain that the Chechen was shooting blind; he was well concealed, and the rounds weren't getting even close to him. He couldn't see their impacts, but bullets make a different sound when they're far enough away not to worry about. The *hiss* of their passage was a lot different from the *snap* that a bullet made when it passed close by.

He searched for the muzzle flash. There. He spotted it just as the Chechen's mag ran dry, so he could only guess when he peered through the darkened scope. Four rounds elicited a scream and a *thump*, and more return fire roared up the mountainside, smacking into dirt and tree boles but still high and off to his right.

Flanagan still got down and shifted positions, careful to move as silently as possible and keeping as many trees between him and the enemy as he could. He heard another scream, and the renewed burst of fire suddenly stopped. A last *click* silenced the scream. Gomez had counted coup again.

Then he had to throw himself flat as a veritable storm of automatic fire raked the hillside. There were a lot of trees between him and the shooters, but they were getting closer than they had before. And this wasn't just one or another shooting back at shadows, either. There were at least four guns rattling out there in the dark, muzzle flashes strobing in the shadows under the trees, a few green tracers skipping off tree trunks. He made himself as small as he could.

*There are more than just six.* The volume of fire was too high. Some other fighters had come up and joined the first group.

The fire slackened a little for a few seconds, but the remaining incoming was still heavy enough that he didn't dare move. Looking off to his left, he saw Gomez crouched behind a tree, as bullets smacked splinters and chunks of bark off the far side of the trunk.

A moment later, the fire increased again, though it seemed a little wilder, as if the bad guys weren't as sure of their targets. Then it slackened slightly again.

*They're breaking contact.* It was as good a break-contact drill as he'd ever seen the bad guys execute. The Chechens' reputation as good fighters was certainly intact, despite the cat-and-mouse game they'd been playing, taking greater advantage of the shadows and the cover of the trees than the Russians likely ever had.

He keyed his radio. "Kodiak, Woodsrunner. You might want to speed things up. The bad guys know the game is up, and they are coming your way."

"Roger that." Brannigan's voice was icy calm. "We are driving out in the next two mikes."

"Copy. We'll fall back and circle around, meet you at the mouth of the valley." He let go of the PTT and ran to join Gomez, who just gave him a thump of a fist on the shoulder as he knelt next to him. He'd heard.

"Gambler, Woodsrunner. Head for the mouth of the valley. We'll link up on the move." He could already hear Curtis grumbling in his head, but there was nothing for it. They just had to roll with the punches.

Together, he and Gomez started to bound up the hillside, back toward the crest of the ridge, keeping the bigger trees between them and the incoming fire—which was starting to slacken again as the Chechens received no return fire.

They had to move fast if they were going to get out of Mazimchay with the rest.

# CHAPTER 25

Santelli watched the road over his AS Val's red dot sight, chewing at the inside of his cheek.

He'd been a little worried that his fears and newfound insecurities—that he'd never had to deal with before, in the Marine Corps—might become a distraction on the mission. But right at the moment, he wasn't even thinking about home, or his family, or even the possibility that the entire mission might be a setup. The sector in front of him was his sole focus.

When the chips were down, Carlo Santelli still had it.

What he *was* thinking about was getting out of there. *And* what was going to happen after that. He didn't think that a gold cache big enough to buy *nukes* was going to be easy to transport anywhere. And as huge and powerful as it was, he doubted that the An-12 would be able to haul even half of the gold that was supposed to be there, with or without passengers.

Add in Dmitri's presence...he hadn't been happy to see the Russian gangster again. He knew he wasn't alone, but he was slowly and methodically putting pieces together in his head, and he didn't like the picture that was taking shape.

*If the Russians don't have the lift for half a billion dollars' worth of gold—or however huge this was supposed to be—then what's the catch? Is it really gold we came for? Or something else? Heroin, maybe? Is that the setup?* He would have snorted if he wasn't already deeply conditioned to stay as silent as possible on security—or in an ambush position, which was more like what they were doing.

But all of that got pushed to the wayside as he saw movement ahead. He lifted his rifle a little ways and peered through the gloom, trying to identify what had just caught his attention.

There. A short, boxy Lada pickup was moving slowly up the road, its lights off. He could see movement in the back, and he caught a glint of light on metal. The lamps on the farmhouse behind him had flashed off a gun barrel. There were several fighters in the bed, their rifles laid over the top of the cab.

*How many Chechens are in this piss-ant little village?*

He leveled his Val, peering through the sight, putting the red dot in the vicinity of the cab. Better to stop the vehicle first, then worry about the shooters. And the best way to stop the truck was to kill the driver.

He fired four shots, the subsonic 9x39mm rounds barely lifting the muzzle at all. The suppressor was quiet enough that he actually heard the windshield break, just before the truck suddenly swerved off the road, as the shooters in the back started yelling. It bounced off the dirt surface of the road and slammed head-on into a tree.

Santelli was already up and moving. Sure, he was supposed to be on security, but he was out on the northwest corner, close to alone, and the rest of the Blackhearts were back behind the house, either at the barn, or in the trees and hedges around the barnyard. And while he might have come across to some as unimaginative, Santelli firmly believed—just as Brannigan did—that sometimes the best defense was a good offense. Keep the enemy off balance, and they won't be able to penetrate your security because they don't know exactly where it is.

They'll be too focused on staying alive.

He ran as fast as his short, thick legs could take him to the next bush. A little voice in his head was wishing for NVGs, but he'd never been as attached to the technical toys as some shooters he'd known. When he'd been a young grunt PFC, they might have had one set of NVGs for a squad. The rest patrolled, night or day, rain or shine, with the bare Mark One eyeballs they'd been issued when they'd been born.

It had been a long time, but Santelli figured it was like riding a bike. Once his eyes had adjusted, it all came back.

He dropped to the prone behind the bush, leaning out slightly to get a better view of the truck. The shooters in the back had recovered from the impact quickly, and were already on the ground, their weapons up, spreading out to either side of the road. Santelli didn't give them enough time to get into cover. He flipped the Val to auto and raked the Chechens and the truck with a long burst, dumping the magazine into them, bracing the mag against the ground and leaning into the stock to stabilize it as best he could.

The Val chattered, rounds smacked into the sheet metal of the bed with *bangs* much louder than the reports of the shots themselves, and two men crumpled, one biting off a scream as a bullet ripped through his knee and his leg collapsed under him.

The trigger *clicked* without recoil, and Santelli hastily rolled behind the bush, ripping the magazine out and reaching for another one, cursing the Russian refusal to make a rifle with a last-round bolt hold-open. He rocked the fresh magazine in and racked the bolt, the *clack-clack* sounding horrifically loud compared to the sputtering *clicks* of the rifle's fire.

One of the Chechens must have heard it, too. An AK spoke with a stab of flame and a rattling roar, bullets ripping through the branches and kicking up dirt as they reached for Santelli's hiding place.

***

Brannigan heard the shooting and knew they were out of time. With Flanagan's diversion over, and the surviving Chechen fighters falling back to the village, and with what sounded a lot like reinforcements coming from the west, they had to move, or they were never getting out of Mazimchay alive.

"Mount up. We'll sort out what's going where and how when we get to Balakan." He circled around the GAZ-66, yanked open the door, and hauled himself up. "Get in!"

Jenkins clambered behind the wheel, staring for a moment at the Cyrillic-marked dash and the stick, which was behind the seat and the padded cover over the engine. He pushed at the pedals and tried turning the key. Nothing happened.

"Tell me you've driven a stick before, George." Brannigan was about to lose his patience.

"I have! I've got it in neutral and the clutch is down." Jenkins was already starting to sound a little panicked.

The other truck had started, its chugging rumble competing with the two other vehicles behind it. "We're the last ones, George." Brannigan rolled down the window.

"There's a battery kill switch behind the engine!" Wade, behind the wheel of the second GAZ, was already ahead of him. Brannigan gave him a thumb's up.

Jenkins had heard, and he was searching behind the engine compartment. "Got it!" He flipped the switch, and a yellowish light came on at the top of the dash. A moment later, he had the big truck running, and was grinding the transmission into gear.

Brannigan winced a little at the noise, but there wasn't time to finesse the gears. Jenkins stomped on the gas and they surged out of the barn, even as Brannigan cranked the window down and stuck his Val out, ready to engage as the firefight out front intensified.

***

Flanagan and Gomez weren't running, but they weren't moving slowly and deliberately, either. They stepped it out through the woods, hardly even bothering with the tree-to-tree, cover to cover sort of movement they'd maintained on infiltration. Things had changed, and they needed to cover ground.

The fact that the two of them still moved with a great deal less noise than most was a testament to their skill in the field.

They threaded their way down through the woods, keeping to the military crest as much as possible, a few yards below the actual crest of the ridgeline. And while they were moving fast, that didn't mean that they weren't scanning and listening as they went.

Gomez had moved up in front, taking point as he'd been trailing Flanagan on the way in. Now he stopped, throwing up a clenched fist. Flanagan froze immediately.

The rustle of movement up ahead wasn't overly loud, but it was still noticeable. Then Flanagan caught a glimpse of a figure moving cautiously through the trees, up on the ridgeline itself and slightly ahead of them, moving in roughly the same direction. If he'd been relying on his naked eyes, he probably wouldn't have been able to see Curtis, much less identify him, but with his plundered NVGs, he could just make out the man's build and the way he moved.

He keyed his radio. "Gambler, Woodsrunner."

The man up ahead paused, confirming the identification. "Send it."

"We are about fifty yards behind you and down to your right. Hold what you've got; we'll come to you." Gomez was already moving before Flanagan had finished speaking.

It took less than a minute to reach Curtis and Hank Brannigan. The two of them had found a particularly large oak to shelter under, each down on a knee, back to back, covering as much of their surroundings as they could. Gomez and Flanagan still got within a couple of yards before they were seen.

"Friendly." Gomez's whisper was low but penetrating. He stepped around a tree, even as the younger Brannigan swiveled his Val toward him. "*Friendly,* kid."

"I see you grabbed some 14s, too," Flanagan whispered as he took a knee next to Curtis. "You still make as much noise as a herd of elephants." He was only half-joking. Their situation had his nerves stretched taut, and every stray noise got under his skin.

Curtis sputtered, though his voice was still pitched low, even as the staccato reports of gunfire rattled down below. "I was in a hurry, coming to try to bail *you* out, Joseph!"

"Who said we needed bailing out?" Flanagan felt the corner of his mouth tug upward despite himself. He was glad that Curtis was there and still in one piece. "The two of us killed almost a dozen between us and the rest ran before you could even get here."

"Ungrateful…" Curtis shook his head. "Well, Oh Great Woodsman, I guess you're on point, then."

"Naturally." Flanagan stood up, stepping in front of his old friend. "Can't have you bumbling into things."

Curtis muttered under his breath, but he fell in behind Flanagan. He turned and found that Hank was still on a knee, and he stepped back to tug the younger man to his feet. Gomez would take rear.

"Keep close," Flanagan whispered when Curtis turned back to the front. "We've got to move quick." All the kidding was over. He was back to being deadly serious. They weren't out of the woods yet.

Curtis thumped his shoulder by way of answer, and Flanagan turned back down the hill, stepping off a little bit slower than before, but not by much.

Below them, the fight only intensified.

***

Burgess was already moving before the trucks surged out of the barn. He'd had to make a decision as soon as the enemy vehicle started approaching from the end of the valley: stay in place and hold security, or move up to support Santelli? His first instinct had been to do the latter. Santelli was just one man, and he was closest to the road. And they hadn't seen or heard any movement coming from the flanks.

Technically, he knew the right answer was to stay put until it was time to roll out. Leaving a sector unsecured could easily lead to them getting flanked.

But he'd learned fast, even before the Blackhearts, that sometimes you had to go against the textbook answer, especially when working with a small team. There are always tradeoffs when you don't have a platoon or two on the hit. They had less than a squad, and Santelli was under fire.

Tradeoffs had to be made. So, he made one and rolled with it.

He still stayed in the shadows, even as Santelli curled into a ball behind a bush as the Chechens he hadn't already shot returned fire wildly. Burgess had to throw himself flat as bullets *snap*ped overhead. The burst wasn't aimed at him, but it was still close enough to damn near take his head off.

Instead of waiting for the fire to slacken so that he could run to the next bit of cover, Burgess kept moving, low-crawling as fast as he could toward the next tree. He could see more of the road now, and the three or four Chechens crouched behind the crashed truck, one of them spraying the trees with AK fire. He couldn't see Santelli.

But he could see the enemy, and as long as Santelli wasn't in his line of fire, that would be enough.

He got to the tree, paused for a moment behind it as a couple of stray rounds smacked into the trunk with heavy *thunk*s. He flipped the selector down to the automatic slot, then rolled to his left, found his sights, and dumped half the mag into the knot of men behind the truck.

The Val's accuracy was impressive, given its compact size, relatively short barrel, and the subsonic ammo. From what he could tell, the entire thirteen round burst went right into the middle of the group, punching through flesh and bone alike. Screams erupted and the fire abruptly stopped as the man closest to the corner slumped forward, his Kalashnikov bouncing off the back of the truck with a *bang* before he fell on his face.

Then Burgess was up and moving, dashing toward a massive tree that loomed over the road. A fast series of *click*s and more impacts smacking into and through the metal of the truck bed announced that Santelli was alive and kicking.

Then the roar of engines closed in, and more fire smashed glass and punched holes in sheet metal. The lead GAZ 66 pulled up and Jenkins stuck his head out, even though it was doubtful he could see Burgess in his hiding place. "Get in!"

Burgess broke out of cover a half a step behind Santelli. He was a little surprised to see four trucks; he'd expected one. But he'd been working in the world of private military companies—both completely legit and what might be termed slightly shady—for years, and he had long since learned to be flexible.

He clambered into the back of the GAZ right behind Santelli. He almost barked his shins on the pallet strapped down in the bed. Santelli *had* stumbled over it, and he was swearing viciously as he dragged himself up onto the bench, only to lose his balance again as the truck lurched back into motion. Burgess grabbed him and helped him up before he fell over the tailgate. Behind them the other three trucks were closing in, blacked out but close enough to be impossible to miss. He could even just make out the shape of a figure—it might have been Krivov—hanging out of the passenger side window of the second GAZ with a Val held ready.

Burgess watched Krivov as they hurtled toward the end of the valley. The Chechens might be the greater threat, but

Burgess hadn't lived this long by trusting his allies. His friends, yes. His allies?

Never.

Four trucks laden with gold bars raced out of Mazimchay.

Behind them, high up in the hills, IR lights were already moving.

# CHAPTER 26

The gunfire in the village had died down by the time Flanagan and the others got close to the road, but they definitely weren't out of the woods yet.

Flanagan had sped up on the way down the hillside, even though he could hear Curtis and Hank stumbling and cursing under their breath behind him. Even with NVGs, it was still awfully dark under the trees, and not everyone was as sure-footed as he and Gomez were. He had seen some of the lights moving up the mountain through the trees as they passed through a small clearing, and knew what they meant, especially when he could only see them through the 14s. No curious farmer or miner was going to be up in those woods with IR. The Chechens had more fighters in the vicinity.

Either that, or the Russian double-cross was coming sooner than they'd expected. He had to assume it was a double-cross, since they hadn't been told to even expect Russian forces anywhere in the vicinity.

But the more he thought about it, the less likely it seemed that they were Russians. They weren't placed right to be the Russians pulling a fast one. If the Russians wanted to turn on them, it would make sense to cut them off, not start a stern chase down out of the mountains. No, he was pretty sure the lights were coming from another Chechen force descending from higher up the mountain.

Which meant that they needed to move fast. Even if everything went smoothly, and Brannigan and the others had eliminated the last of the resistance in the village, if Flanagan, Gomez, Curtis, and Hank were late to link up, it might give the enemy enough time to close the distance.

And Flanagan had seen something from up near the Chechen outpost they'd eliminated that told him that they weren't finished in Mazimchay yet.

He couldn't be sure. Even as he threaded his way through the woods at just short of a jog, he was second-guessing himself a little. But he'd thought he'd seen a couple of trucks set up next to the road near the southwestern end of the village, along with what looked like an ancient UAZ van. It wasn't *necessarily* a checkpoint or an ambush, but it very well might be.

And if it was a checkpoint, that alone could slow or stop the trucks long enough for the pursuing force up in the mountains to catch them.

He kept going for another two hundred yards, slowing just as the trees started to thin out again. Then he lowered himself to a knee behind a tree and looked back, just in time to see Curtis almost pass him. The shorter man was clearly getting winded—Curtis was a weightlifter and bodybuilder; he'd never been much for cardio even when they'd been squadmates in the Marine Corps, all those years ago—and was about to pass by where Flanagan had taken a knee, without noticing.

Flanagan rose smoothly and intercepted him. "Bring it in." He wouldn't ordinarily risk talking at this distance—the checkpoint was now only a hundred fifty yards away, and he could dimly hear radio calls and see some movement. One of the bad guys had accidentally triggered a light, too; he'd seen the flash. But even with Curtis and Hank running with night vision, he needed to coordinate the next few moments without hand and arm signals. This could be tricky enough; he didn't want to risk a misunderstanding, which he'd seen from using hand and arm signals on NVGs in extreme low light before.

Curtis took a knee next to the tree, and a moment later Gomez had corralled the younger Brannigan and brought the four into a tight circle beneath the oak's boughs. Flanagan pointed toward their objective, which was starting to catch some slight illumination in the green circle in front of his left eye, as the first beams of the lead truck's headlights filtered through the trees. They were running out of time.

"Skirmishers right. Stay low, move from cover to cover, don't open fire until I do. Mario, you still got any grenades?" He kept his voice as low as possible; he probably couldn't be heard a few feet away from their tiny circle.

"One." Gomez's voice might have been a breath of wind in the treetops, but Flanagan caught it anyway. His every sense was at its peak, the adrenaline coursing through his veins.

This was why he was still out here doing this. He'd never felt so alive as he was right then, when that life could be snuffed out in a heartbeat.

"Okay. Grenades first, then we finish the rest with guns. Ready?" He got thumbs up from each of them; even Hank Brannigan just held up his thumb rather than say anything.

Flanagan slung his Val carefully so that it shouldn't clank—the Russian sling wasn't the greatest, but he'd jerry-rigged it with a couple of knots so that he could tighten it down—and pulled one of his two remaining frags out. Then, once again moving with as much stealth as he could muster, he left the cover of the oak and started forward.

He was able to get the first twenty yards or so in a high crouch, stalking step by step toward the checkpoint with another tree between him and most of the enemy. Then he sank down to his belly, low-crawling through the low shrubs, weeds, and grasses between him and the road.

Behind him, the other three had spread out, and soon were all down in the shrubs and weeds, creeping toward the road, as the lights from the northeast intensified, and the Chechens hissed last-minute coordination as they got into position to try to stop the escaping trucks so that their compatriots in the hills could sweep down on them.

Flanagan could hear the double *clank* of a heavy machinegun being prepped, the bolt hauled back and the charging handle pushed home. The lights were getting brighter. He couldn't wait any longer.

He lifted his head to get a better view. He was still over thirty yards away—a long throw for a frag. He was sure he wasn't going to be able to get close from the prone. Fortunately, none of the bad guys were looking in his direction; they were all focused on the road and the oncoming trucks.

The man behind the DShK on the back of the pickup truck was getting on sights, his hands on the spade grips, and his thumbs presumably on the butterfly triggers. There was no time left.

At the risk of making noise and exposing himself, Flanagan heaved himself up, getting one knee and one foot under him, yanked the pin out, let the spoon fly, then hurled the grenade as hard as he could at the pickup. It was going to fall short—he could tell that almost immediately—but it was still on track to do some damage.

And he was still within the wounding radius.

He threw himself flat, already reaching for his last grenade. A moment later, the frag detonated with a *whump* that rattled his teeth. A split second later, a second explosion echoed it; Gomez had been right behind him.

There was no time to catch his breath. The trucks had just loomed out of the trees ahead, their headlights bathing the checkpoint in brilliant white light. Smoke was still rising from the double grenade detonation, and the Chechens were momentarily stunned, even though he was pretty sure that they hadn't managed to kill any of them. The explosions had come from a quarter they hadn't been expecting, though, and it made them hesitate for a few seconds.

That was long enough for Flanagan to pick himself up again after the deceptively soft patter of shrapnel had died down, unsling his rifle, and start slamming pairs of 9x39mm into bodies currently clearly visible in the light of the trucks' high beams.

He shot the DShK gunner first. He actually had to flip up his NVGs, as they were getting whited out in the glare. Quickly reacquiring the target, he caught a glimpse of the man, dressed in civilian clothes but wearing a plate carrier and helmet, slapping his hand back on the spade grips and crouching down to find the sights just before Flanagan put the first round into his side, just below his ribcage. The man almost collapsed at the hammer blow, folding around the impact and letting go with one hand, though he still held on to the heavy machinegun with the other. But Flanagan's finger was already tightening on the trigger, and the second round went in through his clavicle. He crumpled into the bed, the DShK's muzzle swiveling to point at the night sky as he fell.

The faint chatter of AS Vals around him heralded the deaths of the rest. Surprise counted for a lot. And the Chechens hadn't quite figured out where their attackers were coming from.

Maneuver counted for a lot, too, especially in the dark.

He searched the checkpoint, scanning for movement. Nothing stirred as the trucks closed in and the suppressed gunfire died down. He flipped his NVGs down to get a better look into the shadows.

Just as the green circle settled in front of his eye, he saw one last Chechen behind the truck that mounted the DShK. The man was in a low crouch; from his body language, it looked like he had been cowering, terrified, as the bullets had rained down and snatched away the lives of his comrades. But now, alone, he was starting to move, and it looked to Flanagan like he was reaching for a weapon.

Before he could do anything, though, Gomez's Val chattered nearby, and the young man was knocked onto his face. He didn't move again.

Then the trucks were looming close, rapidly approaching down the road. "Woodsrunner, Kodiak. I assume those explosions were your doing?"

"They were. Checkpoint appears to be clear. We are sweeping through." Flanagan was rising to his feet as he spoke, his Val still pointed at the trucks.

"We don't have time. Boris doesn't speak Chechen somehow, but we got one of their radios, and it's pretty clear that they've got reinforcements coming. We'll keep guns out, pause just past the kill zone to pick you up, then drive on." Brannigan's voice was brisk. "We're not seeing any further movement. Let's make it quick."

Flanagan wasn't sure of the wisdom of it, but sometimes speed and audacity counted for a lot. He just hoped they hadn't missed another bad guy who was on the other side of the technical.

They had.

A rattle of automatic gunfire thundered, muzzle flash flickering from somewhere on the other side of the gun truck.

Barely feet away from the second GAZ 66 in line.

***

Brannigan saw the strobe of flame from the Kalashnikov's barrel off to his right. It looked so close that he was surprised he didn't feel the heat.

He didn't feel the rounds ripping through his side, either, which was good. Nor did he hear them hitting the side of the truck. He didn't stop to think about it; he just swiveled in his seat, glad that the Russians had at least made the GAZ 66's cab big enough for gigantic Slavs, and aimed at the flash. He dumped a good chunk of the magazine in the general vicinity of the shooter, and the shooting stopped with a scream. Then they were past, and he didn't have a shot anymore.

"Status!" He barked the single word into the radio; he didn't know who might have been hit, so he didn't use callsigns.

"Boris is hit." Wade's words were clipped; he was trying to drive, talk on the radio, and—presumably—treat Krivov at the same time. "He's alive, but he took a round."

Brannigan might have heard Krivov cursing in Russian in the background.

"Hold up and let Joe and the others get in." Jenkins stomped on the brake and stopped the truck with a lurch, fortunately remembering to stomp on the clutch at the same time. Dark figures erupted out of the brush and ran toward the trucks.

Jenkins leaned out and pointed toward the rear vehicles. "There are more seats back there."

But Flanagan jumped on the running board and hauled himself up to look in the driver's side window. "There's an old UAZ van up the road about a hundred yards. It might be nothing, but from where it's sitting…"

"You think it's a VBIED?" Brannigan hardly had to ask. After the resistance they'd encountered so far, not to mention the mines and IEDs in the woods…

"More than likely. Hold what you've got here, and I'll stalk up there and see if I can find a pressure plate or some other kind of trigger. *Don't* drive past it yet." He really didn't need to make that last admonition. But under the circumstances, Brannigan sure wasn't going to call him out for it. Instead, he just nodded.

"Go." He craned his neck to peer through the side mirror. He couldn't see the IR lights that Flanagan had, but he had heard the radio traffic. The Chechens weren't done yet.

He just hoped that the vehicle wasn't an IED. If they had to try to get through the trees to avoid it, there was no way they were going to evade the Chechens. They'd have to ditch the vehicles and run.

And then what would the Russians do?

***

Flanagan moved fast, though he got off the road first. If there was one IED, there were probably more, and if there was one thing that Flanagan had learned a *long* time ago, regardless of how much the regular Marine Corps had brain-dumped it in favor of body armor, was to *stay off the trails*.

He wove through the trees and bushes, moving as fast as he could while still being able to see some detail through the NVGs. He was looking for tripwires, pressure plates, or anything else out of place.

He was immediately glad that he'd been alert. He stopped just as he felt the slight pressure against his shin. He couldn't see anything when he looked down, but he could feel the wire stretched taut against his leg. Carefully, hardly daring to breathe, he eased his leg back, reaching down to find the wire with his fingers, keeping his muzzle high.

The wire was about a foot off the ground, stretched tightly between two trees. He turned his head toward first one, then the other. There. It looked like they'd tied a full satchel of Semtex or similar explosive to the tree. Probably seasoned with nails, screws, bolts, and whatever else they could find to use for frag. Fortunately, he hadn't pulled the igniter—he'd already be dead if he had. Careful to keep his fingers on the wire so he didn't lose track of it, he stepped gingerly over it and kept going.

His heart was hammering in his chest, and he felt his limbs go faintly rubbery from the adrenaline dump. That had been too close.

*And I'm going* toward *the possible VBIED. I really should make sure I never,* ever *tell Rachel about this. She'd have a heart attack.*

He avoided any more traps on the way to the van, then carefully got down low and stared at the road from the end, painfully aware that if it was remote detonated, he was still far, far too close. Especially if the vehicle was full of explosives.

He stared as hard as he could, but he couldn't see any wires leading out onto the roadway. Taking a deep breath, his pulse pounding and his mouth as dry as the Sahara, he circled the UAZ van, carefully checking for any wires or other triggering devices.

He didn't find anything. No pressure plate, no "string of pearls," which was a line of small contacts strung out across the road, no tripwires. At least, there were no tripwires across the road. He did find another one behind it, stretching into the trees, where another IED was tied up where it could blow another six-foot crater in the landscape if someone had crossed that wire.

He tried to see inside the cab. There wasn't enough illumination to see much. He couldn't tell if there was a cell phone wired in or not.

There was nothing for it. He looked back up the mountain. The IR lights were still moving. He wondered if they were using IR-filtered flashlights, or if they just had IR weapon sights turned on permanently. Either one wouldn't surprise him, after spending most of his adult life in various Third World warzones.

He keyed his radio. "Kodiak, Woodsrunner. No pressure plate, no other physical trigger that I can find."

"Roger. We're coming to you. If we get blown up, well… Van Zandt should reimburse our families."

Flanagan hoped that Santelli wasn't listening to the radio that closely.

The trucks trundled forward, slowing a bit as they got closer to the van. Jenkins, at least, was clearly more than a little nervous to be driving past a potential bomb of that size. Not that Flanagan could blame him; standing that close to it was making him more than a little nervous.

The lead GAZ suddenly surged forward, passing the van as quickly as possible. Flanagan held his breath, knowing that if the van went boom, he'd never even feel it.

It didn't go boom. The next four got past, and they slowed a couple hundred yards down the road—not quite out of the blast radius, but close enough that he didn't have to run a quarter mile to catch up.

Flanagan ran anyway. IR lasers and floodlights flickered through the trees behind him, and a few bursts of gunfire rattled, bullets passing by overhead. The Chechens were coming.

It was time to go.

# CHAPTER 27

They didn't actually go out via the main road. That would have been suicide, since they would have needed to go right through the Azerbaijani border checkpoint. With the explosions and gunfire up in the hills, it was a miracle that the Azeris hadn't shown up in force yet.

In fact, as they neared the turnoff onto the logging road that Krivov had assured them *should* get them out, Brannigan could have sworn he saw several large armored cars moving up the road from the southwest. They'd moved fast enough so far, but the inevitable Azerbaijani response was on its way. Hopefully they hadn't been spotted; Brannigan had had Jenkins turn the headlights off, and had gotten a pair of NVGs from Flanagan for him to drive with.

"Right here." Brannigan pointed. Jenkins squinted as he slowed, but he didn't quite turn yet.

"Are you sure that's a road?" Jenkins kept looking from the oncoming lights of the Azerbaijani border patrol and the dark, narrow slot in the trees.

"It's all the road we're going to get, and this truck was designed to go offroad. Now get us moving!" Brannigan was watching the oncoming armored vehicles, too. And they were closing in faster than he was comfortable with. He had no doubt whatsoever that the Russians would hang them out to dry if the Azeris caught them.

Jenkins cranked the wheel over and dropped several gears, sending the GAZ 66 trundling toward the trees. He was cursing under his breath the whole time. Brannigan couldn't be sure if the former SEAL was more worried about getting caught by the Azerbaijani border patrol or getting the truck stuck.

And as they got closer, it did feel like the heavily-laden diesel was about to bog down. Fortunately, Jenkins worked the transmission and cranked the wheels right and left, keeping them moving. They still scraped a tree branch as they passed under the eaves of the forest.

The tightly-spaced convoy threaded their way onto the logging road, sometimes barely fitting between the trees. So far, there was no sign of further pursuit. Brannigan was listening carefully for a firefight to break out between the border guards and the Chechens, but nothing happened. The only thing he could hear was the rumble of the diesels and the creak of their suspensions as they threaded their way up the mountainside.

Getting over the crest was tricky; there wasn't any more room than there had been below, and the narrow road turned sharply as it crossed the ridgeline. He found himself holding his breath as they made the turn, but Jenkins managed it without getting hung up or otherwise smashing into a tree.

He couldn't watch the other three trucks as they followed; the rear-view mirrors were quickly cut off by the trees. His was actually smacked against the cab by a branch as they went by a little too close, and he wedged it back into position, glad that it hadn't shattered from the blow.

The weight of the gold in the back was making maneuvering even more difficult. Jenkins was visibly fighting the wheel at every turn, no matter how slight, and the suspension groaned with every bump. The others couldn't be doing much better, particularly not that Mercedes.

The road didn't turn much on the way down the other side of the ridge, which was at once a blessing and a curse. A blessing in that Jenkins didn't have to try to maneuver around the switchbacks; a curse because it was pretty much a straight shot downhill, and with the load in the back, the GAZ 66 wanted to pick up way too much speed going down. Jenkins had it in first gear, and he was still riding the brake all the way. Brannigan was glad the truck was a military model; the taillights were dark with the blackout switch on.

Unfortunately, the Matra and the Mercedes were civilian models, without any blackout lights.

Even without NVGs, he'd started to get some of his dark adaptation back, and he could see the lurid glow of the other trucks' brake lights behind them, filtering through the trees. There would be no hiding that if anyone was watching the hillside, and he hoped they hadn't used their brakes much on the way up the ridge. If they had, there might well be a nasty surprise waiting at the base of the hill, in the shape of a group of Azerbaijani INKAS Sentry vehicles.

Despite Jenkins' efforts to keep their speed down, the GAZ 66 was moving at a good clip as it reached the bottom of the hill and the clearing just before the road. He had to fight to get it turned to follow the treeline, and it felt like they *almost* tipped over as he made the turn.

The ground wasn't all that good for driving with a load of precious metals, either. Even from the passenger seat, Brannigan could feel the soft ground trying to give way under the truck's tires.

Jenkins stayed as close to the treeline as he could, circling around the clearing before lurching up onto the road. Brannigan twisted his head to watch the right, where he could see the bright glare of the border checkpoint's lights. But he didn't see any oncoming vehicles. Apparently, the border guards were concerned mainly with the disturbance up in Mazimchay, and they had directed all of their attention there.

"We need to make tracks." He leaned out the open passenger's side window, searching for the Mercedes and the Matra. They hadn't gotten stuck yet, but it looked like the Mercedes was struggling. He really hoped they didn't have to try to recover it.

*We won't. Not under these conditions. I'll burn it and let Krivov tell his bosses that we couldn't get it out. I'm not trying to recover a civilian box truck full of gold with eleven men this close to a border patrol checkpoint.*

But whoever was driving the Mercedes—Brannigan thought it was probably Javakhishvili—knew what he was doing. Deftly gunning the engine where needed and maneuvering to keep from letting the wheels dig into the softer ground, he got the box truck across the clearing and up onto the highway. The Matra handled the terrain a bit better, though it had to go straight across the clearing. The path alongside the treeline had become too rutted and torn up.

"Let's go. Gun it." He could have sworn he'd already heard aircraft. The Russians might be early.

Jenkins didn't need to be told twice. He opened up the GAZ 66's engine with a roar, quickly working through the gears—at least, as quickly as he could get the heavily-loaded truck, which wasn't that speedy to begin with, to accelerate. The other vehicles followed, the second GAZ 66 taking up the rear.

Brannigan watched the rear view as best he could, watching for any pursuit. So far, the highway behind them remained empty.

He didn't expect that to last.

But the expected Azerbaijani pursuit didn't materialize during the roughly ten-minute run to the Balakan airfield. He didn't doubt it was coming, but hopefully the shortcut over the mountains had delayed it enough that they could get away.

There wasn't one An-12 sitting on the strip. The Russians had brought two. They must have been anticipating the size of the haul. The only issue would be loading it. Even with forklifts, it would take time to transfer almost nine tons of gold bullion. And as he looked off to the north, he could see headlights moving. The Azerbaijanis had probably figured things out in Mazimchay, and they were on their way.

They tore through the entrance, where shadowy figures carrying A-545 rifles waited on security. The Russians were on the ground and waiting.

One of the figures stepped forward as they slowed. The headlights revealed the vaguely Asiatic *Spetsnaz* trooper who had accompanied Krivov in Sochi, dressed in plain green fatigues and carrying an A-545. He stepped up to the truck, climbed on the running board, and pulled himself up to look in the window. "*Mayor* Krivov?"

Brannigan jerked a thumb back toward the rear of the column. "He took a round on the way out." If the Russian understood, he didn't show it; his face was still blank and impassive. He clambered down and headed toward the rear. Brannigan got out and followed him. If Krivov had been hit badly enough, this could get really complicated, really fast.

The climbed up on the passenger side and spoke quickly. Krivov replied, and Brannigan breathed a *little* easier. If he was talking, he couldn't have been hit that bad. A moment later, the Russian climbed down and trotted back toward the gate. Krivov stuck his head out.

"We need to get the trucks inside the airport and begin loading." He was clearly in pain, but he was coherent. "Our crew chiefs will drive the GAZs onto the aircraft. Anatoly's people will be here to take the Matra and the Mercedes shortly."

"What about us?" Brannigan felt his stomach tightening, his awareness sharpening. If there was any point this was going to go bad, this was probably it.

"We need your team to help with security. Anatoly's people have bribed the Azerbaijani authorities, but their interference is only matter of time now." He grimaced. "And the Chechens will have local agents who will be alerted."

Brannigan had to agree. That didn't make him comfortable with the situation. The Russians were separating the Blackhearts from the loot, and therefore from the birds. He couldn't care less about the gold at that point; those aircraft were their lifeline out of there.

But there wasn't much he could do except risk a firefight with the *Spetsnaz*, with the Azerbaijani police closing in.

Of course, that might happen anyway, depending on Krivov's and Pichugin's plans…

He jogged back to the front truck and clambered back into the cab, pointing forward. "Head to the edge of the strip." Jenkins complied. He was clearly getting more comfortable with the Russian truck; maneuvering through the gate and to the edge of the airstrip, behind one of the massive An-12s, was considerably easier than navigating that logging road behind them.

It took only a couple of minutes to get all four trucks lined up next to the strip. Russians were already waiting, clambering up onto the running boards and gesturing for the Blackhearts to get out. "Do it." Brannigan wasn't any happier than the rest, but he also wasn't sure how well his guys were going to be able to maneuver the trucks onto the aircraft. It wouldn't help anyone if they insisted on loading themselves, and the planes crashed because they screwed it up.

They clambered out, their weapons still held at the ready. None of them were inclined to let their guard down, he saw. Good.

Krivov's Asiatic lieutenant pointed them toward the southeast end of the strip, behind the two big transport planes where they were lined up to take off, their props still turning. There wasn't much cover there, and Brannigan was suspicious, but nodded and started in that direction, intending to get security set in where they could watch the Russians as well as the perimeter.

The strip was flat as a pancake, and there weren't any convenient equipment cases or bunkers to use for cover. He ended up setting in right at the edge, just inside the relatively dense strip of trees and bushes that bordered the strip. It put them even farther from the birds, and he didn't like that much, but the alternative was to be out in the open, which would be worse if things went south.

He stayed mobile, moving back and forth along the line of the Blackhearts, constantly keeping one eye on the loading operation. The GAZs had turned out to be barely too big to fit in the Antonovs' holds, so a forklift had been brought out, and was even then loading the gold from the rear GAZ onto the second An-12.

The *Spetsnaz* were staying close to the planes and the front gate. And the longer Brannigan watched, the less he liked it.

A couple of vehicles came in the gate. He watched carefully; that hadn't been part of the plan.

"Who the hell are these guys?" He'd paused next to Santelli, who was also watching the Russians. The old Sergeant Major didn't trust their Russian allies any more than Brannigan did.

"At a guess? Dmitri's boys. Though given how everything else has settled out on this op, that doesn't necessarily make me any more comfortable." He checked how much ammo he had left. Three magazines of the five they'd inserted with. It wasn't much, but it was enough for a good fight.

But the anticipated attack didn't come. The newcomers got in the Matra and the Mercedes and drove away. The Russians finished loading the gold in the rear An-12 and moved on to the front.

Brannigan's eyes narrowed. With the gold loaded on the rear aircraft, men were already getting aboard. And his team was still almost three hundred yards away.

"This is it." He looked down the line. "Everybody up! Get ready to move!"

But a moment later, all hell broke loose.

Three vehicles came careening through the gate as the forklift moved away from the lead An-12, just far enough to be out of the way before the operator jumped out and ran to the bird. The rest of the *Spetsnaz* troopers were right on his heels.

The three oncoming vans ignored the An-12s and the Russians, turning a hard left as soon as they came through the gate and barreling toward the end of the strip where the Blackhearts had set in. They stopped right at the end of the actual airstrip itself and the side doors flew open.

Flanagan had taken his captured NVGs back as they'd gotten off the trucks. He saw what was coming a fraction of a second before any of the rest except for Gomez. "*Get down!*"

Brannigan threw himself flat as dark figures piled out of the vans, dropped to their knees, and opened fire. Strobing muzzle flashes flickered in the dark, as the two An-12s started to taxi, their ramps coming up and their engines bellowing.

Bullets raked the trees over their heads, shattering branches and *thud*ding into tree trunks. A burst went over Brannigan's head with a harsh series of loud *crack*s.

Then the entire line of Blackhearts, without a word, returned fire.

Their weapons were considerably less noisy and flashy than the enemy's. They clattered and sputtered in the dark, muzzle flash all but entirely eliminated by their suppressors.

The Blackhearts were all better shots than their adversaries, and they had the advantage of a better view of their targets. Most of the enemy shooters were up on a knee, backlit by the single streetlight above the terminal, and they were in the open. The Blackhearts were in the prone, with only the darkened line of the bushes and trees behind them, making them much harder to see.

The first volley smashed half of the attackers off their feet. Brannigan shifted targets from the first man he'd shot, tracking in on another who was suddenly running for the back of the middle van, as the newcomers' fire died down to almost nothing. Another pair hammered that man in the side, and he staggered, but got behind the vehicle.

Then the fire redoubled, as the shooters found some shelter behind the vans. Brannigan returned fire, then shouted at Bianco. "Base of fire here. Joe, Mario, Wade, and Tom, with me. Flank left!"

It was already too late, and he knew it. The first An-12 was already in the air, and the second was accelerating down the strip. They'd been left behind when the shooters had shown up.

And he was pretty sure that had been part of the plan all along.

He sprinted down the treeline, staying behind the men who had stayed in place, still trading shots with the attackers, who had suddenly found themselves pinned down in a very poor position. Brannigan stretched out his legs, pounding toward the thinner line of trees and bushes that bordered the strip to the west, knowing that this was likely futile, that they still didn't have any cover, and that they had a long way to go to get to the Georgian border even if they survived the next few minutes. But it wasn't in him to just quit. He'd fight through until he killed everyone trying to kill him and his, or until he went down, and if it turned out to be the latter, he'd have an honor guard of corpses to precede him.

Reaching the treeline, he turned and ran along it, digging deep as his lungs and his legs alike started to burn. It had been a long time since he'd slept or eaten last, and it was starting to take a toll. Grit and anger were the only things keeping him going by then, and he was pretty sure the rest of his boys were in the same boat.

He got about as far as he dared and threw himself flat, turning to face the bad guys as he did so, already finding his red dot with his eye before he'd even quite hit the ground. The shooters were still concentrating their fire on the end of the strip; either they hadn't noticed his flanking maneuver, or they were too dumb to realize what had just happened.

His finger was tightening on the trigger when four big, blue armored vans rolled through the gate. The Azerbaijani National Police had just arrived.

A couple of dozen armed men in green and black uniforms and body armor piled out and opened fire almost before they'd hit the ground, tearing into the shooters who were suddenly completely exposed in the open around the three vans. Bullets shredded flesh and splashed blood against the white metal of the vehicles, where they didn't miss bodies and punch holes in the backs of the vans themselves.

"Fall back." The Azeris were focused on the shooters for the moment. They had to know the Blackhearts were there—the recently deceased had been shooting at *something*. But they might have the tiny window of time they needed to get away. "Meet at the corner to the south."

But even as he let go of his radio, a pair of vans pulled up on the road just on the other side of the treeline, and the doors slid open. All four Blackhearts swiveled, their weapons coming up, prepared to sell themselves dearly.

"Come my friends! We do not have much time!" Dmitri was in the passenger seat of the lead van, leaning out the open window and waving them forward. "Those fools bought us a few minutes, but the Azeris will be coming soon."

Brannigan didn't trust Dmitri as far as he could throw him. None of them did. But the choice was currently between going with him or quite probably getting rolled up by the Azeris after *two* major firefights. Even if they ditched the weapons and gear, he doubted they were going to get out of Azerbaijani prison before they were all old, bent, and gray.

"Let's go." He held his position in the trees, watching the Azeri police surround the three vans and the corpses scattered around them while Flanagan, Wade, Gomez, and Burgess quickly clambered into the windowless back of the van. A moment later, he followed, hauling the door shut. The van surged into motion, stopping again shortly thereafter.

Half expecting the door to be locked, Brannigan yanked on it. Somewhat to his surprise, it slid open; he piled out, looking for the rest of the Blackhearts.

Santelli had most of them getting into the rear van, then he sprinted toward Brannigan, who held out a hand and hauled him inside. Then he slammed the door shut and banged on the side of the van.

Moments later, they were racing away from the airfield, leaving nothing behind but bodies and some very stirred-up Azerbaijani National Police.

# EPILOGUE

The drive was a long and uncomfortable one, made worse by the uncertainty that weighed on each of them. *What happens now?* No one in the back spoke. They just waited, hands on their weapons, braced against the walls of the otherwise stripped van, while the miles rolled away and the night got steadily older.

The two back windows in the rear doors hadn't been completely obscured, but they were covered with translucent film so that no one looking in could see any detail. That went for anyone looking out, as well, but it did mean that they could see the world outside slowly getting lighter. Dawn was coming.

The sun rose and the day brightened. Brannigan still couldn't tell where they were. He tried to peel the film back on the rear windows, but it proved futile. It was stuck firmly to the glass, and even when he got one corner to come away, the adhesive marred the view enough that he still couldn't see much.

His watch said that it was almost noon by the time they finally stopped. They heard the passenger door slam as the engine died, and then the side door rolled open, revealing Dmitri with his wide shark's grin. They were in a large, empty warehouse, a rollup door clattering down toward the floor behind them. "Welcome to Tbilisi, my friends."

Brannigan stepped down out of the van, his Val still in his hands, trying not to groan as he finally stretched his cramped limbs. He scanned the warehouse carefully, dreading what would happen if they got into a fight in their current condition.

But it appeared to be genuinely empty except for the two vans, a brown Lada, and Dmitri and his drivers. He looked down at the Russian mobster. "I'd ask how the hell we got here, but I doubt you'd tell me."

Dmitri grinned even more widely. "Trade secrets."

Brannigan nodded. "Thought so."

Dmitri circled a finger to indicate their surroundings. "You have a radio or phone to call your friends?"

Brannigan nodded again. He'd made damn good and sure to keep the sat phone with him. "So, now what?"

Dmitri shrugged. "You call your friends. We disappear." He lifted his eyebrows suddenly, and then rummaged in a pocket. "Oh, yes. This." He held out what looked like a small flash drive, with a swing-out cover that had the word "Ledger" etched on it.

"What's this?" He didn't immediately reach for it.

Dmitri held it out waving it slightly to get him to take it. "Bitcoin wallet. It has your share."

Brannigan's eyes narrowed, and they were icy cold as he stared Dmitri down. "There wasn't nearly enough time to get any of that gold transferred into Bitcoin. You knew this was going to happen."

"Of course I knew." If the Russian was intimidated, he didn't show it. "I was paid to make it happen. But you are here, you are alive, so it all worked out, *da?*"

But Brannigan wasn't going to take the hint and just let it go. He could feel the rest of the Blackhearts gathering at his flanks. They weren't willing to, either. "So, was this the plan all along? Get us to do the dirty work and then leave us to the Azeris? What does that accomplish?"

Dmitri's face went blank for a moment. He fished a cigarette out of his jacket pocket and lit it, then squinted up at Brannigan through the smoke.

"What do you think it accomplishes for Russia if eleven Americans are caught—or their bodies identified—in the Caucasus, armed and conducting military operations?"

The words hung in the air for a moment, the enormity of what had just happened sinking in. "So, *that* was the whole point? We got played from the get-go? We were just sacrificial lambs to justify more Russian paranoia about the US?"

Dmitri shrugged. "It was part of it. Denying Abu Mokhtar a good bit of his funding was part, too. He is clever. He does not use banks or digital means of paying. He has been keeping his operation supplied with gold, diamonds, drugs." He took a deep drag on the cigarette. "Taking his gold was still the, how do you say? The primary objective. You were… an added bonus. Pichugin's stroke of genius."

Brannigan nodded grimly. Pichugin hadn't struck him as a fire-eating *Spetsnaz* commander. "Who is Pichugin? Really?"

"He is GRU. If this operation had worked in both aspects, he would now be a General."

"Were there ever really any nukes?" Santelli's voice was low and deadly.

Again, Dmitri shrugged. "Maybe. I do not know. I think perhaps they were an extra carrot to get your government to help."

"Oh, that's just great." Santelli looked like he was about to explode. "All this, risking our necks, just for some damned Russian ploy."

Javakhishvili looked positively murderous.

"So, if this didn't work, won't you get in trouble with Moscow?" Brannigan's voice was even and measured, his eyes boring into Dmitri. "After all, if they paid you to make sure that we didn't escape…"

Dmitri grinned, though the expression didn't quite meet his eyes. "Oh, I was never supposed to be in Azerbaijan for this. I will simply blame it on the incompetents I was able to hire. I can even turn it back on them. I was told they were connected to the Night Wolves. They were supposed to be good fighters." He shrugged again. "They failed. Just got themselves shot to pieces. Not my fault."

He turned toward the Lada, waving a hand farewell. The fact that he turned his back on eleven pissed-off men with rifles said something about how secure he figured his position was.

"Dmitri." Brannigan's voice was hard. Still, the gangster turned slowly, his expression unconcerned. "Why? Why'd you pull us out?"

For a moment, the affable mask slipped. Brannigan wasn't sure exactly what he saw in its place. Dmitri was an enigma.

The mob boss looked him in the eye. "It was business. When a man like you gets off Khadarkh on his own, it tells me that he is formidable. If he was left behind again, and I was involved, he might decide that the second time was enemy action." He grinned again, a shark's grin. "I can get around governments and their police. But a man like you could be very dangerous. A man like you might ignore loopholes I can use with governments. I cannot afford to run from a man like you forever. And I did not trust the incompetent *mudaki* I hired to actually kill you."

He turned back to the Lada again with a wave. "Enjoy your share, my friends. Until we meet again."

## LOOK FOR MORE HARD-HITTING ACTION SOON, IN:

## BRANNIGAN'S BLACKHEARTS

# WAR TO THE KNIFE

A border city is in the grip of a ruthless criminal…

…And he might be working for even more sinister backers.

But will killing him be enough?

Ramon Clemente was a general in the Colombian Army. Now he has seized the city of San Tabal, deep in the jungle on the border between Venezuela and Colombia. He hasn't sworn allegiance to Venezuela, but he is turning the city into a drug-financed Communist hellhole.

And his connections with narco-terrorists has put a bullseye on his back.

Since he's got the Colombian authorities thoroughly penetrated, no one has managed to get close to him. So Brannigan's Blackhearts are going in dark, undeclared to the Colombians, to kill or capture Clemente.

But the Americans and the Colombians aren't the only ones who want Clemente dead.

He's made enemies much closer in his grab for power.

And Brannigan and his boys will discover just what is at stake if they kill Clemente and leave.

# AUTHOR'S NOTE

Thank you for reading *Enemy of My Enemy*. A bit more of a return to the straight-up mercenary action story this time. Having an arc is all well and good, but this series was always intended to be a *bit* more standalone. There will be more like this in the future.

To keep up-to-date, I hope that you'll sign up for my newsletter—you get a free American Praetorians novella, *Drawing the Line*, when you do.

If you've enjoyed this novel, I hope that you'll go leave a review on Amazon or Goodreads. Reviews matter a lot to independent authors, so I appreciate the effort.

If you'd like to connect, I have a Facebook page at https://www.facebook.com/PeteNealenAuthor. You can also contact me, or just read my musings and occasional samples on the blog, at https://www.americanpraetorians.com. I look forward to hearing from you.